I0670078

SUSAN E. FARRIS

Nuts About You
Midnight Bluff Book One

SWEET STORIES WITH SOUTHERN SASS

First published by SF Consulting 2021

Copyright © 2021 by Susan E. Farris

All rights reserved. No part of this publication may be reproduced, stored or transmitted in any form or by any means, electronic, mechanical, photocopying, recording, scanning, or otherwise without written permission from the publisher. It is illegal to copy this book, post it to a website, or distribute it by any other means without permission.

This novel is entirely a work of fiction. The names, characters and incidents portrayed in it are the work of the author's imagination. Any resemblance to actual persons, living or dead, events or localities is entirely coincidental.

Susan E. Farris asserts the moral right to be identified as the author of this work.

If you would like to use material from the book (other than for review purposes), prior written permission must be obtained by contacting the publisher at susan@susanfarris.me. Thank you for your support of the author's rights.

First edition

ISBN: 978-1-73-645235-6

This book was professionally typeset on Reedsy. Find out more at reedsy.com

Contents

Dedication

For Dawn and a phone call
that gave me the courage to change my life.

Free Short Story

Get a glimpse of Cress and Jake's life after the Happily Ever After in "**All I Want for Christmas**."

Jake and Cress just want to spend a romantic evening together at Midnight Bluff's Christmas Festival. And this year, Jake has big plans for Cress' present.

But when things keep going wrong, he has to embrace the giving spirit of the season and accept the help of his neighbors in order to pull off a Christmas miracle.

Read "**All I Want for Christmas**" today:
https://susanfarris.me/free-reads/.

Nuts About You

Susan E. Farris

Midnight Bluff Book One

Chapter 1

 press stared at the bubbles in her champagne as she
held it up toward the chandelier. She slowly swirled
the glass, watching the small sparks of light slide up
the side. It might have been premature to order the bottle,
but she knew what tonight meant for her and Grant. And
Lord knew, she needed something to celebrate after today's
disaster at work.

Her engagement would *thrill* her mother. Well, she'd at least
be pleased with the prospect of a wedding to plan. She had
decidedly mixed feelings about Cress' choice for her future
son-in-law.

She took a big gulp and winced as the carbonation burned its
way down her throat. Around her echoed the chatter of a full
restaurant. Candles flickered on the white linen tablecloths,
their light glimmering a thousand times over in the elegant
cut-glass goblets.

The softly sobbing notes of a violinist floated from the
corner. Uncomfortable in her stiff silk dress, she squirmed

in the slick chair in the center of the room. As happy couples conversed in hushed tones around her, she sat alone at a table for two, fiddling with her silver cross necklace. Taking another gulp of her champagne, she rolled her shoulders and tried to relax and listen to the elegant music.

Well into her second glass and still alone, Cress eyed the roll on the plate across from her, considering nabbing it. The two glasses of champagne were going straight to her head, and she didn't want to be drunk when Grant got here. Whenever that was. It should have been half an hour ago. She speared the roll and slathered butter on it.

Just as she shoved the last flaky bite in her mouth, Grant plopped into the seat opposite her, his dark blond hair falling into his hazel eyes. Cress eyed his work slacks and colorful Polo, but shrugged off his work-casual appearance. At least he was finally here.

She grinned and leaned forward, grasping his hands. Her nails looked perfect after her trip to the salon for those outrageous French tips he was always telling her to get, and she hoped he noticed. She would have to get them taken off in the next day or two; fake nails were wildly impractical out in the field, but she would do anything to make this night special for him.

He coughed and sat back, pulling away to wave down their server as he swiped at his nose. "Could we get some more bread, please?"

Belatedly, she realized there were crumbs scattered all over her plate, and she surreptitiously swept them away underneath the server's bemused glance.

"How was your day?" she asked, trying to sound chipper, but she could already feel some of the bubbliness from the champagne wearing off beneath his abrupt manner.

"Decent. Finalized a proposal for a small town in Vermont—a revitalization project that's going nowhere—but my supervisor's happy and gave me the green light to put out a call for contractor bids on it." With a loud sniff, he rubbed at his eyes. Always with the rubbing and swiping and sniffing around her. Was she made of ragweed or something?

Deciding to put her attitude aside and try again, she took his hand. "Sounds like you had a productive day."

He shrugged. "Did you get that promotion to project lead you were gunning for?" He tilted his head and studied her. She swept her thumb across the back of his hand, wanting tonight to be just about them and their future. Not about her failure. Again.

"C'mon. Let's toast to a beautiful evening." She poured him a glass of champagne, bubbles fizzing over the back of her hand as she spilled a bit in her haste.

Grant took the glass from her before she could spill more. "Cress. We've talked about this. Did you at least put your application in?"

She drew back her hand, offended. "Of course." Cress hunched her shoulders, not wanting to relive her humiliating day, but knowing if she didn't offer some details, he'd pry them out of her bit by painful bit. She'd rather get a bikini wax.

"Dr. Gregory doesn't think I have a 'tough-enough personality' to handle the entire team." She bit her lip to keep from adding to the thought that maybe he was right.

Dr. Gregory had all but laughed at her application, despite having the endorsements of most of her senior teammates. He'd given the promotion to their new, and highly charismatic, teammate Jim without so much as even looking through her file.

She didn't blame Jim for being well-liked, but she *did* blame Dr. Gregory for dismissing her out-of-hand. He'd refused to consider the depth of her knowledge of hickory decline, her reputation as a meticulous researcher, and her long-standing relationships with everyone not only on their research team but across their field in the Northwest. Her body flared hot and angry at the thought of his scoffing, the little hairs pricking up on the back of her neck.

Still, Cress knew she was not the most outgoing of the group. Even if she was laser-focused on their research, on the rare occasions she was in the office, she wasn't one to join in for drinks after hours or gossip around the dented-up tables in the break room. When people wanted to talk, they sought her out, but she didn't seek others.

Maybe that was her weakness. She'd rather be in the forest than at a fundraising formal, but you needed both skill sets to be a good leader. Grant's congested voice broke through her rabbit trailing thoughts.

"That's such bull. You have the most field experience and have published more papers than anyone else on that blasted team. Heck, more than two or three of some of those guys combined. Who did they give it to, if not you?"

This night was quickly turning from the romantic evening she had envisioned to another grilling about her career decisions.

She hugged her arms to herself and whispered, "Jim."

"Jim? The new grad. He's been there, what, a year?"

The promotion going to Jim was an insult, and she knew it, but Dr. Gregory had announced without forewarning this afternoon. There was nothing she could do without looking petty. She dropped her eyes and didn't respond, hoping he'd let the topic go. Sometimes, Grant would relent if they were out in public. But tonight, he persisted.

"Honey, did you even try to stand up for yourself?"

She looked up at Grant. Disappointment pinched the corners of his eyes. But it wasn't disappointment *for* her; it was disappointment *with* her. An icy blast of air washed over her from the overzealous air conditioning, and her breathing hitched. What was happening to their romantic evening?

She shook her head and swallowed, trying to focus on what really mattered: them. "Let's not worry about that. There will be other opportunities." Picking up her glass, she held it toward him unsteadily. "Let's just celebrate us tonight."

But Grant was shaking his head, wiping at his nose with his white linen napkin. "Honey, I don't think there is an 'us' anymore. That's what I wanted to talk to you about."

She set the glass down, spilling a few sticky drops onto the table and watching the moisture wick into the pristine cloth. Her ears rang.

"What are you saying?" She pressed her trembling lips together and stared down at her lap, willing herself not to cry, to not make a scene in the middle of this beautiful restaurant. Her mother's words rang in her ears. A lady did not draw attention to herself by pitching a fit in public. But all the day's rejections came crashing down on her in one thunderous heap and she felt her voice crack.

"You take me out to dinner—which you're late to—at the most romantic place in Wisconsin, just to break up with me? I thought you were proposing!" Her voice ticked up shrilly and a few tables near them glanced over sympathetically. "This is the most humiliating day of my life!" Grant shot a nervous look at the glowering maître d', and she lowered her voice to a stage whisper. "Why are you doing this?"

"Come on, Cress. You can't be surprised by this, can you?" Grant clasped her hand. She snatched it back, and he huffed. "Look, we're both always working. But you're not even trying to go anywhere with your career, not really, while I've steadily been climbing in mine. And you bring home all those plants. That you know I'm allergic to."

"We don't live together, Grant!"

"Yes, but I'd like to come over to your apartment or even be around you without sneezing my head off. It's like you purposefully roll around in pollen."

"I'm a doctor of biology. I work with plants. I'm outside, in the forest seventy-five percent of the time." She circled her hands exasperatedly. "You knew this when we started dating. I can't exactly change my career because you won't take Claritin."

He sat back in his chair and gestured at her. "Where is *that* fire with your career? You'll let me have it, but heaven forbid you stand up for yourself at work."

"I don't want to be known as a shrew at work!"

"And I don't want to be shackled to someone with no ambition."

Cress sat back, hands over her face. That wasn't it at all; the politics—she couldn't believe he understood her so little. She took a few deep, steadying breaths and looked up at him. "Well then, I guess there's nothing more to say."

"Come on, Cress. Don't be like that. I just don't think that we're a good fit is all."

Ice flowed through her, crackling through her stupidly

expensive French tips clutching the table. *Don't be like that.* Grant was the one dumping her. He didn't get a say in how she reacted or felt.

She didn't have to make a complete spectacle of herself, but, by the mighty Mississippi, she was going to have the last say this time.

She stood and grabbed the champagne from the ice bucket. "Fine. If that's how you feel, then thank you for your time, and I wish you the best." She raised the bottle in a mock salute. "I hope you find your fit one day. Thank God it won't be me." She stalked out of the restaurant. Grant could have fun with the bill when he found out she'd ordered the most expensive bottle on the menu.

* * *

The empty bottle fell to the floorboard with a clink as Cress leaned her forehead against the steering wheel and sobbed, snot bubbling out of her nose. She swiped at her face and her fingers came away black with mascara and eyeliner. Disgusted with herself, she dug in her console for her stash of napkins and tried to mop up her face even as more tears threatened.

How could life have fallen apart so spectacularly in one day? The promotion she had worked years for handed to a newbie and now this…

A miasma of humiliation and rejection fogged her brain as she sniffled again. Her mind swirled with all the time she had spent with Grant. Seven years of brunch dates, late-night movie showings, strolling through the botanical gardens.

Her stomach roiled at her idiocy, thinking he could be the love of her life as they had laughed and argued together for so long. She was a doctor, for Dolly Parton's sake. She shouldn't be this foolish. Had she really just been a check box for him on his climb up the ladder? A smart girlfriend to show off at parties? A pleasant way to fill the time?

She cursed her stubborn heart for leading her down such a useless road. Her mother had been right: her career was a waste, her love life was meaningless, and it had been a mistake to move all the way from the lush fields of the Mississippi Delta out here to the backwoods of Wisconsin. All to save some stupid trees. Stupid, beautiful trees.

She leaned her head on the cool steering wheel, longing to be in the woods with just her sleeping bag and rucksack. The only place she ever felt at home was among trees. Trees were so much better than people. They didn't tell her she was a weirdo or not ambitious enough or not girly enough. They just sank their roots into the homey soil and raised their branches to the sun and wind, happy to be completely, utterly themselves. A lone tear tracked its way down her chapped face, and she sat back up.

Trying to breathe deeply, she hiccupped and felt the acid creep of indigestion from champagne on an empty stomach—a decision she was already regretting. There was no way she could drive home to her depressingly empty apartment like this.

With a resigned sigh, she kicked off her heels and reached into the backseat for her spare hiking boots. Thankfully, she always kept a set of gear in the car. Tugging them on, she yanked the laces tight, then swung open the door. Standing was a struggle all on its own, but she'd done this to herself, so she would get herself the half dozen blocks to her apartment. Which was an easy stroll on a good day.

Today was not a good day. A few hundred yards from the restaurant parking lot, she leaned up against the glowing plate glass of some late-night store, wind plastering her hair into her face, as she blinked at the absurdly spinning sky.

Her eyes watered against the lights and the tittering stars as the creeping hysteria of the pity party wound back up her throat. All she wanted was for someone to come and take her hand and lead her home—a champion in the dark.

A tippy tapping on the glass arrested her downward spiral. A tiny little paw pressed to the window. That paw belonged to the sweetest little cocker spaniel puppy she had ever seen. Despite the wind, Cress melted into his warm, brown eyes underneath a quizzically cocked brow.

Who kept a pet store open this late at night? But the chipper face of the puppy spun before Cress, distracting her from rational thought.

He shook himself and sat down, tongue lolling out, and seemed to nod at the door, a command for her. She shook her head, trying to clear it, and he wagged his tail, patiently waiting. Standing up, she pressed a sweaty hand to the glass but hesitated. She'd never had a dog before, much less a puppy. But it was so tempting to have a little friend that would be loyal no matter what.

What if she screwed him up like she did everything else? Dogs didn't care about perfection; they just wanted food and love. That she could do. He scratched at his shoulder and yapped at her, tongue still lolling. She laughed, hiccuped, and reached for the door.

* * *

Glaring morning light filtered through the blinds and hit Cress in the face with a smack. She groaned and rolled over. She tried to sit up, but yesterday body-slammed her back into the bed. With a pitiful gasp, she collapsed back into the pillow, ready to pretend the world didn't exist. She just wanted to disappear into a little fantasy bubble where her granny hovered in the next room with sweet tea and biscuits, ready to hug her to her lavender-scented bosom and make it all better.

However, reality crept in with the light and a head that throbbed so badly her ears ached with a high-pitched whining that wouldn't go away. She needed water. Badly.

As sunlight filtered through the leaves of the ferns hanging above her, she peeked through her fingers at the sink on the other side of her tiny studio apartment. It was only a couple dozen feet away. A few steps. She could make it if she moved slow. And didn't trip over a plant.

Holding her forehead, she slid out of bed, easing around the monstera that had gone through a growth spurt that summer. Her feet landed in a frigid puddle. The whining inched up in pitch and tippy tapping echoed toward her. A tiny white and brown puppy appeared at her feet, his whole body vibrating from his wagging tail.

"Oh, no. Oh, no!" she croaked. She tiptoed to the bathroom for towels, trying not to spread what she was ninety-nine percent sure was pee all over her floor. The whining puppy followed her. The last thing she needed was a dog in the middle of the shambles of her life, chewing on her surely poisonous plants. From the tiny bathroom, she threw a towel onto the puddle. The puppy pawed at her feet, anxious whining continuing.

"What? What do you need?" she asked, exasperated, and he ran to the door, looking up at her with mournful eyes. Understanding clicked, and she yanked on her robe. A fuzzy memory hit her, and she dug through her purse. A leash fell from it, and she snatched it up and pocketed her cell phone and keys.

Feeling bedraggled and bewildered, she headed toward the sad little stretch of grass out front of her apartment building. Spotting the stretch of dusty green, the puppy drug her forward and squatted, relieved. Realizing she had nothing to take care of him except the leash, Cress hung her head and groaned. As the wind whipped around her, she hugged the robe to herself, wondering if she had enough Crisco in the pantry to make Granny's biscuits.

She could use a taste of home right about now, and, to her chagrin, they would suffice for a cheat breakfast for the bundle of energy yipping at her feet until she could get showered and make it back to the pet store for some puppy chow.

Her cell phone rang, and thinking it was Grant checking on her, she nearly hung up on it before she saw the caller ID.

"Hey, Gramps." Her voice rasped out, and she coughed, trying to clear it.

"Well, you sound like you've seen better days."

"Hello to you too."

"Are you ok, sweetheart? I was calling to see how that big promotion went."

A knot clenched in her throat. "It didn't. They gave it to someone else."

"You're the brightest one in that place. If they can't see it, do you want to be working for a bunch of goonies like that?"

Cress' voice cracked as she chuckled, and she ended up

hacking and coughing for a solid minute. She really should have brought a bottle of water with her.

"Are you sure you're not coming down with something?" Gramps asked when she finally stopped coughing.

She strolled down the strip of grass, letting the pup sniff at all the interesting smells. Champ, his name was Champ. That's what she'd called him last night as she'd drunkenly toted him home. It was coming back to her now.

"No, Gramps. The only thing I have is the worst hangover of my life and a case of puppy-itis."

"What the heck is that?"

She tittered as Champ snapped at a butterfly. "It's what happens when you stumble into a pet store while you're drunk."

Over the line, he sucked in a breath. "*Ooooh.*" A pause followed. "What are you going to do with the little fellow?"

Champ rolled onto his back, wriggling back and forth in the grass. She grinned as his ears flopped back and forth. "I guess I'm a dog owner now. It helps that he's awfully cute."

"Sounds like a plan." A long silence followed. Cress frowned. It wasn't like her grandfather to linger on the phone. His check-ins were regular and brief and consisted mostly of chit-chatting about her job and the weather. Gramps wasn't a big fan of Grant either, avoiding the topic unless Cress brought him up.

"What's up, Gramps?" She pulled a hand through her oily hair, longing for a hot shower. She smelled like she'd slept in a bar's dumpster last night instead of her bed.

He cleared his throat, the sound rasping over the poor connection. "Well, this is just awful timing, but I was calling with a favor to ask."

Like she needed any more complications in her life. She sighed as she looked up at the scant clouds floating overhead. But it was her Gramps. She tried to keep her voice neutral. "What is it?"

"It's sort of my own job offer for you." The world froze at his words as she peered at the grass at her feet, shaved so close to the dirt that she could see its roots. Even the acrid scent of the asphalt parking lot seemed to fade as he spoke.

"I'm here by myself, running the orchard. And it's just getting to be a bit much for me—I haven't been able to keep things up the way they need to be kept. The harvests are getting to be finicky. I was wondering, with you working with trees and all, if you'd want to come help me. Maybe one day take over the family business? I can't think of anyone else I'd rather have. And well, if you don't, I'd have to sell."

She sucked in a breath. "I don't know, Gramps. That's a lot to take on. I have my career… " A career that had just tilted toward fizzling out. "And pecans are a little different from hickory." She knew she had her dad's old reference books somewhere, but they would be outdated by now. She'd need to find new ones.

"Same family of trees, though. You wouldn't be too far outside of your specialty."

"Still a lot to take on. And I'd be giving up my career." Her objection sounded weak even to her, but Gramps was a big believer in letting people decide things for themselves. An image of the old farmhouse, her entire family around the dinner table, wavered in front of her, but she pushed it aside. She needed to think logically.

"Look, I don't need you to decide right now. I have a potential buyer, and even though I don't like the guy, it's a generous offer. I have to let him know by the end of the season, so you have a little time. Talk to Grant, but promise me, you'll think on it."

Something clicked in her mind. Her career hadn't grown the way she'd planned. And her relationship... "Grant won't be a problem. We... We're not together anymore."

He whistled. "I'm sorry, sweetheart. I'm sure you're not happy."

She sniffled. "Not really, no." Champ wound himself in a circle around her feet, wrapping her legs with the leash. She sighed, pinned to the spot but without a free hand to unravel herself.

"You've got deep roots, baby girl. You'll weather this storm." His words warmed and encouraged her. Gingerly, she lifted one foot free from the entangling leash.

"I hope you're right, Gramps. Right now, it seems pretty bleak." There wasn't much left for her here anymore. If she stayed, she'd be stuck in a dead-end research role for an untold number of years before another promotion opportunity came back open. If it opened. At that point, would she still have enough fire to go for it, or would she be too burned out? Shaking the other leg loose, she picked up Champ and tucked him under her arm.

Gramps' voice crackled over the line. "That's just because you're in the thick of it. You've got no distance from it. No perspective."

No distance. Everything was just heaped on top of her right now. She frowned as she studied a Bradford pear at the entrance of her apartment building. Earlier that summer, she'd warned the building manager they were planting the sapling in the wrong place; there wasn't enough rich soil to

14

sustain it and the heat radiating from the side of the building would scorch the tender leaves. He'd scoffed at her and planted it there, anyway. Now the tree languished, stunted, one side brown and dead. It wouldn't last another season in that spot.

As much as she loved her career and her colleagues, she'd felt herself languishing here. Dr. Gregory and the board had passed over her again and again for promotions and grant recommendations. Maybe it was time for a transplant.

Maybe it was time to return to native soil.

"Hey, Gramps?" Her voice whispered over the line.

"Yes, darling."

"I'm coming home."

Chapter 2

J ake threw the stack of fence posts over his shoulder and slammed the tailgate of the truck. Rusty paint flaked off and showered down into the bed, and he turned with a scowl. One of these days, he would sandblast the old truck down and paint it properly, but that would have to wait for the off-season. If they ever had an off-season.

He headed for the corrugated tin barn that rose ahead. Rounding the corner, he nearly collided with Bo. The old man clucked at him as he dodged under the posts.

"You know, Vada could have one of the guys deliver a whole passel of those out here for you. Just keep a bunch stocked up." Bo followed him into the barn, his voice ringing off the walls.

"But then I wouldn't have an excuse to run into Midnight Bluff and stop by the bakery." Jake patted his middle, which was getting a little pudgy from all of Willow's danishes. It was also his only chance to check on Vada lately and keep his promise to his late wife to make sure her sister didn't work herself to death.

Bo chuckled. "If you're not careful, Ruffin is going to have you running extra drills on the weekends."

"Eh, I'm not afraid of him. Besides, with me doing the heavy lifting for two around here, I can still run circles around him."

Bo coughed and looked away as Jake ducked into a storage corral. His chest tightened, knowing he's said something wrong. Leave it to Jake to go insulting the man who'd saved him over and over again. It's not like Bo had asked to be hit with a severe case of rheumatism.

Clearing his throat, Bo rubbed his hands together. "Listen, Jake, about that. I'm hoping you'll have help here soon."

He finished stacking the posts against the wall of the corral, taking his time arranging them so they wouldn't slide and fall. He bit the inside of his cheek as heat spread through his chest.

"I have help. Mac and Franklin are great guys. Hard workers. And they know this place almost as well as I do."

"You know I'm not talking about Mac and Franklin."

Jake's shoulders pinched at his tone. He really didn't want to have this discussion again. The orchard was his home now, his only home, and he didn't want some stranger coming in and messing with how he ran things. Trying to sound lighter than he felt, he grabbed a diamond sharpening stone and a pair of shears.

"Well, we could always use another pair of hands around harvest."

Bo huffed and took the tools from him, setting them back on the shelf. Jake turned to another and began pulling down chemicals to mix for spraying in the next couple of days.

"Jake. Hold still for a second."

His hands already on the containers, Jake paused, looking

over his shoulder.

"I called my grandchild, the biologist, the one who works with trees. And she's agreed to come out here and help me run the orchard."

Jake set them back down and turned to face Bo. It looked like he would have to face this sooner rather than later. "I thought we had talked about this? And we'd left it at you would teach me so I could take over the orchard, and I'd bring on a couple more guys in a few years and you'd retire."

Bo shook his head. "That's where you left it, but I had objections. The main one being that my joints can't take more than one or two more seasons. We don't have the time. And honestly, the orchard needs a lot more help than you or I can give it." Shoving his hands in his back pockets, Bo stared up at the rafters. "I haven't been able to maintain it since Hank died and it needs a heck of a lot of work that I just don't know how to do." His eyes darted to the ground. "And my grandchild works with hickory decline—got a Ph.D. in it—she can get us back on our feet."

Jake pinched his lip as he studied Bo's evasive looks. Something more was weighing on him, and he wasn't saying it. It wasn't like Bo to withhold on Jake. With a sinking feeling, Jake asked the question that had been bugging him since their first conversation, and the one Vada had just echoed in town.

"Are you sure it's just that? It doesn't have more to do with trying to keep the farm in the family?" He shoved his hands in his pockets and hunched his shoulders. He and Bo were tight, that was for sure, but they weren't blood, and at the end of the day, that was what seemed to matter most around these backwater Mississippi Delta towns.

"Jake, you know I don't care two figs about that kind of

thing!" Bo's face flushed. Raising an eyebrow, Jake waited in silence. "Oh, all right. It wouldn't be right if I didn't try to pass the orchard along to family first. Lord knows, Leora would tan my hide me if I didn't—not after everything Hank did for me and Elena, God rest her soul." He held up his hands. "But it's not only that. I meant what I said about the orchard needing help to produce a good yield again."

Jake leaned against a stall. "The last few years have been pretty dismal. But it's just weather."

"It's more than weather, Jake." Scuffling his feet across the concrete, Bo shook his head. "We've done all we can between watering and fertilizing. I've just got this feeling that the trees themselves ain't right. If we don't get someone in here who can pinpoint what's going on, there won't be an orchard left for anyone." He clapped Jake on the back and headed for the door. "And I might as well sell to Mr. Glower."

With an *ugh*, Jake straightened and followed. "Pretty sure that bastard is waiting with bated breath for us to go belly up so he can buy the land at auction for a penny."

Bo shot him a sharp look. "Mr. Glower is a decent man. He wouldn't do that. If we had to sell, he'd stick to his original offer."

Jake crossed his arms and snorted. "Jessayin', he seems pretty intent on becoming the next land tycoon around here, and he's none too gentle about how he does it. Jumping in right when farmers are down on their luck."

"He is forceful. I'll grant you that." Bo rubbed at his chin. "Still, we could do worse than selling to someone we know." He clapped Jake on the shoulder. "But I don't think we'll have to, with Cress coming."

Jake nodded, wanting to avoid talking about Cress. "Van's

turned into a nasty piece of work these last few years. Vada told me he made an offer to Tate Sessums the other day. If he takes it, that's 'bout half the small-time farms in the county Van's bought out already."

"Oh, come off it! Mr. Glower drives a hard bargain, but he's no action movie villain." Bo strolled through the rear entrance of the barn. Jake followed him.

"I'm just saying, it's mighty convenient that Van always seems to make a 'generous' offer right when a farm is struggling with a run of bad luck."

Bo clucked his tongue. "I've known Mr. Glower since he was in diapers. He wouldn't be a good businessman if he didn't take advantage of an opportunity when he saw it." With a sigh, Bo looked out over the orchard. "Still, with the catfish processing plant gone, there soon won't be much left of Midnight Bluff without the family farmers. If we can't hold out, I don't know who can."

Beside him, Jake surveyed the rustling trees, lined up in orderly aisles stretching as far as the eye could see across the gently rolling fields. Peace spread through him in a soft wave, as it always did underneath their boughs. This place was worth saving. Even if it meant putting up with a snobby city person. But that didn't mean he wouldn't try to get Bo to see things his way first.

They settled onto a couple of old hay bales. Taking in a deep breath of the clear air, Jake let the silence linger for a moment as he enjoyed the last few rays of the late afternoon sunshine. He didn't want to disturb the stillness with arguing.

As the last ray of the sunset filtered through the leaves, sliding from gold to coral to pink to dusky blue, cricket song filled the air and meadowlarks dipped and dived overhead, whistling and trilling.

Finally, Jake turned, knowing Bo would go in for supper soon and needing to say his piece. "Look, Bo. I know you're worried about the orchard. But I can handle it. I mean, I already take care of all the equipment and I help you manage the fertilizing and spraying. There is a reason you made me your farm manager this past year."

Bo nodded slightly and Jake charged ahead, having saved his best point for last. "I trust your instinct—let's call an arborist in for a look. But I just don't think having some city-slick academic getting underfoot is the best idea if we have as much work as you say we do to get this place back in shape."

Bo burst out laughing, doubling over and resting his hands on his knees. "*Ooh*, Jake, you always say the darndest things. A city-slicker!" He stood, clapped him on the shoulder, and walked off to the house still whooping with laughter. Jake sat there, gaping after him, wondering what in the world he'd said that was so funny.

He could handle the orchard on his own and he didn't need some prissy academic to help. He'd show Bo that when his grandchild got here, whoever she was. She was probably pale and stooped and wore glasses from reading too much. No way she'd be able to keep up in the orchard. She'd most likely poke about a bit and make a few whiney suggestions, then disappear inside to make declarations from the air conditioning like some annoying but ignorable oracle. He nodded to himself. He could wait this out. Patience was all he needed.

Jake stood and stretched, his back crackling after a long day spraying fungicide up into the branches of the trees in the west lot. His shoulders ached from another day spent on the tractor, keeping the air blast sprayer going as quickly as possible. There was just so much ground to cover by himself. As he wearily trudged toward his cabin, the baying of his hounds in their kennel resounded across the twilit fields. He took a deep breath and opened the door to a cabin empty and still.

Chapter 3

The early afternoon sun glinted off the pond behind Gramps' house. The deep blue water rippled gently in the breeze, the long cattails bobbing and swaying. Cress drew in a deep breath and let it out slowly as she soaked up the golden light and the glorious twittering of blackbirds in the distance. The pecan trees shimmied and shifted in a light afternoon breeze, the warm smell of greenery and earth rising to her in a heady wave through the open window.

Eagerly, she slung the door of her truck open. After days pulling the U-Haul down lonesome stretches of highway with nothing but her thoughts and bursts of static from the radio to keep her company, no amount of RedBull or coffee could touch the exhaustion weighing down her eyelids. As she stepped from the truck, her knees crackled and threatened to lock up. Gingerly, she straightened her legs and then bent to touch her toes.

With a groan, Cress reached toward the clouds, flexing her stiff fingers. She eased her head side to side, relieved to feel a small pop in her sore neck after hours on the road. Kneading at her shoulder, she gazed at the trees before her, their trunks thick and dark and stretching forward in inviting shady rows. Behind her, Champ whined and pawed at the window, eager to be released.

Pulling his leash from her pocket, she reluctantly turned and reached for the handle. She supposed the poor little guy needed a potty break before she found somewhere to stash him while she unloaded. Before she could snap the leash to his collar, he wriggled from her grasp and bolted in a silky streak of white and brown for the trees.

"Champ, no!" With a gasp, she dashed after him, desperate to not lose sight of his furry little butt among the unmowed rows of trees. On a four-hundred-acre farm, it would be nearly impossible to find such a small puppy.

Delighted to be running free, he wound among the trees, Cress sprinting to keep up. She rounded a large trunk, panting, and skidded to a stop. Champ lapped at the chin of a chuckling farmhand, safely captured in his arms.

As the man turned to Cress with the squirming and dancing puppy tucked under his elbow, her jaw dropped. He had that farm-boy physique with lean hips and built shoulders, a tan line ending at his shirt sleeves—and a bleached white T-shirt that had seen better days. His dark hair desperately needed a cut and flipped out from the back of his John Deere baseball cap. He seemed to be mid- to late-thirties and had a bit of scruff on his chiseled jaw. He would have been just an average good looker. Except for his eyes. Those meltingly soft brown eyes. They made her want to sag against a tree and fan herself with one glance. He caught her staring and scowled.

Cress shook herself. What the hay? She didn't even know

his name. How could this Adonis be mad at her already? He cleared his throat.

"Looks like you lost this," he growled and shoved Champ to her. Mutely, she accepted the now-whining puppy. "You should keep up with your pets better. With all the equipment and pesticides we use around here, he could get hurt."

She clipped Champ's leash on and set him down, where he wrapped himself around her legs. As usual. With a sigh, she looked up. Eventually, he'd untangle himself. The farmhand was watching her wordlessly, the scowl still branded between his eyes. What bee was stuck in his bonnet?

Still didn't stop her from being a decent human being—or "heaping coals" as Mom said. Holding out a hand, she smiled broadly, being sure it crinkled the corners of her eyes—her best "let's make friends" smile. It worked every time. "Thank you for catching Champ. He's a handful. I'm Doctor Cress McBride, Bo's granddaughter." The Adonis' scowl only deepened.

He reached out and shook her hand, giving it one swift pump up and down, squeezing so hard she swore the bones crackled.

"Jake Wilder. Bo's farm manager." He ground the words out between his teeth. Cress decided immediately he must have had spoiled milk with his cheerios this morning because he was just being a sourpuss at this point.

She widened her eyes, going for excitement. "Oh, that's great! We'll be working together a lot then. You must know everything about the current state of the orchard." His posture stiffened, and he gave a brief nod. "Once I get settled in, I'd love to pick your brain about what's going on. It's always best to start with the current practices and history. And you would know best."

He shrugged and turned away. As he began walking toward the barn in the distance, he said over his shoulder, "That's easy. We've had a bad run of luck with the weather the past couple of years. I've adjusted the water flow from the wells and upped our zinc fertilizer to compensate."

Cress stepped out of the leash and hustled to keep up with his long strides. "So, you don't think there's anything else that needs to be done?"

His voice floated back to her. "Not really."

She stopped and looked around. The trees in this section were at least twenty years old and about thirty-five feet apart, which meant they'd only been thinned once. By now, they should have been thinned twice and be roughly eighty feet apart. She studied the branches for the telltale signs… yep. Branches from adjacent trees overlapped and knocked into each other, cutting down on airflow, causing poor pollination and making mildew much more likely. That probably meant any spraying was way less effective, too.

Absorbed in studying the trees, she squinted to get a better look. The leaves looked funky. She stepped closer and stretched up onto her tiptoes, snatching a handful. They were sticky and spotted black and brown. It was just a matter of time before they started falling.

She looked around incredulously. This wasn't just a case of a couple of years of bad weather. What this orchard needed was a complete overhaul, from spacing and pruning to its spraying and fertilizer protocols. Possibly some replanting as well. Her heart sank. She hadn't known it had gotten as bad as this. Her dad had loved this orchard; he'd put all his time and energy into it.

Jake had halted as well and stood studying her. He scratched at his chin and shifted his weight.

"So, what's the verdict, Doc?" He smirked at her. So that's how it was going to be. He thought she was all flash and no substance because of some academic title. Wasn't the first time she'd run into this, working with loggers and forest rangers on research projects. They took one look at her petite frame and name badge, and the jokes started rolling in.

But this was her home.

An angry flush licked its way up her chest. She stalked toward him and slapped the leaves into his hand. "You can't tell me you think that this looks like healthy growth! Bad weather. Bull shit." His face went blank as he looked from the leaves to her face and back.

"It's just some spots."

"Healthy leaves don't have spots! They're not sticky and curling either! You have pecan scab and mites at the very least." She took a deep breath and forced herself to speak calmly as she rubbed at her temples, Champ's leash dangling from her arm. For once, the puppy sat obediently by her feet. "Who monitors the orchard?"

"I do the maintenance work, mowing, and harvesting, along with two other guys. Bo does the marketing and accounting. Every once in a while, he comes out and stares at them for a bit."

"But no one monitors?"

He crossed his arms. "They're trees. They grow. They put out nuts. They shed their leaves and they do it all over again. We trim any broken or galled limbs. Why should we need to 'monitor' them more than that?"

Cress groaned and tapped the leaves in his palm. "Because

of stuff like this." She looked around, wondering what else she would find. "We've got to stay ahead of this stuff, or it can get so entrenched that yields go down to almost nothing."

Jake twitched his head to the side, rubbing his ear against his shoulder. He remained silent, lips stubbornly pressed together. Cress rubbed at her forehead. "I take it yields are already going down?"

He gave a curt nod. "Still could be just the weather."

She wanted to smack his stupidly handsome face. But she needed to play nice. They would be working together, after all. Swallowing down her frustration, she pinched the bridge of her nose, then set her hands on her hips, willing herself to be calm. It would be disastrous to get into a shouting match with the farm manager on the first day.

Just then, a light dripping sounded at their feet. Champ had hiked up his leg and, with a relieved look, peed on Jake's left boot.

"Champ, no!" Cress tugged him away as Jake hopped awkwardly, shaking the moisture off with a disgusted grunt.

"Doc, you've got to control your dog!" He rubbed his boot across the grass, staring daggers at her.

"Sorry! Sorry!" Cress snatched up a now dancing and yapping Champ, determined there would be no more antics.

Jake scrunched his nose before he rubbed at it and shoved his hands in his pockets, along with the wad of leaves. He took a deep breath and let it out slowly. "C'mon. Let's go find Bo. I'm sure he wants to see you." It looked like he was trying to play nice, too. At least for the moment.

Cress looked at the wriggling puppy in her arms. "You're going to get me in trouble one of these days, aren't you?" Champ yipped and licked her chin. With a groan, she followed

Jake.

* * *

They found Bo in the equipment barn, directing Mac as he repaired the tines on a harvester. Jake hollered at them over the clatter of tools and the two men straightened. Bo broke into a wide grin, his teeth glowing in the dim light of the barn at the sight of his granddaughter. Jake clenched his fingernails into his palms as the irritated look melted from her face and a radiant smile took its place.

Cress brushed past him, the scent of ocean water lingering behind, and rushed to hug her grandfather.

"Sweetie! You're here early. And who is this little fella?" Champ yipped at Bo's words and licked at his beard, delighted with the new texture. Bo chuckled and rubbed his head.

"I was just happy to get here. It was slow going, what with hauling that trailer." Jake stood back and watched as she kissed Bo's cheek and set Champ down to wind in circles around her legs again. She really should choke up on the leash a bit more to prevent that. "I thought we'd never make it."

"Well, you're here now and we've got everything arranged for you to have the guest suite upstairs. You'll have plenty of room and privacy." He patted her arm. "I know this is different from having a place of your own, but we'll make do."

Cress grasped his hand. "It's perfect, Gramps." Gramps. She called him Gramps? Jake shot a look at Mac, who also watched them bemusedly. The two men shrugged at each other.

Bo gestured at Jake. "It looks like you've met Jake. And this is Mac." He jerked a thumb toward Mac, who gave a little wave from his awkward hunch on the floor next to the harvester.

Cress returned Mac's wave and glanced at Jake, her smile tightening. "We ran into each other in the orchard." Jake shrugged and bobbed his head. He couldn't say he was thrilled with her, either.

Bo's eyes flashed between them, taking in Cress' drawn-up shoulders and Jake's crossed arms. A tense silence hung in the air. He rubbed his hands together with a clap. "Well, there will be time for more getting to know each other later. For now, let's get you settled." He waved for Jake to follow.

The three of them set out from the barn, leaving Mac to continue working. As they peered into the back of Cress' U-Haul, Bo whistled. "You sure have a lot of plants."

Cress nodded. "Comes with the territory. Plus, I like plants."

Jake snorted; the back end of the trailer was filled with a sea of green. This chick had a serious obsession. There might have been moving boxes underneath them somewhere. Bo and Cress looked at him quizzically. "It's just a lot of green stuff," he stuttered. Why did he always have to say the stupidest thing?

Bo turned back to the trailer and studied it for a second. He bent down and scooped up Champ. "All righty, then. I'll be on puppy sitting duty. Keep him out from underfoot. You kids have fun unloading."

Cress punched his arm. "Uh-huh. Taking the easy job."

He held up a hand. "Hey! These old bones can't handle stairs like they used to." Turning away, he grasped Jake's arm and shot him a look.

Jake rolled his eyes. Yeah, he got the drift. Play nice. He snatched up a huge plant with monstrous leaves and headed toward the house. Cress trailed behind him, a pot cradled on either hip.

"Be careful not to hit the stems on anything! That plant bruises easy."

He waved an arm to acknowledge he'd heard, then propped the screen door open. This was going to be a long afternoon with her bossing him around. He groaned and hefted the plant onto his hip, bracing himself. But he was careful not to bash the ever-shifting greenery against anything. The last thing he wanted to do was destroy some rare Bolivian cactus or whatnot.

Surprisingly, they worked in silence. He'd figured she'd take delight in bossing him around, but she was content to let him do his own thing. Their footsteps echoed on the stairs as they carted up first armful after armful of plants, then boxes of books, clothing, and other miscellanies to her new rooms. Cress merely pointed occasionally when she wanted something heavy set down in a particular spot, but mostly, she just nodded at Jake's questions and left him to his own devices. He reveled in the quiet.

After bringing up the last load, Jake stood surveying the piles of boxes and sea of plants drenched in late afternoon sunlight. Shiny, dark leaves bobbed in a gentle flow of air as the A/C kicked on. He swiped at his face as a ticklish bead of sweat ran down his jaw.

Cress plopped down onto the floor and unceremoniously hacked into a box with a pair of scissors. "Thanks for helping. I know you must be tired." She waved him off, but he stood rooted to the spot as she pulled out pieces of a metal rack and began clicking it together, already oblivious to his presence. There was still a lot of work to be done. Some of these pots came up to his knee and weighed about the same as a baby calf. And this wisp of a girl had just nonchalantly dismissed his help? He stood watching her, bemused.

"What are all these things anyway?" He nudged a pot with his foot. Bright purple striped leaves on delicate trailing stems spilled over the sides.

"That is an inch plant." She wiped a strand of hair out of her face. "Here in the South, it's pretty common to call them Wandering Jews."

"Not a very polite name."

She shook her head. "It's not. That's why I call it an inch plant." With a huff, she stood up and began sliding and snapping more shelves into place on the vertical bars. He reached over and held it steady for her as she fidgeted with the base until it sat even.

"Thanks." She nodded at the big plant that he had toted in first. "That one is a monstera. It takes a while for them to get that big, but I've been babying it for a couple years now." Flipping one leaf back and forth, she nodded to herself. "Looks like it survived the journey all right."

She pointed at the shelf she'd just assembled, then at a bay window. "Since you're standing there, would you slide this shelf in front of that north-facing window?" He blinked. How had she known that was north? Did she have a compass somewhere? Ignoring his gaze, she pulled more shelving pieces out of the box and what looked like a bunch of fiddly straps as he slid the shelf over to the spot she'd indicated.

While he centered the tall shelf, she began wrapping the straps around one pot, then wandered around the room. He blinked as he realized it was a macrame hanger. Eve used to have one just like it before... He coughed and looked away, blinking at the memory of her fern hanging on the front porch.

Cress hoisted the plant with trailing vines and heart-shaped leaves colored with gold and green variegations. "This is a pothos. It likes bright light, but nothing too hot."

He chuckled. It looked like he was in for a biology lesson, after all. Guess he'd brought that one on himself. Jake began picking up plants at random and putting them on the shelf. "You're going to be living in a jungle up here, Doc."

Laughing, Cress set the pothos in its hanger on a side table and stepped over to him. "That's the idea. But plants feel homey to me." She rearranged some plants he'd place on the shelf, moving some into direct light and others into shade and spacing them further apart. As he looked, he could almost tell by the delicateness of their leaves, which needed to go where. More carefully, he continued loading plants onto the shelf.

She continued as she handed him a plant with long flat leaves that stood straight up. "There's just something comforting about being surrounded by green growing things. Don't you think? That is why you work in an orchard, isn't it?"

He rolled his shoulders as he fiddled with a pot. "I don't know. Never gave it that much thought." He knew one plant with its arch of snow-white blossoms. He had bought Eve one for Valentine's Day one year. It was all he could afford to get her with the medical bills piling up.

Gently, he moved the orchid to a higher shelf. It wouldn't do for Champ to get ahold of that; he was pretty sure they were poisonous. "Around here you just kinda take any job you can get. And Bo, well, I owe Bo a lot." He cleared his throat and glanced at her, but Cress seemed preoccupied as she studied the ceiling by the other window, a screwdriver in hand. "I guess I do like being out among the trees, though."

She hummed her assent as she stepped up onto a wobbly

33

chair. His heart twisted down into his stomach, and he set the plant down with a clatter. This chick was clueless.

"You're going to hurt yourself. Get down and give me that."

With a startled look, Cress hopped down from the chair, and his heart slowly settled into its normal rhythm. "I've hung plenty of plants before." Her voice was low and petulant.

He shot her an unconvinced look. "With what? Silly putty? Because that sure isn't going to do it." He nodded at the little screwdriver.

Crossing her arms, she scowled at him. "Usually, I have a drill. But it's buried in one of these boxes." She waved her hands at the stacks surrounding them.

He rubbed at the back of his head. It would take forever to find it. "I've got a drill. It'll only take me a second to go get it. Why don't you unpack some clothes or something? Just no more climbing on the furniture while I'm gone, ok?" He turned to the door. "Last thing I need is you breaking your neck the first day on the job."

As he hurried to his cabin, Franklin waved him down with a broad grin, his white teeth blazing in the sun against his bronze skin. "Yo, how's the new boss lady?" He scrubbed a hand across his forehead and rested a pair of lop-jaws, newly sharpened blades shining on his shoulder.

Jake shoved his hands into his pockets and rocked back onto his heels. He did not have time to be gossiping like some old biddy. "She's different all right. Not what I imagined for a city kid."

Franklin gave him a puzzled look. "City kid? Naw, bro. You turned around. She grew up here--was in my class at school. Everyone had a crazy crush on her, but she spent most of her time in this orchard with her daddy, Hank." He shuffled his feet. "She moved away for college the year after he died. Guess you wouldn't have known that being a few years older than us. Wouldn't have run in the same circles."

Glancing back at the house, Jake cleared his throat. Dropped out of school a few years ahead of them is what Franklin meant, but then again, he was being kind. "I guess not." Jake crossed his arms. "My mistake."

Franklin shrugged. "Could happen to anyone."

A small wisp of guilt stirred behind Jake's breastbone, but he shooed it away as he waved at Franklin. "Well, I got to go grab some tools. Bo's got me helping her get unpacked and set up." Jake shifted, taking a step toward his cabin. "You got it covered out here?"

"Putting this up," Franklin hefted the lop jaws, "Then me and Mac were about to go check the lines. Make sure they're in good shape before we hit that hundred-degree heat next week." He grinned. "Now helping a pretty lady is the job I'd like to have!" Franklin punched his arm and turned to go with a good-natured laugh. "Leave all this to me, man."

Jake wagged his head and headed toward his cabin with a scoff. Pretty lady. More like a massive pain in his butt. Although he would admit he'd gotten more than an eyeful of her backside going up and down the stairs earlier, and it was … nice. He shook himself. Cress was trouble, plain and simple. No matter how good her butt might look in a tight pair of jeans.

* * *

Cress tossed another armful of shirts into the dresser. Heavy footsteps sounded behind her. She shoved at the overstuffed drawer, willing it to close now so she wouldn't have to rearrange it later. Marie Kondo, she was not. Jake strode over to the window with a drill in one hand and a step stool in the other. She shoved desperately at the drawer again. When had she had the time to accumulate this many plaid and denim shirts?

With a screech, Jake unfolded the stool and climbed up onto it. He nodded her over with a bob of his head. She gave the drawer one last useless push and crawled over a stack of boxes filled with books.

"All right, Doc. Where do you want this thing to go?" He held up a sturdy-looking hook screw.

"Stop calling me that!" she snapped. "My name is Cress, not Doc! We're not living in a cartoon." He grinned at her and she scowled back, irritated by his immature antics. What would possess a grown man to pester a co-worker he'd just met was beyond her. Cress studied the ceiling and pointed at a spot that was decently bright but where she wouldn't hit her head on the dangling pot—hopefully. The sooner she could get him out of here, the better.

Wordlessly, Jake drilled a pilot hole, popped in some fancy sort of anchor, and swiftly twisted in the hook. He gestured for the plant. Gingerly, Cress handed the pot in the macrame hanger to him. Much more deftly than she had expected, he looped it up, adjusting it to eye height without being asked. He was full of surprises.

As he climbed down from the step stool, Cress quipped, "You're quite handy with that. Like you've done it a time or two or something." Suddenly, she realized how close they were standing in the room crowded with boxes and plants. So close she could feel the heat emanating from his skin and see the dark of his pupils against the smoky quartz of his irises.

He chuckled, the sound coming out strained and raspy. "Something like that."

An awkward silence cocooned them. Cress glanced around and popped her knuckles, one palm into another.

"Well, I guess I should get back to unpacking. Don't want to be swallowed up in this sea of boxes forever." Why was he hanging around, anyway? Surely, he had better things to do around the farm than babysit her.

She felt his eyes boring into her face, making her feel flushed all over, every nerve ending in her skin tingling almost painfully. His voice curled around her, soothing and energizing at the same time, like a hot cup of coffee.

"Are you sure you don't want help with anything else?" He glanced at her closet, where the doors hung agape, revealing her dresses and a couple pairs of slacks sitting crooked on their hangers among a startling number of coats. The floor was littered with a heap of shoes and hiking boots. "Organize your closet, perhaps?"

She gestured at the door to the hall, wanting his flustering presence to be gone. "Hardy-har-har. Thanks, but I've got this." She took a step back and nearly flipped over a stack of boxes, barely saving her balance and her dignity.

As she righted herself with a shuffling stumble, she added for emphasis, "It's mostly just fiddling with plants and chucking books onto shelves from this point, anyway." With a wave, she shooed him out and turned away, saying, "You'll be bored with me in five minutes if you stayed." And she nailed the landing by hopping over a small potted plant she hadn't seen, twisting her ankle.

"Oh, I doubt that." He lingered in the hall just outside her door, smirking at her.

She lifted her hands and dropped them in an exaggerated shrug. Her ankle was screaming at her. "Why are you still here? Go! I've got stuff to do, and you do too!"

He held up his hands and retreated, his footsteps echoing down the steps. In the quiet that followed, Cress took a deep breath and pressed a hand to her chest. Why in the world was her heart racing? It must be that energy drink she chugged on the drive. Yeah, that was it.

She heard the screen door slam downstairs and glanced out the window. Jake strode across the yard toward the orchard, his white T-shirt blazing in the setting sun. Just as he was about to disappear into the trees, he glanced back at the house. Cress leaped back from the window and tripped over a box, face-planting onto the bed.

Well, at least he hadn't been in here to see her do that. She rolled over with a groan. Could her first day have had a more embarrassing start?

Chapter 4

An ache lanced through Cress' shoulder blade and shot down her back. Sluggishly, she set the armful of books down on the built-in bookshelf and slid into the chair she had just emptied to rub at her shoulder.

Looking at the path she had cleared from the door to her bed and closet, she shrugged, then winced as another lance of pain spasmed down her back. Yeah, she was done for today. This would have to be good enough.

A delicious smell of spices and roasting meat wafted up the stairs, making her mouth water. Her stomach growled, reminding her of the long-gone peanut butter sandwich she'd had for lunch. A clatter of dishes echoed up from the kitchen and she smiled, imagining Lynn, Gramps' feisty housekeeper, clattering about as she set the table and shooed Gramps away from the various pots simmering on the stove. Cress looked down at herself, shirt plastered to her stomach with sweat, and shook her head. She'd have to get cleaned up for supper or risk getting swatted by Lynn.

Slowly, she eased to her feet and dug around in the bureau, looking for clean clothes. A knock sounded at her open door, and she slammed the drawer closed on her fingers in her haste to keep Jake from seeing her Walmart tighty-whitey specials.

Gramps stood in the door, coughing to cover up a laugh as she shook out her hand. "Your mother will be here in about an hour." He glanced around the room. "Where's Jake?"

"Mom? Jake?" Cress shook her hand again, willing the throbbing to go away. "What are you talking about?"

Gramps raised his bushy eyebrows. "Supper? I must have forgotten to tell you when you got here. Your mother wants to welcome you home. I figured supper tonight would be better than her throwing a big bash on Saturday with the Ladies' Auxiliary."

"Oh God, yes." Cress shook her head. "Yeah, I just need a few minutes to get ready. And brace myself."

"Good, good." Gramps nodded and rubbed his hands together. He wasn't very fond of Leora's overwhelming presence, either. "Before you hop in the shower, would you go tell Jake?"

"Why would Jake come to supper? Besides, he's a bit annoying." Cress turned to her closet to pick out the least wrinkled dress she could find. Her stomach fluttered at the thought of Jake and his irritatingly smoldering eyes.

Gramps stared at her, a serious look tightening his lips. "Because he's my farm manager and your new coworker." He tilted his head. "You're going to be running this farm, and that means learning how to get along with the people on it, too. No matter how annoying you find them."

Cress held his gaze for a moment, his soft blue eyes uncharacteristically firm, then nodded. Gramps' face softened, relenting. Cress saw that Gramps had a point. Jake knew this farm forwards and backwards. Even if he was clueless about the trees, he would know the history of the land and equipment for the last ten years far better than she would.

If she didn't murder him first for smarting off about her "academic" education. She sniffed.

"All right. Where do I find him?"

Gramps beamed and nodded. "He's probably out with Franklin, checking the irrigation lines before we lose the last of the afternoon sun. Head towards the well and follow the main line west until you see them."

* * *

Jake swung the door to his cabin shut and closed his eyes as the arctic blast of the A/C washed over him. Even though he kept the tiny window unit set at seventy-four degrees, after a long day out in the orchard, it was heaven compared to the swampy humidity of a Mississippi summer.

With a flick, Jake turned on his prized Dolby stereo before he peeled off his shirt, chucking it carelessly at a hamper in the corner. He just wanted the sticky thing off of him. Kicking off his grass-covered boots as well, he collapsed into the threadbare wingback chair he hadn't bothered to replace since he moved in. Sure, it smelled of dust and mothballs, but it was comfy and that was good enough for him.

He flicked on a lamp and pulled the wilted wad of leaves Cress had flung at him earlier from his pocket and focused on them. The brown spots he'd always thought were due to the sun now stared up at him accusingly. He rubbed the greenery between his fingers, grimacing at the tackiness. They were unquestionably tacky. Could it be from bugs and not dew? Was he really that clueless?

He glared at the leaves morosely. He'd been such a fool to think a high school dropout could run an orchard. No matter how good he was with a wrench. With a snort of disgust at himself, he slapped the leaves down on the coffee table and turned away.

He couldn't dwell on this or he'd drive himself crazy. He needed a distraction.

Snatching up his book from the side table, he flipped to the spot he'd left off and settled in for a quiet evening of scaring himself silly with the master of horror himself, Stephen King. Just as he was getting lost in the twisted plot, a loud howl ripped through the twilight, making Jake jump and drop the book. More howls followed as a chorus of excited hunting hounds ricocheted through the cabin.

With a sigh, Jake flipped the book off the floor and onto the coffee table, smoothing the mussed pages, and stood, his back popping like bubble wrap. He kneaded at it as he strode over to the door and peeped out.

Cress stood beside the kennel's run, wiggling her fingers through the wire. Zeus, his massive American bulldog, melted against her hand, drool pearling from his jowls. A smile played around Cress' face as the other dogs barked and leaped at the fence, tails blurring in an excited fan.

Jake threw open the door. "I'd be careful if I were you. That one is liable to lick you to death."

Cress jumped back from the fence, tripped over herself, and landed with a *whump* on her bottom in the grass. Choking back laughter, Jake pressed a hand to his mouth. The hounds sent up a unified wail. She shot him an aggrieved look, then her eyes darted away, and she rolled her shoulders. She was kind of cute when she was being such a klutz. Jake shook himself at the thought.

"I can see I am in such mortal danger." She winced as she stood, rubbing at her tailbone and swatting blades of grass from her rear end. She studied the dogs, holding out her hands to let them sniff her some more.

"Is there a reason you're harassing my dogs?" Jake wanted to get back to his book, but that would be impossible as long as the hounds were raising such a ruckus.

"Harassing?" Cress shot him a glare, then dashed her eyes back to the dogs again, cheeks flushing. A puff of breeze flitted over Jake's chest, raising the hairs on the back of his arms, and he realized he was standing in front of her shirtless. Cress' eyes stayed glued to the dogs, and she kept her shoulders turned slightly from him even as she refused to leave.

She was embarrassed. By his chest. He grinned and walked over to her.

He was going to have fun with this. He ducked his head to catch her eyes. "Surely, you didn't come all the way out here just to pet my dogs."

"Actually, I went all the way out to the west section first. Then Franklin sent me back here." He blinked and looked her up and down. A sheen of sweat glistened on her forehead and rimmed the collar of her shirt. Her cheeks were flushed, and she looked like she was a little winded.

"Why would you trek all over creation just to pet on my dogs?"

If looks could kill, he'd be dead, buried, and forgotten by now. Cress dropped her scalding gaze as she pressed her lips together and rubbed her palms against the side of her legs.

"Gramps sent me to ask you to join us for dinner. My mom is coming, and Lynn is making some sort of fancy roast." She took a deep breath, and he watched as her shoulders lowered. He sucked his lips in, trying not to chuckle. She was a live wire, all right. He'd have to keep that in mind. She wriggled her fingers through the fence at the dogs as they whined and clambered over each other for attention.

"A roast, huh?" Jake's mouth watered at the thought of Lynn's roast, which was so much better than another one of the TV dinners stashed in his freezer, but he hesitated. He didn't want to get up in the middle of a family thing. He stared at Cress, still avoiding looking at him, torn. Just then, her eyes flicked up to him and over his shoulder. Her eyes widened.

He realized belatedly that he'd left the door standing open and now the notes of Dean Martin's "Sway" drifted across the lawn.

"Rat Pack fan, huh?" She closed her eyes and hummed a few bars as he rubbed at the back of his neck. He couldn't tell if she was making fun of him or trying to be nice.

Eve would have teased him mercilessly if she'd caught him listening to Dean Martin, but Cress was still humming along. He shook his head. Why was he comparing Cress to Eve? Now, he found himself turning to pet the dogs through the fence with a noncommittal grunt.

After a moment, Cress turned toward him. She looked up at him with those big green eyes, biting her lip. "Look, I get that it's dinner with my family, but the roast Lynn has in the oven smells amazing and Gramps will tan my hide if I don't at least try to persuade you. Why don't you come?"

Jake hadn't been to a family dinner in ages—not since Eve had died. He just hadn't felt like there was a place for him anymore with her family, despite Vada's repeated invitations.

He scratched at his hair, thinking. It sounded nice—dinner with Bo, even if Leora was going to be there. And Cress stood looking up at him with those sparkling eyes.

"I don't want to intrude..." he answered reluctantly.

She cut him off. "Oh! You won't be intruding. Truth be told, I kinda need a buffer. My mom's coming and she's a bit..."

"Of a strong personality." Jake grinned. He knew Leora well. He held out a hand. "You got yourself a deal." He chuckled as Cress took it, a deep blush rising from her cheeks down to her collarbone. "Man, you can make me haul boxes upstairs more often if you'll invite me to dinner."

Cress quirked her head at him, smiling and blinking. "I might just have to do that."

* * *

As Jake opened the door of his cabin thirty minutes later, he tugged at his cuffs, already feeling stiff and uncomfortable in the heat in the button-up shirt he knew Leora would expect. He glanced at the half-finished Stephen King novel, abandoned on the tufted wingback chair by his bed.

He was already regretting this decision. And all for a pretty pair of eyes. His gaze drifted to the picture of Eve from their honeymoon on his bedside table, and he looked away quickly. With a groan, he slammed the door and strode across the yard.

"You look nice," he began as Cress opened the front door. He yelped as she yanked him into the front hall. Leora's distinct trill echoed down the hall from the living room as Cress shoved him into the kitchen, and not too gently either.

"Hello to you too," he muttered, voice drawling sarcastically as he pretended to rub at bruised ribs. Lynn glanced at them and rolled her eyes as she continued to dress an enormous roast with sprigs of parsley and thyme.

"You're late!" Cress hissed. His eyes flitted up and down the green silk dress clinging to her curves. She paced in front of him, hands pressed to her stomach and shooting skittery glances down the hall. She was flustered. A corner of his mouth hitched up in a teasing grin.

"It takes effort to look this good." He waved to his collared shirt, clean jeans, and polished boots. Well, at least he'd knocked all the mud off. Cress paused her nervous fluttering and turned to him. Her eyebrows shot up as she looked at him, taking in his favorite pair of "dress" jeans. He did a slow turn, grinning goofily, for effect. Cress sucked in her lips, clearly trying not to laugh.

"I'm sorry. You look nice," she hiccupped, on the edge of a giggle, "Thank you for coming. My mother. She just puts me so on edge." She flicked her wrist toward the living room.

"Some mothers have that effect." He patted her shoulder, the slick dress warm under his fingers. "But I know Leora. She's fierce all right, but she's not that bad." Cress looked up at him, brow pinched, and shook her head silently, hair swishing around her jaw. He offered, "C'mon, let's grab a bottle of wine to take in there and loosen things up a bit."

"She'll only take a mint julep."

He held up his hands. "I'm pretty good with a cocktail shaker."

Cress nodded slowly and blew out a gust of air, lips buzzing. "You're right. I'm letting this get to me too much. Let's make a batch of juleps and get this over with."

He chuckled. "That's the spirit." As he turned to raid the

liquor cabinet, she grabbed his hand, her palm soft in his. His breath hitched in his throat, and he froze, paralyzed by the warmth of her touch. Despite his better sense, he leaned slightly into her.

She looked up at him, eyes green as the leaves on the trees outside. "Seriously, thank you, Jake, for coming." She squeezed his hand once and let go, leaving him feeling cool and empty as she walked away.

With a muffled curse, he grabbed the bourbon and shut the cabinet. Behind him, Lynn laughed softly and shook her head at him.

"Keep flirting like that and you're a goner." Lynn grinned. Jake stomped out of the room.

* * *

Perching nervously on the edge of the settee, Cress offered to top off her mom's sweet tea. Leora leveled a cool gaze at her, then at her nearly full glass.

"Really, dear, anymore and my cup will run over." Leora sipped delicately at her icy drink as she looked back at Cress, beads of condensation already rolling down the cut crystal. The conciliatory jug of mint julep sat at Leora's elbow, steadfastly ignored. Cress' stomach twisted into a nervous, burning ball.

It was going to be one of those evenings. She knew it. Her mom was mad she hadn't told her she was moving home. The decision had been so fast, it hadn't even crossed her mind until she was on the road. It wasn't like they talked on the phone every day... or even every month.

But by the time she'd dialed, her mother's hurt feelings had come pouring out, disguised as thinly veiled barbs.

Now Leora held out the glass, a faint kiss of vermillion lipstick on the rim. "Of course. I suppose it's the least you could do since you're here now." Cress leaped to the pitcher.

Jake's hand was already there, and she nearly clawed him in her frustration. He did not understand the situation he was getting into the middle of.

A saccharine smile dripped across Leora's face. "Jake. Ever the gentleman." As Jake filled her glass, she turned to Cress, primly crossing her ankles. "Now, here is the picture of chivalry." She gestured to Jake, who shifted uncomfortably in his chair. "Speaking of chivalry, when will that handsome Grant be joining us? I can't wait to see my future son-in-law."

Jake sputtered into his julep, and Cress shot him a glare. She cleared her throat and began flicking the nail of her ring finger against the nail of her thumb, an old, nervous habit. "He won't. Be joining us, that is."

"Oh, is he coming into town later?" Her mother eyed her with a glimmer and Gramps slid down into his chair with a shake of his head. Heat blazed up Cress' neck. Her mother was playing games now. Leora knew very well Grant wasn't coming at all; she just wanted Cress to say it out loud so she could have her "I told you so" moment.

She curled her fingers into her palms, the nails digging in sharply. "No, he won't be coming at all. We broke up." She snapped her jaw shut and silence fell. Down the hall, they could hear Lynn setting the table, china and silver clattering against the mahogany. Jake and Gramps looked between her and Leora like they were ringside at a boxing match.

Finally *tsking*, her mother shook her head. "Pity. Though you know I never really had high hopes for that one, despite

48

how handsome he was." She waved a hand airily. "Yankees never quite live up to expectation."

Rolling her eyes, Cress retorted, "He's from the Northwest, Mom... We've been over this before!" She crossed her arms.

"Don't be touchy! I'm just saying he wasn't smart enough for you, geographical differences aside." Leora sniffed and settled her shoulders. "I don't know why you ever thought you had to move a million miles away in the first place."

Cress looked out the window, fists clenched. "It doesn't matter now, does it? I'm back," she bit out. Jake leaned forward and poured a julep, gently pressing it into her hand. Her shoulders relaxed. She shot a thankful look at him, grateful that he'd broken the tension in her with such a simple gesture.

Leora watched, head cocked. "Yes, you are," she murmured. "Everything is just the way it should be." She clasped her hands. "Now, what on earth have you done to your nails? It's like you just don't care anymore! Tomorrow, I'm going to call Stacy and set up an appointment for the two of us to have a proper manicure."

Cress groaned and stared forlornly at a photo of her dad. In it, the three of them lounged on the grass enjoying a picnic. Her mom looked relaxed in a pair of cutoff jeans. She glanced at her mother, still rattling on about French tips, and sighed. It was going to be a long night.

* * *

Next to Jake, Cress drooped in her seat, slouched against its back like a vase of flowers left to wilt in the sun. Leora surveyed her majestically from the head of the table, shoulders held back and chin held up. Leora did everything majestically,

Jake observed, from the delicate sips she took of her mint julep to how she waved Bo over with a flick of her wrist to carve the roasted beef tenderloin at his own table. It must be exhausting to stay that put together all the time.

Jake gulped from his second julep as he watched Leora study Cress with narrowed eyes. After praising Jake for everything from his boots to his beverage-making, Leora barraged her daughter with questions. Everything was up for commentary, from her nails to her choice of post-grad placement. Cress had barely got a word in edgewise during the rising tide of words. The onslaught had not subsided even as they sat down to dinner, rather, momentarily quieted by the necessity of chewing.

After Lynn had arranged the table, she'd settled into a seat beside her husband John, whom Bo had invited for the evening as well, ignoring Leora's side-eye. John was a tall man with a kind face and was a lawyer in the nearby city of Cleveland. Studying the table, Jake realized Lynn and John were seated in between Leora and Bo, just as Jake was seated in between Leora and Cress. It looked like everyone had their buffer for the evening.

Leora shook her hair back with a prim swish as she sawed at her slice of beef. "Darling, isn't your back just aching from sitting like that?

Shrugging, Cress slid up a bit. "I'm quite comfortable."

Leora sniffed. "I can't imagine how."

Silently, Cress sat forward and rolled her spine into a rigidly straight line. She shot her mother a tight-lipped smile. Jake cleared his throat.

"So. Leora, I hear the Ladies' Auxiliary is organizing a charity auction this year to get Main Street paved."

Leora smiled, her startlingly white teeth appearing behind her berry lipstick. "Aren't you on top of things? Yes, it's time to do something about those potholes before someone gets hurt."

Cress cut in, "Paved? Do you mean to do away with the brick?"

Jake kicked himself. With these two, the only safe topic seemed to be the weather. Which they'd exhausted forty-five minutes ago.

"Cress, dear, things around here aren't like what they used to be ten years ago. The brick is in a terrible state. It would be expensive to repair, which the town simply can't afford. Better to pave over it." Leora took a bite of beef, chewing slowly as she focused on her daughter's flushed face. Jake shoveled in a mouthful of green beans as Cress glanced between him and Leora.

"But the brick streets are iconic. You can't just get rid of them!"

Leveling her with a cool stare, Leora retorted, "Iconic to whom? With all our children leaving, we're struggling to keep the town alive." She cut another bite of tenderloin. "Besides, *I'm* not getting rid of them. The entire town council voted on it. Since our application for the revitalization grant was turned down, we're on our own, so we have to do the best we can."

Jake decided he'd try one more time. "Does the council have any more plans? To help revitalize the town?"

Chewing thoughtfully, Leora finally swallowed, then replied, "Emma Jean, Patty, and I have talked about tearing down the old playground and turning it into allotment gardens. We're proposing it to the Ladies' Auxiliary as our

Fall Project next week and are hopeful to get the council's approval on it at the beginning of next month. With the number of retirees we have in town now, we think we'd have enough subscribers to make it worthwhile."

Cress drummed her fingers on the table. "That's not a bad idea. All that equipment has been a death trap since I was little." She sighed. "Have you run the numbers to see what your initial investment and the breakeven point would be, along with yearly fees, to keep up with common area maintenance?" Jake looked at her, impressed and a little proud.

A glimmer in her eye, Leora raised her glass to her lips. "I see dating Grant wasn't the complete waste I feared it would be." She took a sip as Cress' knuckles whitened around her dinner knife. "Are y'all trying the long-distance thing or is he out of the picture completely?"

Jake coughed as Cress dropped her knife onto her plate with a clatter. "Like I said, we broke up." She reached across him for another roll, her hair brushing against his chest. "And I'm a biologist who specializes in trees. I've had a lot of experience working with gardens and nurseries."

Unperturbed, Leora countered, "But the economics of fixing a town is decidedly outside your area of specialty. It's Grant's. Pity. We could use the insight of someone like him."

What was with this ex? Curling his toes in his boots, Jake resisted the urge to "stretch" his legs. Hard. Straight into Leora's shins. Jake could see Cress' fingers dig into the roll, leaving dimples at the words. She dropped it onto his plate with a soft thump before grabbing another for herself and leaning back into her seat.

With a slight shrug, Cress said, "I'm a fast learner. I picked up a good bit from him."

Leora speared a green bean with a tiny jab. "I would hope so, after five years of dating." Jake shot a look at Cress, who murderously stabbed one of her beans over and over again. Five years and no ring? What was wrong with that dude? Did he not have eyes? Cress glanced up at him as if she could read his thoughts. For a split second, he could swear he saw the glint of tears. Then her face smoothed as she turned to her mother.

"It was seven. And we both wanted to focus on our careers. He's done very well." She set down her fork and clenched her hands in her lap.

"Yes, what was the name of that last town he worked with? The one that declared bankruptcy last year?" With a tiny nip, Leora bit the green bean in half and sat staring at her daughter while she chewed.

"That was part of his strategy. To help the town get federal funding." Cress set her forearms on the table as she poked at her potatoes.

"And it worked out swimmingly. Meanwhile, how many papers did you publish?"

Cress whispered, "Four."

"Darling, give yourself some credit. That was last year alone." Leora shook her head, looking stern. "You've done more work in your field in the last five years than some have in a lifetime." She picked up her glass with the closest expression Jake had seen on her face to a scowl all evening. "You've been passed over for promotion after promotion. You must have more backbone. Stand up for yourself. Not sulk in…" she gestured around the room, "… some backwater." Jake bristled at the tone, but Leora continued, her voice low. "I raised you tougher than that."

With a teeth-baring grin, Jake clapped Cress on the back, as he grinned down at Leora. "Well, I for one am glad she came to this backwater. She's going to help us get this place back to the way it was during its glory days. Hank would be proud." Cress stiffened, and he dropped his hand.

Staring at Cress, who had dropped her eyes to her plate, Leora took a sip then said with a smile, "Cress always was top of her class." Smile disappearing as suddenly as it had come, she speared another green bean. "Her father and I wanted more for her than to be scrabbling around in dirt all day."

Jake tightened his fists underneath the table. Next to him, Cress mumbled, her voice so quiet he nearly missed it. He tried not to smirk, but Leora's sharp eyes caught everything.

"What was that?"

Cress looked up, cheeks pale. "I said I like dirt." Jake wanted to give Cress a high five, but he was pretty sure Leora would stab him with her steak knife.

Mother and daughter sat staring at each other for a minute. With a sniff signaling a truce, Leora turned back to sawing at her beef, the silence stretching uncomfortably in the room until Bo broke it by striking up a rousing debate with John over the best chess strategies.

Next to Jake, Cress exhaled quietly and disconsolately prodded at her green beans. Dark circles ringed her eyes and her shoulders slumped. Jake broke off a piece of his roll. He tapped the table gently, trying to catch her eye, but she was absorbed in the bean's mutilation. Finally, he poked her side, startling her into looking up.

Surreptitiously, he flicked a crumb from his roll across the room, seeing if he could land it in the hall. Cress pressed her lips together and snuck a crumb from her plate. With middle finger and thumb, she thumped it toward the hall. The shot went wide and ricocheted off Bo's water glass with a ping. He looked around, confused. A delicately clearing throat interrupted their giggling.

Leora sat, fingers twirling about the rim of her goblet, as she studied them, looking amused. She raised one eyebrow, and Cress hastily folded her hands into her lap, cheeks flushing.

"Cress, dear, why don't I pick you up this Sunday for church? We used to always go together." Leora said the words with a conciliatory purr, her eyes carefully fixed on her plate.

Picking up her fork, Cress began poking at her green beans, mashing one after another into a paste. "Oh, I was planning on getting some rest after my first week… "

Jake understood that. The first week of any job could be brutal, much less one with the hours and tasks of a farm.

But Leora cut her off. "That's nonsense. You'll be on farmer's hours from here on out. Sunday church hours *will be* 'sleeping in' for you. Might as well get used to it." Beside her, Lynn rolled her eyes; Jake shared a look with her. "Everyone will expect you to be there now that you're back. Don't want you looking like a heathen your first week here."

Cress spoke quietly. "I don't see how taking one Sunday to get a little rest makes me a heathen. There will be plenty of others."

Leora sniffed, the corners of her mouth turning down momentarily. "You've been around intellectuals too long." She pointed her knife. "Just because you can, doesn't mean you should. Every opportunity to worship is a blessing." She added, "Besides, we have a new minister and a much more modern worship service—I think you'll like it."

"I never had a problem with old-fashioned services!" Cress' eyebrows drew together in consternation. A shimmer at her collarbone caught his attention; it was a silver filigree cross on a delicate chain.

Leora waved the knife as she ignored her daughter's outburst before returning her attention to her plate. "And church is by far the best place to find a husband. With *Grant*," she said the name with a grunt that signaled her distaste, "out of the picture, that's where you should head." She waved the knife. "Unless you *want* to end up an old maid on this farm." She eyed Jake and Bo.

Now Jake wanted to stab Leora with his steak knife. They were widowers, not old bachelors. He stared back at her with the dirtiest glare he could muster up as Bo crossed his arms.

Cress groaned. "Oh, my God. If I say that I'll come to church with you, will you drop the subject of Grant, please?"

"Someone's touchy." Leora smiled, waving a hand smoothly through the air. "But yes, if you come to church with me, I won't bring him up again. Consider him forgotten."

"Thank you." Cress slapped her palms on the table. "What time do you want me to be ready?"

"Nine o'clock." Leora smiled over her cup. "We can't miss Sunday school."

Cress picked up her fork and poked her green beans again. "Of course not."

Jake refilled Cress' glass, glancing at her with a sympathetic smile. He mouthed "You all right?" She patted his knee under the table as he set the jug of sweet tea down and sat back. As far as family dinners went, Jake had to admit, this one had more than its fair share of drama. He'd forgotten how much he missed that.

* * *

Dishes clattered in the sink as Lynn scrubbed up after dinner, steam fogging up around her. Cress set a teetering pile of plates next to her and swiped a wisp of hair out of her face with a loud sigh.

Lynn twinkled at her, the corners of her eyes crinkling. "Cheer up, dear. The evening is almost over." She picked up a plate and dunked it into the soapy water. "Want to help me dry?"

Cress picked up a tea towel. "If that is a blatant excuse for me to not go back in there for a few minutes, I will gladly take it."

Lynn chuckled and handed her the sparkling plate. They continued washing and drying in companionable silence for a minute before the clack of heels on hardwood interrupted them.

"Oh, there you are!" Leora's trill made Cress grit her teeth. "I was wondering where you disappeared off to. We were missing you in the living room."

Jake hovered in the doorway behind Leora, shooting an apologetic frown at Cress as Leora leaned a hip against the butcher block island. She tapped her fingernails, waiting for a response. Cress slowly wiped off a plate.

"I was just helping Lynn for a minute. I'll be right in." Her mother did not approve of ignoring guests. And with Leora as the star guest, Cress' stomach turned queasy at the thought. She wondered what little tantrum she was about to throw. .

Leora turned a saccharine smile on Lynn. "Oh Lynn, you must be so tired, what with cooking all day and then staying this late. Why don't you head on home? I'm sure John would love to have you all to himself for once."

Lynn shot a skeptical look at Cress, then the pile of plates and pots left to be done. Leora waved a hand breezily. "Don't you worry about that! We'll take care of everything. It will sparkle in the morning when you get here."

A side-eye at Leora's expensive manicure and baby soft hands revealed Lynn's thoughts on the matter, but she silently removed her apron and slipped from the room, brushing past Jake, still hovering in the doorway.

Cress looked at her mother, her expression flat. "That was very generous of you." She let the silence hang.

Leora tapped her nails on the butcher block again. Cress let the silence hang; Jake looked between them nervously, but wisely didn't speak. Finally, Leora dropped her palms on the countertop with a little pop. "Well, it's clear I've worn out my welcome for the day. I think I'll head out too." She paused. "It would be nice if, for once, you acted like you were glad to see your mother, Cress."

Cress bit back all the retorts that danced on the end of her tongue. She stepped forward and kissed her cheek. "Drive safe."

An inhale so soft she almost missed it caught in her mother's throat and a shadow flitted over Leora's face, cracking her perfect mask. Cress blinked and the haughty look of a socialite was back, cool and collected, chin up and lips pursed.

Leora turned and stepped from the room, glancing over her shoulder. With a thousand-watt smile, she called, "Sparkling!"

Cress listened for the catch of the front door, then threw down her towel.

"Aargh!" She ran her hands through her hair, clenched them into fists, and tugged.

"Whoa." She had forgotten Jake was still standing there. Embarrassed, she let go of her locks and dropped her hands. "That is a lot of pent-up rage." He stepped forward hesitantly, hands up. "Now, I'm just guessing, but I'd say that we're dealing with some Mommy issues here?" She couldn't help giggling at the absurdity and nodded. He leaned forward. "In my professional opinion, and tell me if I'm wrong, this stems from a long cycle of you trying to be a dutiful daughter and her not approving of any of your decisions?"

She sighed, rubbing the back of her neck. "I'm not the debutante she wanted."

His eyebrows shot up. "Oh, the horror."

"Something like that. No education or career in the world can make up for that offense." She hung her head. "I don't know why I even try. We don't get each other and never have." Shrugging, she picked up the sponge and plunged her hands in the scalding water. How did Lynn stand this temperature? "It only got this bad though after Dad ... after Dad died. I had no buffer." She glanced at Jake, who had picked up her abandoned towel. "With him around, she couldn't critique me without critiquing him."

He took the plate she handed him. "A farmer and a debutante. Seems like a weird match."

Cress soaped up another plate, remembering how tender they had been with each other, sharing jokes only they understood, cuddling in front of their soap operas, doing life together. She and Jake worked in silence for a few minutes while she thought, washing and drying dishes in sync. Mom had moved back to Cleveland after Dad died, but she'd never complained about the country when he was alive.

She bit her lip and spoke. "They were each other's person,

ya' know? She brought him a little glamour, and he brought her down to earth." She drew the sponge over a plate, wiping away bits of food. "They gave each other balance."

Jake nodded, frowning thoughtfully. She looked up at him. "That's the kind of love I want to find someday, don't you?"

He made a strangled sound. "Sure." A tapping sounded on the floor behind them and a little *yap*. Letting the subject drop, Cress turned to see Champ behind her, dancing with excitement. He barked again, grinning at her. She laughed and bent down.

"You escape artist!" He scooted away from her, yipping. She took a step toward him, and he leaned down, bottom high in the air with a playful growl, before barking and shooting off around the island. She held still to see where he would go, and he poked his head back around in consternation at her, ears pressed back. He *woofed* and disappeared again. She scooted after him around the corner to see Jake calmly pick up the wriggling puppy.

"I believe this is yours," he said with a grin as he scratched Champ behind the ear. Champ slumped in his arms, content and drooling.

"Oh, you're getting dog hair all over your nice clean shirt!" She stepped forward to take him, and Jake swung away.

"I've got him for the moment. You relax. It's not the first time I've been covered in dog hair and it certainly won't be the last." He looked down at Champ. "Well, aren't you a handsome little devil?"

Champ pawed at him, tongue lolling. Cress shook her head. "He's cute, but I have no idea how to train him. I can't even get him to walk on a leash without strangling himself." She rubbed one of his silky ears. "And the only way I keep up with housebreaking him is to walk him just about every hour."

Jake nodded. "That's just the stage he's at right now." He chucked Champ under the chin. "Everything just runs right through him as small as he is." He looked at her with a smile that caused goosebumps to spring up and down her arms. His brown eyes danced merrily. "Think of this like potty-training a toddler. You wouldn't expect a baby to understand overnight. It will take him some time to learn too."

She bit her lip and looked back at Champ, unsettled by how flustered she suddenly felt. "I just don't know what I was thinking. I shouldn't have jumped into pet ownership so fast. Although, truth be told, a bottle of wine may have had something to do with it."

"Then maybe you should drink more often! Look how much he likes you." Jake handed Champ to her, their arms brushing. His hands were warm and rough as they swept across her skin. The contact lasted for less than a second, but she felt tingly and flushed where he had grazed her. She focused on Champ's wriggling antics, hoping Jake wouldn't notice the heat rising in her cheeks. Champ wriggled around to lick her chin, and they both laughed. "I think you're doing fine—jumping in seems to suit you."

Jake placed a hand lightly on her shoulder. "He's high-spirited, so he needs lots of playtimes. As far as training, just give him lots of treats and praise him for everything little thing he does right. Tell him no firmly but avoid punishing him—it will just confuse him."

"Uh-huh." Cress' voice squeaked out. What was wrong with her? Jake dropped his hand and took a step back, leaving the air around her frigid. "Anything else I should know?" She peeked up at him from beneath her lashes, trying to get ahold of herself.

Jake leaned against the island, crossed his arms and peered down at her, brows quirked together. "That's about the gist of it." He looked at the sink, with a few pots left to do, and cleared his throat. "Are you OK here? I need to get back to the house." The side of his mouth twitched up and down as he shuffled his feet. "My own pups need looking after."

She nodded, at a loss for any reason to get him to stay and even more confused why she wanted him to. Stammering, she shrugged one shoulder toward the back door. "I've got it. You go on. It's been a long day." She hefted Champ up a little higher and wiggled one of his paws. "Thank you for coming, Jake."

He shot her a lopsided grin. "Anytime." With a last pat on Champ's head, he turned to go, heading for the door. As he pushed the door open, he said over his shoulder, "You're not so bad, you know, for an academic." Irritation flashed through her, and she flung a dish towel at his head as he disappeared into the dark, letting the screen fall closed behind him.

"Goodnight, Doc!" floated back as his footsteps thudded across the porch and away into the night. The jerk. And they had been getting along so well.

Cress sagged against the sink. "What is wrong with me, letting him get under my skin like that?" she asked the insulted-looking puppy as she pressed a hand to her thumping chest.

Champ whined and wriggled from her grasp to dash around the room, his tiny barks echoing in the tiled room. She turned back to the cooling dishwater and the last few pots, straining to hear Jake's hounds howling out their greetings in the distance. As she slowly swirled the soapy water over a tough pan, she hummed the opening lines to "Sway."

Chapter 5

⁓꙳⁓

P ale morning light filtered in through the window. Cress groaned and rolled over, crinkling paper beneath her. She shot upright, straightening her notes. Gingerly, she set them on the side table and slid out of bed, Champ whining behind her on the bed. She picked him up and wound her way through the books scattered across the floor, pages underlined and annotated feverishly late into the night.

As soon as she'd told Gramps she was coming home, she'd realized just how much she had to catch up on with pecan trees and their care. Much more than what her dad had taught her as a child. Wanting to ignore the depression Grant's sudden dumping had left looming over her, she'd been studying anxiously ever since.

As she started toward the bathroom, her back spasmed, and she gasped, clutching at it as she straightened slowly. Between bringing in all her plants and sitting hunched over her books, she could barely move.

Cautiously, she twisted side to side and bent forward slightly until the cramp released, Champ whining in her arms. After Jake's comment about how she was saving the orchard, she'd panicked and begun racking her books again late last night. Apparently, the difference between hickory and pecan was a little greater than she'd let on in her ego-stung boast.

Glancing at her notes, she swallowed. She hoped she had enough knowledge after her cram session to get her through the first part of today's orchard inspection. Any mistakes she made in her recommendations to Gramps could be devastatingly expensive. In her arms, Champ whined again, and she hastily made her way downstairs and outside before she had a nastier problem to worry about.

Birds sang to the rising sun, calming her keyed-up nerves, as she drank in the crisp morning air next to the pond. Delighted at the space, Champ galloped and jumped in a wild zigzag before collapsing at her feet. His little chest heaved with his panting; his tongue lolled to one side.

She chuckled and scooped him up and turned toward the house. Time to get ready for the day.

A little while later, she bopped back downstairs, notes in hand, to the smell of bacon and eggs. Lynn waved to her cheerfully from the kitchen, her dark hair swept back in a no-nonsense ponytail and swathed in not one but two aprons. She paused at the bottom of the stairs, waving awkwardly and unsure what to do. The kitchen had always been Gran's domain; one Cress had always been happy to help with. Should she offer to help Lynn now?

Lynn moved with surety—reaching into drawers for utensils and cabinets for seasonings without hesitation. Just like Gran had. A wave of yearning washed over her, pressing on her chest, and pricking at her eyes. She'd spent so many hours as a little girl helping Gran cook. Now she wasn't sure if she remembered how to pat out biscuit dough correctly.

Gramps' voice floated to her from his study, and she looked around the corner. He waved her in with a smile. A steaming mug of coffee was already in his hand. As Cress settled into a chair next to him at his desk, Lynn bustled in with a mug for Cress, along with a little plate holding a tiny jug of cream and a pot of sugar. Startled at being served, Cress looked between her grandfather and Lynn. Gran would have drug Gramps by the ear to the kitchen to pour his own coffee before waiting on him hand and foot.

Lynn laughed at her expression. "Don't worry, dear. Most mornings I just have the pot ready, and you serve yourself. Since y'all are meeting and this is your first morning here, I thought I'd do something a little extra to say welcome home."

Gramps sat forward in his chair, setting his coffee down. He turned to Cress with a smile. "Lynn has been a lifesaver ever since your grandmother passed." He patted Mrs. Hearst's hand. "She makes sure that I don't starve and that I have plenty of clean clothes. And that I don't burn the house down."

"Or leave it a muddy mess! Seriously, would it kill you to leave your boots outside occasionally?" Mrs. Hearst put her fists on her hips. Cress watched them with raised eyebrows, suspicions forming.

Gramps winked at Cress. "See what I mean? Lifesaver. We must have clean floors."

Cress suppressed a grin at Mrs. Hearst's exasperated eye-roll. "If I hadn't known you for forty years, Bo McBride, I'd leave you to starve."

"You'd miss our banter every morning."

Lynn huffed as she left the room.

Cress shoved Gramps' shoulder. "Way to get your flirt on, Gramps!"

He sniffed. "Mrs. Hearst is just that. A happily married missus." He shook his head. "You met her husband last night, remember? John comes over and plays chess with me regularly." Cress blinked, having completely forgotten the bland-looking lawyer at dinner last night. She'd have to do better next time. Gramps settled back in his chair. "And I pay Lynn well to help around here in an above-board way. Not even a whisper of shenanigans, mind you."

Cress shook her head, disappointed, as she took a sip of her coffee. "Shame. I'd love to see you all fixed up in your old age."

"Old age! Really, kids these days." He muttered as he shuffled through papers on his desk. She smirked into her coffee as he settled down. He shot her a wounded look, but from the quirk of his lips, she could tell he was trying not to laugh. With a *harrumph*, he held out his hand for her notes. She handed them over with a sigh.

He tossed them onto his desk without glancing at them. Quirking an eyebrow at him, she gestured at the stack of papers, and he waved a hand.

"We'll get to them in a minute. Did you get settled in all right yesterday?"

Cress rubbed at her lip, her stomach knotting. "I did. I still have a couple of boxes left to unpack and I suspect I'll be fussing with how I have things arranged for weeks to come. But the lion's share is done." She folded her hands over her lap and glanced out the window at the trees. "I'm anxious to get to work."

"I'm sure you are. You're the sort to get right to it." He leaned forward slightly, a smile playing on his lips, and Cress knew he was about to pry in that teasing way that always drew her out. "And what did you think about Jake? He's a little rough around the edges, that's for sure. But a heart of gold."

Cress shrugged, trying to play it cool. His dark eyes flashed into her mind, heating her cheeks and irritating her. "I'm not sure, honestly. He's a bit of a jerk, if I'm being honest…"

Gramps' eyebrows shot up. "What makes you say that? Y'all seemed to get along swimmingly at dinner."

Cress squirmed in her chair, the warring images of Jake's snide remarks in the orchard clashing with his courteousness last night. "When we first met, he was just …" She struggled to find the words. "…Very condescending. Kept calling me Doc. Like me having a Ph.D. somehow made me too good to get my hands dirty, and he didn't want to deal with me." She shifted in her seat. "I thought we had that straightened out, but then…" She sighed and pinched the bridge of her nose, remembering her outburst. "I think he was trying to tease me when he left last night, and I threw a dish rag at his head."

Gramps guffawed, then patted her knee with a tut at her distressed look. "I'm sure it will be all right." He sat back with a smile. "I doubt he'll hold it against you. It just takes him a while to figure out new people—same as you in that regard." He picked up his coffee cup and shuffled her notes toward him. "But he's hardworking and loyal and knows this orchard backwards and forwards."

Cress frowned. She wouldn't argue the first two points; she didn't know Jake. But that last one—"He didn't know what leaf scab looked like."

Gramps laughed. "Well, not everyone is like you. They can't

spot disease from a single leaf they pluck off a tree. That's why you're here. Jake knows the mechanics of things. How to keep the equipment running, how to get our guys working together and on schedule, how to prune and prep, and the day-to-day running of things."

He slurped at his coffee and glanced at her notes, eyebrows shooting up. "You're here for things like this." He leaned over the pages. "Actually, what is this? It looks like one of Hank's old inspection checklists, but crazier."

Cress laughed and leaned forward to explain, hoping her notes would get them through the first few days. Boots thumped in the hall a few minutes later, and Jake rapped his knuckles on the doorframe. Glancing up from the pages and plates of biscuits, eggs, bacon spread over the desk, Cress smiled, feeling relaxed and welcoming. He blinked at her, confusion crinkling his brow. It was almost adorable.

"Jake! Come join the party. We're celebrating coming into the twenty-first century with our agrarian practices." Gramps raised his coffee cup cheerfully. He grimaced when he brought it to his lips and found it empty. He bellowed down the hall, "Lynn, could I get a refill? And could we get Jake a cup as well?"

Cress winced at his uncouth behavior. She poked his belly. "Inside voice, Gramps. And you could get your own refill—she's a housekeeper, not a waitress."

Jake coughed and turned away to suppress a grin, and Cress pressed her lips together to hide a smile. She glanced at him and caught his eyes as he pressed a hand over his mouth.

"Thank you for defending me, dear! But I was bringing the pot in here, anyway." Lynn appeared in the door with a glare for Gramps, who flushed and mumbled his apologies as she refilled everyone's cups. As she disappeared, Jake leaned forward and squinted at the papers before them.

"What's all this?" His voice rasped out, suddenly tense. Cress hitched her shoulders and crossed her arms.

"Based on my initial glimpse yesterday, the best place for me to start will be with a full tree-by-tree inspection of the orchard." She ran her finger down the chart as she cleared her throat. "I'll assess each tree for mold, mildew, and pest infections, as well as any signs of nutrient or water deficiencies. This chart will help me follow the protocol for each tree."

She steadied herself before looking at Jake. "Do you have a map of the orchard that I can use with details for each row and tree?"

He swallowed. "You're going to do all that?"

She nodded slowly, trying to decide if he was being dense on purpose or just needed to get more coffee in his system.

She watched as Jake blinked at the chart. He swept a hand over it as his face pinched up, like he'd taken a bite of something sour. "This seems a little overkill." He glanced at Bo, who remained silent, hands folded in front of his mouth as he watched them. "Do you need to inspect each tree? That would take days."

Jake said the words so flatly that Cress dropped her hand from the chart, but he continued. "Why not just enhance the spray and fertilizer schedule overall for things you're worried about and be done with it?" She took a deep breath, glancing at Gramps. He gave her an imperceptible nod.

Cress knew she'd need to justify some of her methods, but having to do it this early aggravated her. But she and Jake needed to mesh, or this would never work; she couldn't start by acting like he was a dumbass.

Smoothing her face, she began, "This method will allow us to be extremely targeted in what we do, saving on chemicals and spotting infestations before they spread to other trees." She raised her hands like a pair of scales. As she spoke, she tilted her hands up and down. "Some trees will have a natural resistance and won't need much intervention. Some will be so diseased that they'll need to be removed and replanted with a hardier species to prevent further blighting that section. Most will be on a sliding scale in between and will take a mixture of pruning, spraying, and fertilizing to get them to a point where they can begin yielding fully again."

She let her hands drop and knotted them in her lap at his scowl. "Spraying is a blanket solution when each tree has a unique problem. This way is going to take time. But it's the only way to halt the orchard's deterioration."

Jake shook his head. "I'm still not convinced the orchard is deteriorating. We've had a couple rough seasons with droughts and ice storms. But..." He let his words trail off, clenching and unclenching his fists. She remained silent. She couldn't make him see something so obvious. She could only do her job and trust that in time, he'd see the results.

Gramps spoke softly. "Jake, we've held off calling in a specialist for as long as possible. We've known that something wasn't right." He let out a shuddering sigh. "But after Hank died... I just never had the heart to learn all that book stuff like he did. I couldn't teach you what I didn't know."

Cress' eyes shimmered, and she blinked hard, trying to press down the sudden welling of emotion. She put a hand on Gramps' knee. He patted her hand gently. "We have someone in-house now, with a wealth of knowledge, and we should take advantage of that."

Clenching the edge of his chair, Jake jogged a knee up and down. Finally, he nodded. "Fine. But I'm still not sure about this tree-by-tree plan."

Cress relaxed. She'd anticipated this argument. "It's standard practice even on commercial orchards larger than ours. It will just take some getting used to. I can train you how to do it as well so that it goes faster."

Running his hands through his hair so that it stood out in crazy little tufts, Jake sighed. "All of this is going to be so expensive. Do we have the funds for it?"

Waving away the question, Gramps retorted, "You let me worry about that. You two just figure out what you need and how to do it." He tapped a pen on the papers spread around him. "Jake, would you get Cress our full records and the maps she needs? She'll need as much detail as possible to make accurate decisions."

Cress could hear his teeth grind as he glanced at her. "Sure." He nodded tersely at Bo. "I've got everything on file."

Gramps snapped his fingers. "Perfect! No time like the present to get started. She can train you on the checklist. You can show her the ropes out in the fields." He patted Cress' knee. "Sound good?"

She shot a nervous look at Jake, who sat glaring into his coffee. It looked like their semi-truce from last night was over. At some point, they were going to have to come to terms with working with each other. They might as well get used to it. She shrugged. "Sure."

Gramps beamed at her. "That's my girl! Y'all get going. With you two working together, McBride Orchards will be back in business in no time!"

Cress chuckled, her voice catching nervously in her throat, as Jake slurped down the rest of his coffee with a loud gulp. He clacked down his coffee mug and wiped his mouth with the back of his hand as he stood.

Without looking at her, he strode to the door. He called over his shoulder, "You comin', or what?"

Scrambling to follow him, Cress looked helplessly at Gramps. He shrugged at her. "Good luck."

She groaned as she jogged to catch up with Jake, who was waiting impatiently for her at the bottom of the porch steps. From his already thunderous scowl, this was going to be a long day.

Chapter 6

G rass crunched and swished underfoot as they walked toward the orchard. Cress clutched her clipboard and tried not to glance at Jake as he stomped along beside her, stubbornly silent. The wind in the trees made more noise than he did.

This wasn't how she wanted to start their first day working together, especially not after the way he seemed to thaw toward her last night. Even if she had thrown a dish rag at him. She cleared her throat with a rasp. "Thank you."

He startled, his soft brown eyes finding hers in the morning light. "For what?" He seemed as surprised as she felt for that opening.

Blushing, she stumbled over a branch, invisible in the long grass. He steadied her with a quick hand on her elbow. She coughed, embarrassed by her klutziness. "For saying what you did to my mother last night." She rolled her shoulders, her back still aching from sleeping in a funny position. "About me being smart. Not many people have ever stood up for me like that." She licked her lips. "She has a way of…" She drifted off, unsure how to describe her mother without sounding like an ungrateful brat.

"Unnerving people." Jake finished for her with a grin. "I've had a run-in or two with Leora. Everyone in Midnight Bluff has. Most of Cleveland too."

"That's for sure," Cress muttered. "She's practically the town council and the mayor all wrapped up in one."

Jake laughed. "I wouldn't say that to Mayor Patty if I were you. You might find yourself shanked at the next festival. Or worse, find your favorite treats constantly 'sold out' just as you reach the booth."

"Now that's maniacal." Cress smiled back at him, pleased to see him relaxing.

"Hey, it's a gentle tyranny, but it's effective."

Cress stopped at the first tree, pulling out the map and a clean checklist. A calm washed over her as she glanced up at the soaring branches, then down at her clipboard. This was her element. Here, she didn't have to second guess herself or worry. She could just work.

As she labeled the checklist, Jake peered over her shoulder. "What are you doing?" His face lit up with curiosity.

She tilted the paper toward him happily; curiosity she could work with. "Cross-referencing the checklist with the map. Won't do much good to inspect the individual trees if we can't find our way back to the one we want later." Pointing at the row, she continued. "We'll do this for each tree every year, so we'll have a detailed record."

A sigh slipped from Jake as he surveyed the section. "This is going to take forever." The crease was back between his brows, and Cress hastened to keep him interested and in a brighter mood. Moving usually helped.

She grinned and handed him a stack of checklists. "Well, you can help me speed things up by labeling the sheets for this section." She waved an arm at the trees in front of them and the undulating branches beyond. "Gramps was so eager to send us on our way this morning, I didn't have any time to do the usual prep work I would have done."

She dropped her arm and spoke under her breath. "Ideally, I would do this on a tablet so we wouldn't have to cross-reference everything or re-log this digitally later."

Jake shot her a bewildered glance as his pen scratched across the pages as he struggled to keep the map from fluttering into his face against a breeze that had suddenly sprung up. "What would you want a tablet for? It's not like we have a signal out here."

Shaking her head, she stepped toward the tree and looked up at the branches, squinting at the leaves. "Signal doesn't matter. You load what you need before you head out. Then you log your data for the day. When you get back to Wi-Fi, it syncs everything for you. You'll have a redundant copy in the cloud that you can access from anywhere with which to plan and calculate."

Jake shrugged, clearly unconvinced, and turned back to the map and checklists. Cress looked back at the tree. Here and there, brown spots mottled the leaves, and the ground felt sticky, leaves and grass clippings clinging to her boots like they'd been glued on. She used her pocket clippers to trim off a low-hanging branch. The telltale velvety brown spots of leaf scab mottled the foliage and when she flipped one leaf over, she goggled at the number of yellow aphids on it. Heart racing, she examined more leaves, calming as she realized the infestation wasn't as bad as the one leaf had looked. It was still not a great start.

She jotted down her notes and moved to the next tree, further down the row. After a few minutes, Jake joined her. He shoved the stack of lists into her hand.

"One pile of toil and trouble, as you requested."

She brightened at the reference. "I love Hamlet!" Maybe they could bond over a shared love of reading.

A puzzled look knitted Jake's face. "You mean Macbeth?"

"Huh?" Her mind flitted through the words and her college literature class. "It's Shakespeare, right?"

"Yes, but the quote is from Macbeth." She watched as he tried to repress a smile and failed. Irritation swirled in her stomach as she turned away.

"Whatever, I was a biology major. Not English."

"*Oooh*, she bristles." His teasing tone floated over her shoulder, and she rolled her eyes. What was it about this place that brought out the teenager in her?

He took a couple of steps to come in front of her. "Hey, I'm sorry. I shouldn't have teased you about that. It's just not often I get to one-up a doctor." He held out a hand with a grin. "Friends?"

She studied him for a second, irresolution making her hesitate. "Fine. But no more sassing me about being an academic." She slapped her hand into his.

His fingers wrapped around hers and he leaned his head toward her, mouth turned up but eyes serious. "It's a deal." They froze, studying each other, and Cress was painfully aware of his hand in hers, more than the summer heat creeping up her arm. She could almost swear that she felt the pulse of his heartbeat through their grip and wondered if he could feel hers racing. Abruptly, she let go and turned back to the trees.

He peeked over her shoulder at the completed checklist. Reaching over, he tapped her clipboard. "So, what does all this mean?"

She tried to wave him off, but he stayed put, way too close for comfort. She sniffed. She was going to have to walk him through it, one baby step at a time.

"I'm cataloging each tree's needs…"

He waved one hand in small, impatient circles. "Yeah, yeah. We went over all that at breakfast. But how do you determine what a tree needs? You looked at that tree for maybe two minutes and got all this."

Cress looked at him a little more closely; he was sharper than he let on. "Outside of soil and leaf samples? Once you're familiar with how a tree should look, spotting the things that are off doesn't take that long."

She gestured to the tree. "For instance, from here, that tree looks great. It's got nice dense, dark foliage, minimal leaf and nut shed, and no obvious galls on the limbs or roots." She grabbed his elbow and pulled him closer, his skin warm under her palm.

An image of him standing before her shirtless flashed through her mind, and she shoved the branch she'd trimmed earlier into his hands as if she'd been scorched.

She stuttered, "Now, what do you see? And don't forget your other senses." She should just focus on the teaching. But it was hard to do with him standing there, looking all muscle-y. Muscle-y? Since when did she think like that?

She backed up a few steps and watched as Jake looked around and peered at the branch. "Well, I see those brown spots you pointed out yesterday. Which I'm guessing is the leaf scab you were so hot under the collar about. And these leaves are sticky and have these little yellow buggers on them, which I take it are some sort of aphid and we don't want those."

He removed his ball cap and scratched at his hair with one eye closed endearingly. Cress folded her arms across her chest and nodded, trying to be encouraging but just feeling hugely off-balance with him standing so close. Still. She'd just gotten out of a seven-year relationship. A serious one. She had no business ogling her co-worker.

Determined to stay professional, she edged away as if she was looking at the tree beside them again. "Exactly." She gestured at the leaves, rustling and swishing in the breeze. "This tree has a moderate case of leaf scab and an early onset attack of yellow aphids." He set the branch down and looked around at the rest of the trees surrounding them, absorbing everything she said.

He shoved his hands in his pockets. "Do you suppose the rest of these trees have the same problem?"

Slowly, she nodded, heart pelting out a wild rhythm. If only all men would listen this well. "As close as they're set, it's likely." Pointing to the trees further down the row, she motioned. "And the further in we go, the more likely we are to find that it becomes more severe and accompanied by other things."

He winced, then ran his tongue over his teeth, in a motion that he had no way of knowing she found incredibly attractive, as he settled his cap back on his head. "Looks like we should get started then."

She couldn't agree more.

* * *

Hours later, sweat trickled down Jake's back, itchy and ticklish, as they stood underneath another tree on the far side of the section from where they had started. The sun now blazed high overhead, and he was regretting his decision not to bring some water with him. He'd thought Little Miss Doctor would have called it quits and run for air conditioning long ago.

Impressively, Cress stood at his elbow, looking unphased by the heat, a slight sheen barely visible on her forehead. She looked at him, her eyes running over his sweat-drenched shirt, and grinned. "It's such a nice day out with this breeze. I can't believe our good luck this late in June!"

His eyes goggled. Today might be the day he killed a doctor. She patted his arm, then made a face as she shook her hand free of the moisture. "Don't worry, we'll take a break after this one and go cool off. We'll regroup later this afternoon when it's cooled down a bit." Finally, a little of the heat showed up in her pinkening cheeks like a normal human being.

Swiping at his face, he bit out, "Ya' think?" Maybe her idea about the tablets wasn't such a bad one. Shuffling through all the papers was slowing them down a good bit.

Cress giggled—*giggled*—at his discomfort, then turned back to the towering pecan with a sassy swish of her ponytail. In the noon sun, her brunette hair revealed playful little streaks of red and blonde. She wasn't half bad when she loosened up a bit and stopped acting like she had a stick up her butt. Or the whole freaking tree.

"All right. What do you notice about this one?" Cress waved half-heartedly at the specimen in front of them, a Stuart pecan with what looked like a rough case of scab and mites. Jake shuddered, feeling like he was diagnosing the trees around him with STDs. Cress laughed, and he realized he'd spoken aloud.

"I mean. You're not far off from how they react to these things. But like some STDs, these infestations are treatable." Jake's mind raced through all the different molds, mildews, scabs, and insects they had already covered that day, overwhelm clawing its way up his throat.

His eyes glazed over at the thought of how much he had missed all these years as he spun deeper into his thoughts. Cress snapped her fingers, and he blinked. "What else do you notice?"

Slowly looking back and forth over the tree, he finally pointed at some spongy-looking lumps at the bottom, where the roots met the trunk. They looked knotted and mottled, different from the usual galls he saw made by wasps. "That looks... off?" As he looked closer, he realized the lumps wrapped completely around the tree.

Cress nodded, her lips pressed together. "It's crown gall. I was hoping not to see it."

He looked at her. How much worse could things get? They already seemed to have every disease possible for pecans. "Why?"

"It's caused by bacteria in the soil that puts the rest of these trees at risk anytime they get nicked, cut, or damaged by frost. This tree needs to come down and all of its roots dug up and burned." She held up a hand as he protested. "It will die in another year or two, anyway."

She pointed to the galls ringing the base of the tree. "The bacteria cause those tumors." He flinched at the word. "They disrupt the flow of nutrients to the tree, making them susceptible to a whole host of other problems. You can see it's already weakened by how many other things have infected it."

She shook her head sadly. "It's a shame."

Even in his uneducated state, Jake had to concede that. This tree's leaf scab and mite situation were more advanced than the surrounding ones. Finally, he nodded, rubbing at his nose. "Ok. I don't like it. But ok."

He shook his head, looking up at the old tree. Every fiber of his being hated that it had to come down; he wished for some impossible way to fight for the magnificent old hardwood that had grown in this orchard for decades. But they couldn't risk the other trees. He sighed. "Let's get out of this heat."

Cress nodded, and with a sigh of relief from Jake, they finally turned toward the house. His mind felt like an overheated engine, filled with all the things he needed to learn. Maybe Cress had some books she could loan him? He gazed contemplatively up at her window.

Bo grinned at them from one of the rocking chairs as he peeled off his boots. He pointed at their shoes with mock sternness. "Got to take those off before you tramp mud over my nice, clean floors."

"I heard that!" Lynn's voice floated out to them through the kitchen's screen door. Jake was too distracted to chuckle. With a keen glance, Bo studied him before turning to Cress. Sinking onto the steps, Jake peeled off his boots as Cress and Bo chit-chatted about the morning's doings.

He continued in a contemplative fog through lunch, thoughtfully chewing his bologna sandwich and barely remembering to thank Lynn. Finally, Bo slapped the island they were standing around with a hearty pat and asked, "So, tell me. What'd you find?"

Cress swallowed a bite of her sandwich and licked her lips, eyes darting from Jake to Bo. Jake stared fixedly at his plate, unsure how to answer. Cress plunged in, "Well, we've made good progress in the far east section. I'm hoping we'll be able to finish surveying the first half by the end of this week, and I can begin drawing up plans to alter spraying and fertilizer schedules pretty soon after that."

Bo nodded enthusiastically, his eyes still on Jake's face. "But what have you found so far? Can you," he waved his arm at the orchard, "fix things?" Jake's gaze flicked to the trees, waving in the breeze, and his stomach sank at the realization of the millions of unseen insects gnawing and burrowing away at them. His shoulders slumped. It was all his fault. He'd been reading Stephen King novels when he should have been studying how to run a pecan orchard properly.

Cress nodded and shrugged, her head bobbing back and forth. "It's going to take some time, and I don't think you're going to like everything we have to do. But yes, it's 'fixable.'" She glanced at Jake with a tight smile.

At her words, Bo had stilled. He spoke slowly. "Ok, let's take this one bit at a time." He inhaled. "What have you found so far?"

Cress tapped Jake's arm, motioning for him to speak. Jake ground out the words. "Just about every tree we looked at had some stage of pecan scab. We also found varying stages of yellow aphids and mites. A few casebearers, but not many, fortunately. And we found one severe case of crown gall."

Jake watched Bo's face. As he spoke, Bo visibly paled. "Haven't we been spraying for all of those? Why hasn't it been effective? And crown gall... I... that means there will be more."

Cress held up a hand. "To be fair, you could have a perfectly reasonable spray schedule and it still wouldn't be effective as close together and big as the trees are."

Eyebrows shooting up, Jake turned to look at her. He crossed his arms. "Aren't trees supposed to be… big?"

Grimacing, Cress shook her head. "Usually, they would have been hedged, so they'd top out at forty feet, making your sprayers more effective. And it doesn't look like they were ever thinned past forty feet apart. At their stage of growth, they should be eighty to allow for optimal airflow." Both Jake and Bo slumped against the island, and she pressed forward, murmuring. "Better spacing would allow for better pollination, more air to get to the leaves so they can dry out between rains and sprays and prevent mildew, as well as keep branches from hitting each other and causing damage."

Bo sank his face into his hands. "It's been twenty years since we last thinned. We were coming up on it just before Hank died, but when… well, that just completely left my mind."

A sour ball formed in Jake's stomach. "You're talking about reducing the number of trees by nearly half!"

Cress bit her lip, then stood up straighter. "But from the look of things, you have a third of the nuts forming on the trees that you should have. And I'll bet those aren't filling properly, are they?"

Jake looked at Bo. The old man shook his head. Looking out the window, he whispered, "No."

They stood in silence for a moment, Bo staring out at the orchard, his eyes glistening. Jake seethed. Who was she to make Bo feel like a failure? To come in here and tell them everything they'd done was a disaster? He glared at Cress. From what Franklin had told him, Bo had hung onto this place by his fingernails after Hank passed away. And where was Cress? Off at some fancy college. His chest heaved with angry breaths.

Cress leaned forward and took Bo's hand. "Hey, the orchard is going to be fine. We'll know the nitty-gritty when I finish the survey." She took a breath. "And the property itself is in great shape. Jake's done a good job running the place." Jake simmered down at the unexpected compliment. "The irrigation lines are immaculate. You've got great cover crops, and everything is clean under the trees. That will go a long way in helping things bounce back."

Patting her hand, Bo smiled, his eyes watery. "Your dad would be so proud of you." He looked between them. "Y'all make a fine team." He rubbed his eyes and sighed. "I should get back to the barn and help Mac and Franklin with that tractor. I'll let you two get back to it." He shuffled out the door. Jake listened as he made his way down the steps.

"Did you have to be that harsh?" he said, turning back to Cress.

Cress paused, a wad of sandwich in her cheek. "What?"

"You wrecked him!"

She set the sandwich down. "He needed to know what we're up against. Sorry if I didn't sugarcoat it to your liking!" She threw up her hands, a bright dot of mustard coating her palm.

"You could have been a little gentler, is all I'm saying," Jake grumbled.

"You'd think he was your grandpa from the way you're going on about it." She picked up her sandwich and took an angry bite. Chewing, she explained, "Look, I just want both of you to know that this isn't going to be easy. I can't snap my fingers and make this place perfect. We're looking at three to five years before we see a profit out of this place."

Jake drummed his fingers. Three to five years? He had been

hoping for more like one or two and then they could part ways. She swallowed the bite she'd been chewing. "And that's with an aggressive plan. If we have the funds to swing all the work that needs to be done." Taking another bite, she pointed the sandwich at him. "If not, we'll have to stage each section, doing what we can as we go and praying for no setbacks. It will get exponentially longer."

Jake leaned his hip against the island, already shaking his head. "Well…" but he was lost for words. She clearly knew more than he did in this situation. He sighed and rubbed his hands over his face. "Where do you propose we start next?" The sooner they got to work, the sooner he could get her off his farm.

She set her plate in the sink. "I need to check the Tedder's traps and make sure we don't have too many pecan weevils to deal with."

"Tedder's traps?" he scrunched his nose.

"Yeah, you know. Big. Pyramid-shaped. Made of painted plywood with some sort of cup on top." She spread her hands above her head, then across her shoulders.

He grimaced. "Oh. Those things. I took them down a couple years back. They were hard to mow around."

She groaned and set her hands on her hips. Staring at the ceiling, she blew out a stream of air. "Well, do you know where they are?"

He shrugged. "I think they're in the back of the barn somewhere."

She walked out onto the porch. "Come on then. I guess we're going to spend the afternoon putting them back up."

He took a deep breath and counted to ten. He did not sign up for being bossed around like this. Her voice floated to him through the door, "We haven't got all day!" He clenched his jaw, then walked out to join her.

* * *

Friday evening, they sat around the dining room table, bowls of Lynn's amazing red beans and rice and pages and pages of Cress' notes spread before them. Cress tried not to fidget, but the tension was unbearable. Underneath the table, she jogged her knee up and down.

Jake reached out and placed a hand on her knee, nodding to the vibrating water glasses. As the warmth of his palm raced up her leg, she mouthed, "Sorry."

Gramps took off his glasses and polished them. "All right, Cress. Let's go over this one more time. For now, you want to do... nothing?"

Cress shook her head. "I want to adjust our spray schedule and our pesticides."

Jake shrugged. "Done easily enough."

"Then next week, as we hit July, I'll do some leaf and soil sampling to determine how to adjust our fertilizer and nutrient supplements."

Bo sat back. "That doesn't sound so bad."

Jake rocked back in his chair and shook his head. "Oh, she's not done." Cress shot him a glare. She did not need his comments right now.

"What do you mean?" Bo glanced between them.

Cress picked up a sheet and handed it to him, willing her hand not to tremble. "Like we already discussed, we'll thin and hedge the orchard in January, as well as remove any particularly weak trees. But next month, I'll need to order the grafts we'll replant with to maintain the eighty-foot spacing."

Bo whistled. "This is a lot."

Cress' stomach sank. "We're lucky it's not more." She fiddled with her spoon. "We found a lot of crown gall in the western section."

Chewing his lip, Bo thought for a moment. "Ok. Let's do it. Let's knock this out this year so we don't drag it out."

Cress could feel Jake's chair hit the floor with a thud. "Seriously? You want to get all this done this year?" She looked at him, confused. He'd known what she was going to propose. He spluttered. "That's two-thirds of the western section. We don't have the guys … the money… Where's it all gonna come from?"

Bo swept up Cress' notes and handed them back to her with a smile. "Make copies of these for me, would you, darlin'?" Relief surged through her; Gramps' instincts were spot on. If he agreed with her assessment, then she hadn't totally screwed it up. She clutched the paper, nearly bouncing on her seat with excitement. She supposed she should be apprehensive about all the work ahead, but she was too thrilled to have gotten over this first hurdle.

Gramps looked at Jake. Cress tried not to smile at his consternation, triumph dancing in her eyes. She wiped the smirk off her face when he scowled at her. Bo continued, "I'll handle the money and you two focus on keeping this place running."

"But … " Cress could see a flush working up Jake's chest and neck as he protested.

Bo raised a hand. "Let's not worry over it tonight." He nodded to their cooling bowls. "Not when we've got Lynn's cooking to enjoy."

Cress pressed her lips together, knowing not to push her luck. Jake stared bleakly at his bowl, looking more defeated than angry. Cress blinked in surprise. She'd expected him to argue more. He pushed the beans back and forth, his eyes dim with worry.

She resisted the urge to reach out and rub her hands over his stubble. Despite his gruff manner, he wasn't so bad after all. He cared about the farm in his way—even if he didn't always express it very well.

She tapped his arm, wanting to extend a peace offering. "I need to grab a few things from the Co-Op tomorrow. Is there anything you need while I'm there?"

He gawked at her as if looking through her before his eyes focused. He scooped up a spoonful of the fragrant red beans. "There are a couple of things I need, yeah. I'd be happy to drive, but we've got to leave pretty early." He tilted his head. "I've got drills tomorrow and I do not want to be late to that."

Bo hooted with laughter. "No, sirree. Ruffin will have you running that ladder 'til you puke."

Jake scowled at him, but laughed as well. "Hey! I'd like to see you do it."

Cress looked at them, confused. "Ladder?"

Bo slapped Jake on the back. "Jake is a volunteer firefighter, as if he didn't have enough to do." He patted his shoulder. "Although, I think he just does it to have an excuse to go into town more often."

Good-naturedly, Jake rolled his shoulders. "Somebody's gotta run all those errands for you and Lynn." He smirked at Cress, making her heartbeat speed up. "Besides, Willow's danishes are to die for."

Bo jabbed his spoon in his direction. "At the rate you eat

them, you're going to die for them."

Cress grinned at their comfortable bickering. Everything was working itself out.

Chapter 7

Honking the horn of his truck again, Jake slouched down in his seat as he waited for Cress to emerge from the house the next morning. He'd forgotten it took women this long to get ready. His mind flitted to Eve twisting up her dark hair for the night, the smell of shea butter hauntingly sweet, and he squeezed his eyes shut, trying to block the memory out. They hadn't even left the property yet, and he was already regretting promising to take Cress to the Co-Op today.

He didn't need anything for once, but it had seemed like a good idea last night. The way Cress had smiled, looking at him with those eyes, green as fresh spring grass, her face softening…

He bashed the horn again, only to leap out of his skin at a soft tap on the window. Cress smiled and waved tentatively as he reached over to pop the lock of the side door. She slid into the seat, the heady smell of her shampoo filling the cab with ocean water, like salt and vanilla. Jake tightened his grip on the steering wheel as they pulled away from the house. She yawned and thunked her head back into the headrest with a groan.

"Tell me again why we're going so early?" she scowled as he turned from the gravel road out onto the paved highway. Absentmindedly, she rubbed at her hands, covered in angry-looking scratches and cuts after working out in the orchard all week without a good pair of gloves. After struggling in a pair that was way too large for most of a day, she'd finally thrown them off and gone bare-handed.

He chuckled at her stubbornness and her early-morning petulance. Just like someone else he knew. "So, I can get to the station on time." The real reason was to miss the worst of the town's gossips, but she didn't need to know that. "You do not want to know what Ruffin will do to me if I'm late."

Cress grinned at him. "Oh yeah, the ladder of death. Or intense puking." She yawned again and stretched her arms out in front of her. "But still. I didn't have a chance to grab a cup of coffee—no one's going to be up. Are they even going to be open?"

"Vada runs on farmer time: open at dawn, closed at sunset." If he was lucky, his sister-in-law would still be nursing her first cup o' joe and would miss the fact that he was bringing in a woman. And a dang pretty one at that. He glanced over at Cress, who looked back at him, face calm and eyes heavy with sleep. "Farmer time is your time now, too." Cress just stared back at him, mouth twitching rebelliously.

"Vada... Vada Wilson?"

Jake shot her a sharp look. He kept forgetting she was from around here. "Yes?" How did she know Vada?

A smile cracked her face, like the sun just beginning to peek over the horizon before them. She grabbed his arm excitedly, and he hissed as he jerked the wheel to keep the truck from swerving off the road.

"You have got to stop surprising me!"

"Sorry!" She did not look sorry, not one bit with that luminous smile plastered across her glowing face. "It's just I haven't seen Vada in years. We lost touch back in college—we both just got so busy." He stared at her as she babbled. "Sorry, sorry. Vada was my best friend in high school. When I moved away for college, well, we grew apart." She frowned, lost in thought.

He nodded as if he followed a word. He was several years older than Vada, which would explain why he hadn't known Cress. But he also hadn't made it out of high school. Even years later, he couldn't decide whether failing biology had been a blessing or hindrance. It had let him meet Eve, after all.

Cress' chatter drew him back from his brooding. "I wonder if she ever got married? Or started that ranch?" She wrung her hands together. "I really should have stayed in touch. I've missed so much."

Jake rolled his eyes. Women. He estimated his chances of avoiding the gossip mill grind to be around zero now.

Spotting the town sign, Cress bounced in her seat. "I haven't seen Midnight Bluff in, gosh, ten years—the new highway straight through from Cleveland. I can't wait to see what's changed!" She grinned at him. "Don't tell me! I want to be surprised."

He bit the inside of his cheek, thinking of the shoddy buildings and abandoned storefronts. "Well, this should be an interesting trip for you then." He turned onto Main Street.

"We'll stop by Willow's first for coffee."

As they drove down Main Street, quiet in the early morning air, Cress fell silent, her eyes growing wide and serious. She leaned forward and peered out the window. Building after building stood dark and hollow, faded and curling butcher paper taped across the windows. Once pristine white paint, flaked and peeled in long strips from the timber frame buildings, fell to the ground in powdery piles. In some spots, roofs caved in from years of neglect. Wind rustled through sun-bleached grass and ragweed in open lots, empty of anything but piles of crumbling cinder blocks.

The tires of Jake's truck rumbled over the brick streets, hitting pothole after pothole. After skidding through one enormous crater, Cress burst out, "What happened here?" She pointed at one shop, its butcher paper slowly falling away from the window in long, sagging heaps. "That's Mr. Ed's Sandwich Shoppe. I used to go there every day after school. When did it close?"

Glancing at her distressed face, Jake pointed at a side street. In the distance stood a large industrial building, covered in rust and surrounded by a collapsing chain link fence. "Catfish processing plant closed about fifteen years ago. I'm guessing not long after you left for college."

She pressed a hand over her mouth. "I mean, I knew things were getting tough the last… the last time I was here. But I didn't know it was this bad."

He shrugged. "When your primary source of jobs dries up and your aging, small farmers can't compete with big-agri anymore, this happens." He looked around, the exhaustion and anger he could usually bury welling up. "This has happened all across the Mississippi Delta. With nothing else to sustain it, the small-town way of life is just dying out."

Cress' brow knit and she glanced down at her clasped hands, knuckles white. He scrubbed a hand across his face and sighed. "The mayor and town council's been talking about some revitalization project they're trying to get a grant for, but…" He waved a hand dismissively. "It is what it is, I think."

Jake parked outside the Loveless Bake Shop—one of a few brightly lit, cheerful-looking shops clustered in the middle of Main Street around the Courthouse and Post Office. He could see Willow Loveless bustling around inside, getting ready to start the day. His stomach growled at the thought of her danishes, and he reached for the door handle just as he spotted Cress surreptitiously swiping at her face. He paused and turned to her.

She glanced up at him, eyes misty, and he blinked in surprise. "It isn't right." She spat out the words, and Jake sat back.

"Right ain't got nothin' to do with it. These big companies come in and pull out and they don't think of the impact they have on small towns." He squeezed her hand. "We just make the best of it."

"That might be. But it still ain't right," she whispered, squeezing his hand back. "I should have been here. To help."

"And what would you have done, other than missing out on the education that's helping your grandfather now?" he asked with a chuckle, at hearing the first hint of a Southern accent from her. It was kinda cute.

"I don't know. Sumthin'." She withdrew her hand and crossed her arms, brows knit in exasperation. In the small cabin, he could hear her stomach growl. He shook his head; he knew a hangry woman when he saw one. Best to feed them as soon as possible. Although his own growling stomach told him he wasn't far behind in that regard.

"Come on." He opened his door. She scowled at him. "Just trust me. Come on." She reluctantly got out of the truck, slamming the door a little harder than necessary behind her. "Pastry and coffee will have you feeling more optimistic about this whole situation. And the Loveless Bake Shop has the best in the Delta."

The smell of warm bread, butter, and sugar washed over them as they stepped into Willow's like a wave of crystallized happiness. Bells jingled above them as the door swished closed. Willow kept a string of Christmas bells strung over the door to alert her to anyone entering, in case she was in the back. Jake heaved a satisfied sigh at the sight of his favorite danishes glistening with cream cheese and icing in the case.

"Howdy!" Willow chirped from behind the counter as she slid a tray of dainty petit fours into the case. "Want your regular, Jake?" Her eyes widened at the sight of someone new. She stuck her hand out. "I'm Willow—welcome to town!"

Cress shook her hand silently, then melted back behind Jake underneath Willow's bright smile. Jake flicked a glance at her lowered eyes and Willow's amused face. He saw what Bo meant by shy now; Cress wasn't just a wallflower—she was practically rock moss when meeting new people.

"Everything's good, so just let me know what you want," he murmured to her. She nodded, but still didn't speak.

He turned to Willow with a shrug. "Two coffees and my usual danish." He glanced at Cress, who was eyeing the ginormous sticky buns. "And let's get one of those sticky buns as well."

"Coming right up!" As Willow bustled around pouring coffees and tucking pastries into bright white to-go bags, Jake watched Cress as she floated around the shop, taking in the gingham topped tables with flower vases and the wine rack on the wall.

"This is a popular date spot," he explained. "Willow usually stays open late on Fridays and Saturdays so couples can stop by for a slice of cake or bread pudding and get a nice glass of wine." He called over his shoulder. "If I'm not mistaken, this is the only place in town that carries an alcohol license outside of the package liquor, right, Willow?"

Her voice floated from the back, chipper and sing-song-y, "That's ri-ight! I barely break even on it, but it's worth it to see so many people having a good time."

She chattered as she re-emerged. "That new Baptist preacher keeps telling me I'm leading the people astray, but even Jesus turned water into wine, so I don't think what I do here counts as debauchery. Eh-spe-cia-lly not when it brings two people closer together." She winked at Jake and handed him his crisp paper bag and coffee cup with an unnecessary flourish. He tried to glare at her blatant hint, but the smell of the warm danish distracted him.

Cress suppressed a coughing fit at his nonplussed look until Willow plopped another white paper bag, warm and fragrant with cinnamon and sugar, into her hands. She reached for her purse, but Jake waved her away. It was her first trip to town in God-knows-how-long; she should enjoy it.

She stuck her nose into the bag with a contented smile. Grinning, Jake paid Willow as Cress pulled the sticky bun out with a happy sigh. With an exaggerated wink and thumbs up, Willow pointed at Cress and mouthed, "Cute!"

Jake made a cutting motion with his hand to stop her theatrics just as Cress looked up. She glanced between them suspiciously. With a shrug, Willow widened her eyes innocently. He wasn't going to avoid the town gossips with Cress; he just hadn't counted on Willow being in on it too.

"You'll have to let me know how you like that, hon!" She handed Cress a cup of coffee. "I've been working on getting my spice mixture perrr-fect and I need taste testers."

Cress nodded, still silent but smiling, as she took a big bite while they headed for the door. She groaned with happiness, and Jake grinned at her.

"I'll take that as a good sign!" Willow called after them just as the door closed with a jingle.

"So that was Willow," he said with a wave at the glowing door. They strolled toward the Co-Op in the brisk morning air. Fog roiled gently through the town square, licking up lampposts and softening the edges of the buildings so that they seemed almost... charming.

Licking her lips, Cress asked, "I don't remember her?"

"She moved here from Atlanta a few years back when the town offered store fronts free of rent for the first two years to entrepreneurs as an attempt to revitalize the town. Been a fixture ever since."

Cress nodded as she munched, mouth full. "She seemed bubbly." Away from the bakery, she was no longer tongue-tied.

"That's one way to describe her." Jake nodded. "She's as sweet as the pastries she bakes. Always helping people out; usually getting herself into trouble while doing it. Ruffin has had to rescue her more times than a cat stuck in a tree."

"Well, I like her. And the sticky bun has nothing to do with it." Cress took another big bite. She spoke around the sugary mass. "Although it is a bonus."

Jake looked at her with raised eyebrows. "Really? You seemed like you wanted to melt through the floor."

Cress took a sip of her coffee, wincing at the heat. "I just don't know what to say around new people. I have no idea what they expect me to do. My mind is telling me to do so many things that I just freeze up."

"That seems rough." Jake looked down at her as she kicked at a loose brick, feeling a surge of protectiveness well up.

"You have no idea." She balled up the paper bag and tossed it into a trash can outside the Co-Op. "Anyway, I manage." She motioned to the door, dismissing the topic, and he frowned, wanting to know more. That would have to wait. "Shall we?"

* * *

As Jake held the door open for her, Cress brushed past him, trying not to be distracted by the clean cedarwood smell of his cologne. Her traitorous stomach fluttered at the masculine scent despite the sticky bun she'd just fed it, and her mind flitted to what it would be like to bury her nose in the nape of his neck and curl up for a nap.

Thankfully, the familiar bite of fertilizer and stench of rawhide washed over them as they strode into the Co-Op, driving such silly thoughts from her head. Cress looked up at the jangling strand of bells above them. Did every shop have these now?

A "halloo" echoed to them from the interior of the store, and they followed a string of flickering fluorescents toward it. Cress surveyed the shelves packed with gloves, boots, and every variety of gardening tools she could imagine. Faded signs drooped from the ceiling promising tackle, feed, seeds, and more above never-ending rows. As they rounded the end of the aisle, Cress spotted Vada leaning sleepily against the side of a hexagonal checkout desk, a coffee mug clenched between her hands.

Cress grinned; her best friend from high school had never been a morning person despite the hours she kept. Vada's dark hair spiraled out in a soft pouf from her head, unchanged since high school. And her ebony skin glowed, even in the dim light, with the same warmth Cress remembered.

"I hope you know what you're looking for, Jake, because you know I'm useless before I've had my coffee." Vada scowled into her steaming mug.

Jake grinned at her. "I hope you're able to perk up a little because I brought you a surprise."

Vada looked up sharply, her eyes darting to Cress hovering behind his elbow. Her mouth dropped into a perfect little O, then a grin, wide and dazzling, dimpled her cheeks. She set down her mug and swung the counter door up.

"Oh my God!" Her voice reached peak squeal as she bundled Cress into an arm-clenching hug. "Is that you, Cress McBride? I can't believe it. Where have you been all these years?"

Cress croaked as she patted awkwardly at Vada's back. "Good to see you too, Vada!"

Vada released her and looked her up and down. "I see you haven't left behind your trusty boots." She motioned to Cress' mud-caked hiking boots, the worse for wearing through the orchard all that week.

Awkwardly, Cress laughed. "Ye-ah. I never got into high heels and things. My mom is still pretty mad about it."

Vada tossed her head back with a delightful roar. "But I loved you for it. Gave me someone to go tramping with." She reached for her coffee mug. "And you weren't precious about your shoes around my horses."

Cress touched her arm. "Say, did you ever start that ranch like you wanted?"

With a wince, Vada shook her head. "No money. Plus, I discovered winters out west are too cold for my blood after I interned on a dude ranch one season." She took a sip. "But I am about to open up an equestrian school out at my parents' old barn. They've let me have the run of the place. Won't be much to look at, at first. But I'll be able to offer stabling and basic riding lessons." She shrugged. "Enough farmers' kids in the area want lessons it should work."

"That's fantastic!" Cress leaned forward, eyes sparkling.

Jake slapped his hand on the counter. "I can clearly see this place has no intention of serving its customers." He grinned good-naturedly at Vada, and she jabbed his arm. Cress looked between them curiously. "I'll go grab what I need." He tapped Cress on the shoulder. "Don't forget your stuff, 'K?"

She saluted at his back as he walked off, sending Vada into a fit of giggles. From the corner of her eyes, she watched him drift up and down the rows of goods, head bobbing in and out of view as he bent for items on the lower shelves. When it came to Jake, it was like her guy-dar was suddenly on high alert.

"Looks like Jake was flirting with you!" she teased Vada. It suddenly felt like she'd eaten gravel for breakfast instead of a sticky bun and she took a hasty swig of her coffee, scalding her tongue.

Vada doubled over laughing. "Jake? No! He's family—my brother-in-law."

"Jake's married? How did I not know that?" Cress shot an

irritated look at the back of his head where he hovered in the pet aisle studying the dog foods. Her heart and throat were in an unexpected wrestling match, and she forced herself to swallow the sudden knot of frustration and disappointment down.

"Oh, probably because he doesn't like to talk about it. My sister died a couple years back. Cancer." Vada studied the swirls in her coffee as Cress blinked at her in shock. Eve had been nearly five years older than them, but Cress remembered her soft eyes and gentle smile well.

"Eve is dead? Oh my God, I'm so sorry, Vada. I didn't know. Mom didn't even mention it to me." Cress touched her arm, but Vada shrugged. She waved her hand as if brushing away cobwebs. Her nose crinkled up in a forced smile.

"Anyway, you're about to find yourself the talk of the town. Shacked up with our most eligible, reclusive bachelor. I hope you're ready to be pounced on every time you come into town."

Cress' mouth dropped open. "Shacked up! We live in separate—What do you mean talk?"

"O-oh, girl! You gon' catch flies like that." Vada took a sip of her coffee as she tittered. Cress snapped her mouth shut. "I'm only teasing you."

"Vada!"

"Jake is the most pine-d for bachelor—tragic history, smokin' hot, hardly ever socializes now that Eve's gone. Makes him mysterious." Vada winked at Cress. "Doesn't hurt that he's one of our volunteer firefighters, too. And you're going to be working with him every day. Just be prepared to be pumped for gossip, is all I'm saying."

Cress crossed her arms. "He's not that hot."

"So, you have noticed!" Vada crowed.

A sack of dog food slammed onto the counter. Jake scowled at them. "Noticed what?"

Cress flushed, and Vada slammed her mug down. "How many times have I told you not to sneak up on me while I'm gossipin'?"

"Your gossiping would be more effective if you weren't so dang loud, woman!" Jake slapped down a pair of leather work gloves and a set of rubber wellies.

Vada eyed them. "Those a mite small for ya'."

"Are these your size?" he asked, his eyes boring into Cress. He'd noticed her shoe size? And how had he known that she needed boots and gloves? He gestured at her feet, and she looked down self-consciously. "You'll wear out those in no time if you keep wearing them around that muddy orchard." His voice was gravelly with irritation, and she wondered what was eating him.

Turning the wellies over, she looked at the sizes stamped into them, then tried on the gloves. The leather was thick but supple and flexed easily. "They'll work," she finally replied. She looked at the bag next to them. "Puppy food?"

"It's for Champ." He leaned an elbow on the counter, avoiding her gaze. "It's higher quality than that expensive stuff you're feeding him and better for his breed, since he's a small dog." She nodded, warmth spreading through her chest at the thought of him looking out for her. It wasn't like she knew how to judge dog food. She'd just bought what the store clerk in Wisconsin had recommended. And it had cost her a pretty penny.

Jake looked at her, irritation on every line of his face. "Is this everything you needed?" He'd guessed nearly everything she'd needed, but she was puzzled by the sudden change in his mood.

Not wanting to argue, she simply shook her head. Looking around, she reached over and grabbed a pair of hand shears from a nearby rack and dropped them on the pile. "That's everything."

Vada cleared her throat in the sudden quiet. "Ok, then." She looked between them.

Jake drummed his fingers on the counter. "Well, come on. Ring us up, Vada, before you tell the whole town the rest of my bloody business." Cress shoved her hands in her pockets, suddenly understanding his tension.

"Jake …" she began. But he gestured at the ancient computer, black screen blinking with glowing green characters behind the counter, and Vada pressed her lips into a flat line and began pecking numbers on the keyboard.

"Need anything else?" Vada frowned at Jake, her expression stern, as he picked at a peeling blister on his thumb. Cress pulled an order sheet for a couple of pecan growing guides she needed from her back pocket, and Vada whistled at the odd order but got everything entered quickly.

"All right, it should be here in about a week. I'll call you when it's ready." Vada tapped her nails on the counter as Jake paid for the rest of their items with the orchard's credit card.

He began hustling Cress toward the door with exasperated shoo-ing motions. Nonplussed at being bossed around, Cress clasped the gloves and wellies in her arms and turned toward the door with a sniff and a flip of her hair. Halfway down the aisle, Vada called out, "Cress!"

She braced her feet against the floor and was satisfied to feel Jake slam into her with an *oof*! Looking over her shoulder, she saw Vada leaned over the counter with a conspiratorial grin as Jake rubbed at his chest.

"Come to the hog hunt at the Wilkinsons! It's in two weeks and I could use another woman in the field with me. And it's great stress relief." She shot a pointed stare at Jake.

Jake hefted the bag of dog food on his shoulder as he rolled his eyes at her. "I am not bringing a newbie on a hog hunt!"

Vada leveled a fierce gaze at him. "I ain't asking you, am I?" She jerked her chin at Cress. "You in or what?"

Cress looked from Jake's scowling face to Vada's bright grin. Despite his recent thawing toward her, Jake still hadn't taken her seriously for a moment since she'd gotten here. If this was a chance to show him she was more than a powder-puff academic, she'd take it.

She grinned back at Vada. "Oh, heck yes!"

* * *

The sun was just making its debut on the horizon, slipping from behind the earth's rim in a showy burst of pink and gold light, glancing through the clouds amidst a burst of birdsong. The bells of the Co-Op clattered behind them as Jake stalked ahead of Cress down the sidewalk.

A dark cloud had settled over him inside the Co-Op. From his position several aisles over in the cavernous store, he'd heard only snatches of the girls' conversation.

But one thing had been clear: Cress saying Eve's name.

The rest didn't matter. He was sure that now she knew enough about him to pity him, and he didn't want to see that look on her face. The way their eyes always scrunched up and their mouths turned down. Like you left a bitter taste.

And worse were the hurried glances and cut off conversations. Like your grief was something catching. He ground his feet into the pavement, gravel crunching beneath his boots.

A huge Ford F-150 drove up onto the curb a few spaces in front of them, and Van Glower swaggered out, a wad of chewing gum already rolling around in his mouth with a wet smacking sound. Jake clenched his fists at the glimmer in his eyes as the older man studied Cress.

With a jerk of his chin, Van greeted them. "Howdy, neighbors! Looks like y'all gearing up."

Cress clutched the boots and gloves, halting on the sidewalk. She cocked her head while raising her chin, giving her the look of an impudent parrot. "Don't believe I caught your name."

She stood, one shoulder forward and one foot back, like a boxer in a ring—if her hands hadn't been full. Jake begrudgingly acknowledged that at least the lady had good instincts for oily snakes.

"How rude of me!" Van held out his hand with a wide grin, brushing past Jake without so much as a sideways glance. "I'm Van. Glower. Neighbor to your grandfather. Hoping to be business partners with him."

Jake watched as Cress awkwardly shifted her pile of gear to one arm to limply shake hands with him. Van enthusiastically pumped her arm up and down so hard Jake thought her teeth would rattle out. "I heard you were coming to town but didn't realize the granddaughter with all the fancy degrees would be so dang pretty, too."

Where Cress' face had been an unreadable mask, Jake watched a wolfish smile slowly spread across her cheeks. A gleam appeared in her eyes as she sized him up while he tucked his thumbs behind a huge silver belt buckle.

She put on a coquettish Southern accent. "Why, thank ya', Mr. Glower. And I can't believe I let my manners slip." Van grinned.

Cress dropped the accent. "Doctor Cressida McBride." At her sharpened syllables, a sinking feeling settled in Jake's stomach, and suddenly that danish from early was burning a hole in his gut. "But you can call me Cress."

Van swallowed as he looked at her too-broad grin. "Cress. Is that like the plant that goes in a salad?" His smile wavered.

She smiled with teeth. "The Shakespearean character." Jake winced as Van rubbed his hands together while he thought for a moment.

"Just like your daddy to name you after a book."

Her smile became tight-lipped. Cress shook her head. "My mother picked my name."

The three of them stood for a moment in awkward silence. Jake let the silence simmer as the sun gently gilded the tops of the buildings.

"Well, we've got to be going. Lots to do around the orchard. Nice to meet you!" Cress nodded to Van and caught Jake's eye. But Van pinwheeled his hands, motioning them to hold up.

"Cress, I'm glad I ran into you like this. There's something I was hoping we could talk about." He cut his eyes to Jake. "In private."

Cress scratched at her nose. "I can't imagine what you'd have to talk to me about, but whatever you have to say to me, you can say in front of Jake." She shrugged a delicate shoulder. "He is my grandfather's farm manager, after all. My business is his business."

Shoving his hands in his pockets, Van grunted assent. "Look, your grandfather has been putting me off for an answer about selling the farm. I can see you're real sharp. And you know as well as I do your grandfather is getting on up there in age. It's a good time for him to sell." He rocked back on his heels. "You and I both know it would be hard to find a buyer for an orchard in a place like this, and I've made him a more than generous offer. One he can retire comfortably on. But I need an answer. Do you think you could talk to him?"

Jake clenched his fists at the audacity. But Cress' face remained smooth as a pond on a windless day. Shifting her weight from one foot to another, Cress looked up at him.

"An answer?"

"Yes. It really would be best before that place gets any more rundown. Don't you agree?" A crinkle formed between Van's brows and almost imperceptibly, he leaned toward Cress, the bulk of his body looming between her and the morning sun.

Jake was standing close enough to see the trembling in the end of her hair. A surge of protectiveness fired through him, and he pressed his free hand to the small of her back. She glanced at him then jutted her chin defiantly at Van.

"You're right." Van smiled at her words, face smooth and unperturbed. "I am sharp. And you know what all those fancy degrees are in?" The smile disappeared from Van's face, and he flushed. Cress continued. "Biology. I'm the leading researcher in hickory decline—which is in the same family as pecan. So, I'm plenty smart enough to turn *my farm* around. So, thank you for the offer, but we won't be taking it."

She stepped around him. Van reached out as if to grab her, but Jake stepped in between them. He put his hand on Cress' shoulder and hurried her away from him. His heart leaped at the thought of this fierce woman going to war for them. And for a second, he believed they now might just have a chance.

Van's voice floated after them, and Cress glanced over her shoulder, eyes slit and mouth pressed thin. Her fists were balled tight as she clutched the gear to her chest like a shield, and Jake squeezed her shoulder reassuringly. "Honey, you got more balls than most men." Van's voice pitched up to carry his words to them as they reached Jake's truck. He slung the bag of dog food into the bed and swung the door open for her. "If you change your mind, I'm real easy to find."

Willow peered out from the bakery as Jake revved the engine and peeled off down the street, jolting over the bricks and potholes.

"Jake." Cress gripped the door handle, lips white.

"God, I hate that guy. How dare he treat you like that?" Jake pressed the throttle harder, and they sailed over holes with a bone-rattling jerk.

"Jake! Please, slow down before you kill us." He glanced at Cress, now clutching her seatbelt with both hands, eyes closed. On the floorboards, the abandoned gloves and boots bounced up and down with muffled thuds.

He eased off the gas, slowing to a more reasonable speed as they bumped and jostled along Main Street. She peeled her hands off the seat belt and pinned him with an icy stare, green eyes flashing.

Glaring back at her, he asked, "You just freeze, huh?"

If looks could kill… "That guy was being an asshole. It's different."

"I guess that's why we get along so well then."

She crossed her arms and glared out the window with a look that was so acidic it should have melted the glass. "Probably." They sat in awkward silence for a few minutes, the only sound the whistling of the air whipping through the cracked windows.

Finally, Cress asked, "Now, will you please tell me what all *that* was about?" Her voice sizzled with restrained anger, and Jake wondered if he touched her if he'd get a little shock of static.

He swallowed, not wanting to talk about Bo's business. A glance at Cress told him he had a powder keg sitting beside him in his truck, though. He rubbed his mouth. "Van is just a bunch of bluster. Don't worry about it."

She uncrossed her arms and turned to him. Her voice cut through the roiling wind. "Bull. I've dealt with enough men like that to know trouble when I see it. And if McBride Orchards has trouble heading for it, I need to know." She leaned toward Jake, and he frowned, stretching his lips down in an exaggerated grimace. "If you don't tell me right now what is going on, I'll ask Gramps. There's more going on at McBride Orchards than a case of leaf scab!"

He gripped the wheel tighter, his elation fading to frustration. Dadgum this girl. She was so dang irritating getting involved in everybody's business. He'd underestimated her ability to stir up drama. For all he knew, that Yankee ex of hers would somehow crawl out of the woodwork.

He gritted his teeth. "Your grandpa's already handled it. Like I said, Van is just being a jerk." At Cress' unconvinced look, Jake explained, "Van made him an offer on the orchard a few months ago. It was a decent offer, especially considering the last couple of seasons."

Remembering Van's face when Bo turned him down made him smile. "But Bo turned him down. Didn't want to sell the family stead. I think he was already considering asking you to come out. And Van has been buying up a lot of the small farms in the area, driving out competition." He muttered, "He's getting too big for his britches."

Cress looked at him, that cute little crease between her brows back in place. "If Gramps turned him down, why does he think he'll reconsider now?"

Jake shrugged, hoping to end the conversation. "Maybe he thought you'd be gullible enough to talk to your grandpa?"

She shook her head, frowning in thought, as they turned onto the highway. Something didn't sit right with her about that idea. Riding in silence, the wind whipping her hair around her face, she stared into the distance as striped fields of cotton and soy spun past them, interspersed with stands of pine. The muddy scent of a far-off storm rolled over them as a thunderhead piled up along the horizon.

"Looks like rain," he commented, pointing to the purple-gray cloud. Nodding absently, Cress tapped her fingers on the door.

"What did he mean 'before it gets even more rundown?'" She shot him a sharp look, and inwardly Jake dog-cussed himself.

He exhaled heavily, and she pressed him. "There is something!" She grabbed his arm. "I swear if you don't tell me!"

He yanked his arm back, her touch still warm on his skin. "All right! Quit grabbing at me." He rubbed at his neck. "Look, the finances aren't in the best of shape. We've spent most of the savings on keeping the farm afloat the last couple of seasons. The harvests just haven't been what they should be. So, things are a bit tight. If we don't get things going right, and soon, we might have to sell just so Bo can retire, or we'll risk his personal savings." He kicked himself mentally as soon as the words left his mouth.

Cress gaped at him, stricken. "It's that bad? Why didn't Gramps call me sooner?" She turned to the window and rubbed her forehead, murmuring, "I can't imagine how worried he must be."

Jake shook his head. "Like I said, you're here now. Everything is going to be fine."

Cress spoke darkly, "Yeah, no pressure or anything. Just save the family farm. Oh, and there's no money to do it with."

Shooting her an amused look, Jake patted her knee. "Bo wouldn't have called you if there was no hope. And he's pretty savvy. I'm sure there's enough money to do whatever you decide we need to do." He swallowed. Then again, what did he know about orchards? He was just a glorified lawn mower, apparently.

He shook his head and looked at her, still staring morosely out the window. "But in the meantime, probably best if you steer clear of Van. Don't want you tangling with him by yourself. This town doesn't need any more drama."

She bobbed her head. "Heaven forbid I give the gossips *more* to talk about."

Her falsely chipper tone told him it was safer not to ask, so he shrugged. "Best thing to do is get the orchard steady enough that he doesn't see us as a 'good investment' anymore."

A stony grin crossed her face, and she cracked her knuckles. "Then that's just what we'll do." He chuckled nervously. The last time he'd seen a determined look like that, he'd been playing touch football with Eve's family, and her cousin immediately slammed him into a fence and broke his collarbone.

"I don't even want to know what you're planning." He slapped the radio on to change the subject. "Whatcha' listen to?"

"Jazz. Blues. Classic rock. Anything with a little soul in it."

He eyed her appraisingly. This he could work with. "All right then. Blues it is." As they rolled down the road, nodding along to the radio, he watched her fingers tap to the beat on her thigh. Her nails were cut short and rimmed with dirt. An overwhelming urge welled up in his chest to tuck Cress' hand into his own. He strangled the steering wheel. His time for things like that was over, buried with Eve.

He'd been incredibly lucky to have found such an incredible woman like he had. He didn't need to tempt Fate by grasping for a second chance at love.

Cress picked up the gloves from the floorboard and tried them on. She wriggled her fingers, the supple leather flexing easily. She smiled at him, cheeks dimpling. "Perfect fit."

His heart sputtered. Dang it.

Chapter 8

C ress put the gloves to her nose and inhaled the musky scent of the fresh leather. Jake had picked out the perfect pair: buttery soft yet strong enough to protect her hands from scraping branches and equipment. With a little smile, she dropped them onto the bed and reached for Champ, whining inside his playpen.

As she hurried outside with him, she frowned up at the towering piles of cumulonimbus clouds; wind whirled through the trees. The sight of Midnight Bluff had shocked her, and her heart ached at the thought of all those storefronts, dark and hollow. As Champ scuttled in the sun-bleached grasses at the edge of the pond, she slipped out her phone from her back pocket and pulled up a number she thought she'd never use again.

Her fingers trembled as she typed.

I have a small-town revitalization project I think your company would be interested in.

She studied the words for a second, then hit send. It wasn't like he'd respond to her anyway, not after she made such a scene. She hadn't heard from him since that night. Before she could put her phone away, it buzzed in her hand, the screen lighting up.

Send me the details.

She inhaled sharply through her nose, the loamy smell of the orchard swelling around her. Grant didn't hate her. And Grant could help Midnight Bluff. A confusion of relief, anguish, and gratitude gripped her heart, making her hunch over. She clutched her phone to her chest and leaned against a pecan tree, a film of tears in her eyes.

It wasn't until the first heavy drops of rain struck her that she shook herself and, collecting Champ from his enthusiastic wallowing in pond mud, hurried back into the house.

* * *

Jake stripped off his gear and collapsed on the cool concrete floor of the fire station's garage, gasping. Ruffin's gravelly voice boomed above him. "Don't tell me you're getting soft now."

Jake rolled to his side then pushed himself up, painfully. "I am not getting soft." He winced as he stood. "You just had me do five extra ladder runs. In full gear. In the rain." Despite his best efforts, he'd been late to drills.

Ok, it might have had something to do with lingering over coffee and Cress' plans for the orchards in the farmhouse kitchen, but he still had a valid excuse.

Ruffin pinned him with a knowing stare, his blue eyes not missing how his gaze wandered to the horizon. "If I didn't know you better, I'd say you're distracted by a certain new occupant of the orchard."

"Geez, does everybody gossip in this town?" Jake wedged his fingers under the edge of a worn monster tire and heaved. He flipped the heavy rubber wheel with a grunt. "Cress is helping Bo get the orchard back in shape. We just work together."

Thomas Pipkin piped up from where he was sitting on a picnic table in the corner with a few other guys. "Yeah, but I heard from Herb in town that she's even hotter than she was in high school." He took a sip from his water bottle, then dashed the rest over his head. "So?" He looked meaningfully at Jake.

Jake ignored the wagging eyebrows of the other guys, even as an image of Cress' perfectly tight… He grabbed the tire and flung it over. "So, what?"

"So, what! Come on, man! You've seen her up close at least a dozen times at this point. Is her as—" Floyd Kelly began before Ruffin chunked a towel in his face.

"Language!" Ruffin ran a tight ship for an ex-Ranger.

Jake huffed as he grabbed the tire again. "I didn't know her in high school. But yeah. She looks fine, I guess."

Thomas set his water bottle down, disbelief on his face. "She looks fine? You've got to give us more than that! This is Cress we're talking about." He glanced nervously at Ruffin, who was fiddling with something on the truck, then made some crude gestures with his hands toward his chest and butt. Jake rolled his eyes and turned away. Mostly to hide the heat in his face.

Again, he grabbed the tire and flung it away from him. "We're done here," he grunted.

Thomas and the other guys groaned. "Spoilsport." They stood and headed into the station for the lunch break.

Ruffin walked over and clapped him on the shoulder. "Still,

it might do you some good to take orders from someone new. And a chick at that."

Shaking his head, Jake swiped at the sweat streaming down his face. "It's not like that. Cress isn't my boss."

Crossing his arms, Ruffin leveled a steely gaze at him. "You're kidding yourself if you think she isn't."

Jake put his hands on his hips and looked up at the sky. "Why does everyone keep trying to tell me how it is with Cress? I'm telling you, it's not like that. She's just helping Bo." He paused and said more quietly, "I don't even know if she's going to stay."

"You're crazy if you don't think Bo isn't going to hand over the orchard to Cress. That girl is going to be your boss one day. Just you wait."

Jake shook his head, and Ruffin leaned closer. "What? You don't believe me?" He studied Jake's face, and Jake squirmed, feeling uncomfortable under his friend's scrutiny. "Oh bro, you better be careful. Don't let this chick get to you." Jake scowled at him as Ruffin clapped a hand on his shoulder. "You already had one great girl in your life. Guys like us don't get a second shot."

Jake slapped Ruffin's chest. "This from the dude who spends an awful lot of time 'rescuing' Willow! Dude, what are you lecturing me for?" Ruffin had the decency to drop his gaze, scratching the back of his neck. "Besides, I'm not an idiot. Cress irritates the fool out of me. No chance anything between us would work." He thought of her that morning staring down Van, and his heart flipped. He swallowed, forcing a blank expression.

Ruffin nodded, his face still serious. "Good. The last thing I need is to be picking up your sorry, brokenhearted butt because you went and did something stupid." He punched Jake's arm.

"Geeze, man! Stop it already. Come on, I'm hungry." They headed into the station for lunch with the others, but as the door swung shut behind them, Jake couldn't help glancing back down the highway in the orchard's direction.

Chapter 9

idnight Bluff Baptist Church glowed in the morning light, the cross-topped steeple pearly white and shining. One of the few buildings in Midnight Bluff not in a state of disrepair, Jake watched sullenly from the cabin of Bo's truck as a steady line of people streamed into the front doors.

"Why am I doing this again?" he asked. He tugged at the buttons on his cuffs for the second time that week. He muttered, "It's not like you're the most regular churchgoer either."

Bo glanced at him, eyebrows raised in amusement. "*We* are doing this because it's Cress' first week back, and Leora will skin us alive if we don't. The family that prays together and all." He drummed his thumbs on the wheel.

Jake grumbled, "That's not the saying."

Waving away Jake's statement, Bo continued, "Besides, after Van's little stunt, we've got to show the town we're all together." He gestured to the crowd. "Send a message."

Jake sighed. "The town doesn't need a message. Van does." After their run-in with Van at the Co-Op, Bo had sussed out that something was up, as both Cress and Jake avoided him. As rain pelted down that afternoon, he'd cornered Jake in the equipment barn while he'd struggled to install the new teeth on the harvester correctly; Mac hadn't gotten them on quite right the other day. With heavy drops pinging on the roof, Bo had peeled the truth out of Jake.

Holding up a finger, Bo replied, "Cress needs us to be with her if he tries to cause another scene." A jolt ran through Jake at the thought of Cress alone with Van. "And the town needs to know that we won't put up with his bullying." Bo slapped Jake's leg. "Sometimes it just takes one person to show the way." He swung the door open and popped out.

"Show the way to what?" Jake hurried after him, flabbergasted with his nonchalant attitude, but Bo continued hustling toward the church.

As they reached the door, a *halloo* behind them made Bo draw up short. As Jake scrambled, trying not to crash into him, Bo turned with a wide smile.

"Why, if it isn't Billy Brooks!" He held out his hand. "I haven't seen you in a coon's age. How're the kids?"

Billy, a barrel-chested man with an imposing girth and owner of the farm bordering their eastern lot, vigorously shook his hand. "They a'ight. Scattered to the four corners of the earth, same as everyone else's."

Jake shuffled to the side as the two men chatted, allowing the slowing trickle of people to pass. Billy darted a look around them, then leaned toward Bo.

"Say, I heard Glower tried to buy you out. Is that true?"

With narrowed eyes, Bo pressed his lips together and *hmmed* an assent.

Billy nodded and explained in hushed tones. "He made me a similar offer. Told me to think on it. Thing is, I want to retire. My daughter wants me to move down to Florida to live with her and the grandkids." He shoved his hands in his back pockets. "But I 'shore don't like Glower. Not after what he did to Lemuel."

They tutted, and Jake rolled his eyes. Lemuel hadn't gotten his contract in writing, and Van had stiffed him on nearly a third of what he'd promised because the property hadn't been in the "promised condition." Coulda' seen that one coming from a mile away with a shifter like Van.

Billy leaned closer to Bo and grabbed Jake's shoulder, drawing him in as well. "Look, we're neighbors, and I've known ya' for years. If you can give me the CMA of the property, I'll sell it to you, lock, stock, and barrel." He patted Bo's shoulder. "With that young lady in there, I know you can turn it into something fine and have a legacy to pass on to the next generation."

Jake studied the pavement, scuffing it with his boot. They'd never have received this kind of offer without Cress. Despite Billy knowing Jake since Bo first took him on, he meant nothing to him, just another high school dropout who worked on a farm.

Even as his own emotions swirled inside him, Jake watched Bo think for a moment, rubbing his lips together. Bo studied the door of the church, where Cress waited inside, then looked at Jake. "What do you think, Jake?"

Jake shrugged, hands clenched. "What does it matter what I think? This is your legacy." He couldn't help the tinge of bitterness in his voice.

Shaking his head, Bo clasped his shoulder. "You're my farm manager. You've been with me for years and you know our business better than anyone else. I trust your judgment. If you say we can't handle it—that's your call." Jake stared at him in disbelief then swallowed. He wasn't even going to ask Cress; he wanted only Jake's opinion.

He looked down at his hands and relaxed his fists. "We can handle it. The only question is money. Between what we're currently doing and the last few seasons…"

Bo shook his head. "I can cover it." He turned back to Billy, who'd stood with his arms crossed, waiting patiently. Holding out his hand, he smiled. "You've got a deal."

* * *

Cress shimmied back and forth on the pew trying to find a comfortable spot for her aching back. Working in the orchard had been brutal the past couple of days, and her tired muscles screamed against the hardwood. A bony knuckle jammed into her rib warned her to be still. Just like when she was a child. She rolled her eyes and continued to twist about until she was slightly more settled.

Her mother shot a look at her, lips pursed into a tight little bud. She'd been peeved with her ever since she'd strolled from the house this morning in jeans and a white linen blouse, fifteen minutes late. On purpose, of course. With no time to change into something "more suitable," they'd gone peeling out of the gravel drive almost as fast as Jake had a few days before.

Around them, the last few stragglers settled into the pews with coughs and crinkling bulletins. Cress turned and waved to Vada a few pews back.

Her mother whacked her knee with her bulletin. "Could you please be still? You're as bad as a fussy toddler!"

"I'm here, aren't I? I was just being sociable." She pulled out her phone and queued up her Bible app. "I thought you would be happy with that."

"What on earth are you doing? Put your phone away!"

"Mother! Chill." Cress held up the screen. "It's just my Bible." She tapped on the screen. "Looks like the preacher has posted his notes for the sermon in the app, so I can save my notes in here, too."

Leora sniffed and snapped open her bulletin. "*Huh.* Don't see why folks can't just use a good old-fashioned Bible instead of all these whiz-bangs."

As the choir filed in, Cress just shook her head and folded her hands, phone silenced and tucked carefully underneath her leg for the moment. The door at the back of the church creaked open, and Bo and Jake hustled up the aisle, sliding into the pew next to Cress. A muted buzz flew around the sanctuary before it was muffled by the choir standing to lead the first hymn.

Jake shot her a smirk as he flipped open a hymnal and belted out "Love Divine, All Loves Excelling" in a surprisingly lyrical baritone. Trying not to smile, she turned her attention to her hymnal.

Just then, a man a few rows in front of them turned his head, catching her eye. With an exaggerated wink, Van Glower nodded at her then slowly turned back around. Her stomach clenched, and she resisted the urge to chunk the hymnal at the back of his head.

With a small tap, Jake shook his head at her. As the choir

bellowed on, he leaned over and whispered in her ear, his warm breath trailing down her neck, "You don't have to worry about Van. I have something to tell you after church." A grin spread across his face, revealing an adorably chipped eye tooth as he sat back.

A shiver ran down Cress' back. She couldn't resist smiling back. "What is it?"

He just shook his head and raised his hymnal, rumbling out the last verse with gusto. Cress looked at the back of Mr. Glower's head, snuck a peek at Jake out of the corner of her eye, and decided she'd save the book chunking for another day.

As the service wrapped up, Bo and Jake slipped from the pew as quickly as they had come in. Leora zipped her Bible back into her ruffled, monogrammed case. She sighed, "We have got to find that man a wife."

Startled, Cress asked, "Jake?"

Scoffing, Leora gestured toward the pulpit, where the pastor stood gathering his notes and polishing his glasses. "The preacher, honey. Pastor Riser? No preacher that young should be without a wife for long. It just leads to trouble."

Cress studied him. Clean-shaven with an inky clipper cut and ebony skin, he cut a smart figure in his three-piece suit and gleaming shoes. "That shouldn't be a problem." She clicked her tongue. "He kinda looks like Derek from Criminal Minds. Just, ya' know, with more hair."

Her mother gave her an appraising look, eyes squinched. "Well, I can always give him your number. You know, if the hair does it for you?"

Shoving her phone in her purse, Cress cleared her throat. "I'm taking some time off … from dating. I think it is best for everyone if this natural disaster stayed away from men for a while."

Shooting a look toward the door where Jake and Bo had gotten held up by a couple of neighbors, Leora *mmhmmed*, the corners of her mouth tipping down in disbelief. Cress rolled her eyes and stood. As she turned to scoot down her side of the pew and beat a hasty retreat, she found herself face to face with Patty Conroy, the town's mayor for the last twenty years.

"Cress, dear!" Patty's voice had the nasally shrill of the allergy-prone. In her hand, she clasped a handkerchief, edges scalloped, and the corner monogrammed with her "mayoral seal." Not that the town had an official seal.

Cress hugged her neck. "Mrs. Patty!" Her voice bubbled with all the enthusiasm she could muster after a long sermon. Patty wiggled her fingers toward Leora, who smiled warmly at her old friend.

"It's so good to have you back, dear! And looking so..." Mrs. Patty waved a pointer finger up and down Cress' outfit. "Modern! You're quite the career woman now, aren't you?"

Being home was bringing out Cress' petty teenage side. She suppressed yet another eye roll and the desire to jut out her hip. "Well, I can certainly tell you everything you never wanted to know about hickory decline and then some."

A trill of laughter pierced her ears. Mrs. Patty grasped her arm. "You always were just the funniest. I'm so looking forward to having you back at all of our little gatherings."

Cress couldn't think of a worse fate than being stuck at one of her mother's soirées. Although, being in this proximity, she supposed she wouldn't have much choice in the matter. She tried to keep her smile from slipping at the thought.

Suddenly, Vada popped her head around Mrs. Patty, hand

on her shoulder, causing her to jump. "Excuse me, Mrs. Patty, but I need to borrow Cress for a second. I've got a question about an order she put in at the Co-Op the other day."

Mrs. Patty squeezed Cress' arm. "Of course, dear! Go ahead. We'll catch up later." Cress wriggled around Mrs. Patty and skedaddled down the aisle with Vada. Behind them, she could hear, "Well, Leora, you must be mighty glad to have your child back in town!" Her mother must be practically glowing with excitement. No one's children came *back* to Midnight Bluff. Although what that meant about Cress...

"Oh, my God! You have no idea how good your timing was!" Cress clung to Vada's arm.

"Oh, don't I?" Vada laughed. "I could see from the deer-in-headlights look on your face that you were not enjoying yourself." She surveyed the thinning room and spun them toward the side door. "Besides, I've been cornered by Mrs. Patty a time or two myself."

Confused by the sudden rerouting, Cress asked, "Ummm, where are we going? The cars are that way." She pointed over her shoulder.

"But so is Lou Ellen Pearce and her minions, and she has been trying to pry details out of me all morning about you and Jake." Vada drug her on toward the side door that would issue them out into the camellia garden, which would be dormant—and empty—this time of year.

"Me and Jake? There is no me and Jake!" Cress sputtered.

"That's what I told her, but she wouldn't believe me." Vada shoved the door open, and they burst out into bright noon light. Right into the middle of a cluster of women.

Before they could retreat, a dozen hands with perfectly pearly manicures pulled them forward. "There you are! We've been looking for you!" The high-pitched, saccharine voice of Lou Ellen filled the air. As the town's queen bee in training, flanked by her ladies in torture, Missy Pipkin and Janie Kelly, dragged Cress forward, Vada mouthed, "I'm sorry! I didn't know!"

Cress just glared at her as she was enveloped by a wall of women who hadn't talked to her since she declared she wasn't going to enter another beauty pageant at the ripe old age of sixteen. Much to her mother's consternation. There was no escaping them now.

Thirty minutes later, she stalked toward the car, smelling of at least fifteen different perfumes from all the hugging. Her cheeks hurt. Hell would freeze over before she'd let those women think she was intimidated by their Botox, blowouts, and sculpted brows, so she'd kept her best "company looks" plastered on until she'd wriggled away. Just the thought of Missy's tittering questions about Jake's "job performance" put another burst of angry speed into her power walk.

In her wake, Vada hustled to keep up. "I said I'm sorry!" she called.

Cress spun. "It was an ambush!"

"It was a coincidence!" Vada held up her hands. "I wouldn't have taken us that way if I had known they were all gaggled up right there."

Sighing, Cress brushed her hair back from her face, trying to let her irritation bubble away. She and Vada had just reconnected; she didn't need to blow up on the one friend she had in this town. "You really didn't know?"

Vada took her arm. "I swear on my horse." Their old promise.

Nodding, Cress turned to the car. She wrinkled her nose. "I

need a shower to get all the old lady smell off me. They're all young, for God's sake. Why do they wear perfume like that?"

"For the same reason Lou Ellen does her hair in a beehive." Vada elbowed her. "It's one of the mysteries of the universe, my friend. Come on, I'll treat you to lunch."

As they ambled through the parking lot toward Vada's truck, the hairs on the back of Cress' neck stood up. A *halloo* sounded behind them, and she whirled around. Van Glower stood behind them, a thunderous scowl wrinkling his brow. Cress hoped Jake hadn't gotten it into his head to say something to him after the other day.

Van put his hands on his hips, affecting a disappointed look. So, this wasn't about Jake. Cress' hackles went up immediately, irritation rippling over her. She was so tired of men lecturing her about what she should do that she was already steaming before he even opened his mouth.

"Cre-e-e-ss," the word dragged, weighted with reproach and a feigned familiarity. "I thought we had an agreement. You were going to talk to your grandfather. And now I hear from our good mayor about some other deal he has working with Billy Brooks. Undercutting me." He shook his head, scowling. "I don't like to be kept in the dark."

"What is this? Some kind of Godfather act?" Cress kept her face carefully blank as Vada's grip tightened on her arm. Other deal? Confusion roiled through her even as she grasped for words that sounded tougher than she felt.

"Our business is our own and I'll thank you to keep out of it." She straightened her shoulders, tilting her chin up. "And I already told you I wouldn't talk to my grandfather. You're either deaf or delusional if you think we're going to sell."

Van chuckled, the sound dark and biting. "Oh, we'll see

about that." He took a step closer, and it took all of Cress' willpower not to cower back. He dropped his voice. "It might take some time. But I think eventually y'all will come crawling back to me trying to sell that pathetic little patch of land." He straightened up with a wintry smile. "And when you do," he stretched his arms, "I'll be here." He pivoted and strode away.

Vada let out a whistle. "What a freaking weirdo. I'll tell you, the last few years, Van's been getting more and more aggressive in his 'deals.'" She air quoted as they turned back to her truck.

"I don't know what got to him, but he's not the same anymore." She patted Cress on the back. "But you're smarter than that jerk. It will be fine. C'mon. Let's get some lunch. Food makes everything better."

Glumly, Cress nodded and followed, feeling like she'd somehow stepped in a fire ant bed, then doused herself in kerosene trying to get them off. One little spark and she was a goner.

* * *

Jake and Bo sat in the rocking chairs on the porch of the main house in comfortable silence with a jug of lemonade between them. Leaning his head back, Jake laid his ball cap over his eyes for a light snooze.

Free from all but the most basic chores, Sundays were his favorite days to relax and shoot the breeze with Bo, just like he would with his grandfather. If his family still talked to him.

He sighed and settled into his wicker rocking chair a little deeper, pushing any painful thoughts away and enjoying the late afternoon sun curling in his lap like a lazy cat.

Just as he dozed off, a rattling whoosh far down the driveway pricked at his ears. He peered through one eye, studying the truck working its way up the drive. From the maroon paint and cracked windshield, he'd wager it was Vada's. Groaning, he sat up straighter and reached for the jug of lemonade to pour an extra glass.

Cress was home.

He looked at Bo, who'd cracked a sleepy eye to study the approaching vehicle. Jake cleared his throat. "So, what are you going to tell her?"

Bo straightened in his rocking chair, brushing invisible lint from his shirt. He shot Jake an irritated look. "I hadn't thought about it yet." Jake just groaned.

As Cress slowly climbed the steps, Vada threw a hand through her window in a wave as she turned the truck around in a wide arc and headed back down the driveway.

"I guess Vada didn't want to visit for a minute?" Jake couldn't tell if Bo sounded disappointed or relieved. He liked to gossip as much as Mrs. Patty did. But for this conversation, it was probably best not to have an audience. And a nosey one at that.

Cress gestured toward the cloud of dust wafting away in the slight breeze. "Said she had some horses to go exercise."

"Ah. That girl's busier than a bee." Bo settled back into his rocker with a grunt.

Jake handed the glass of lemonade to Cress, who took it with a nod. He tried to catch her eye, but she fixated on the glass, running her thumb back and forth through the moisture beaded on the side.

She leaned back against the porch rail and took a little sip, smacking her lips. "So, I hear you got something you want to tell me—about a deal?"

Bo shrugged, playing innocent. "What do you mean?" Jake could have kicked him.

Cress looked at Jake, wide-eyed and disbelieving, shoulders tensed. She looked back at Bo. "Jake said you'd taken care of Mr. Glower and he'd tell me about it later. Next thing I know, Van's got me cornered out in the parking lot, ranting about some deal and how you cut him out."

She put the sides of her fist, glass still clenched in one hand, on the porch rail. "So, want to tell me about it? 'Cuz Van was spitting mad, and I can't say I blame him much right this second."

Bo harrumphed. "Van isn't anything to worry about. It's all taken care of." He waved his hand. "You don't need to worry about it, sweetie."

Jake cleared his throat, and Bo shot him a look. "Just tell her, would you?"

Clasping his hands, Bo began, "Not until the details are…"

But Jake cut him off. Cress wasn't stupid and she was tougher than she looked. "Oh, screw the details." He gawked at Bo, willing him to not be so stubborn for once. "This should be her decision, too."

With a long sigh, Bo swiped at his face. "Billy Brooks approached us this morning about buying out his farm, the one that borders our eastern lot. Because he doesn't want to sell to Van when he retires. I took him up on it."

He clasped his hands and rocked forward, the boards underneath him creaking. "I figured it would be a good chance to expand and give you something to make your own. Jake thought it was a good idea, too. And it would head off Van from expanding into this part of the county. Two birds, one stone. Or so I thought."

Cress squirmed against the railing. "You asked Jake?" Her eyes caught Jake's, a brief flash of surprise and betrayal swirling in them before they slid back to Bo. Guilt wrapped around his throat and squeezed.

Bo fidgeted, twirling his wedding band around his finger. "It occurs to me now that I should have consulted with you, too." He looked up at Cress. "I'm sorry. It's not down on paper yet. There's still time to back out."

Holding up his palms, he added, "I wasn't sure, yet, how to swing the financing anyway, and I'm sure Van will still be itching to buy the land. You won't have anything to worry about."

Jake frowned at Bo. That's not what he was expecting. Bo had been genuinely excited about this idea all morning, so sure it was a home run. To hear him express doubt now shook him. But Cress was shaking her head vehemently as she glanced at Jake. He shrugged and dropped his eyes.

"That's not what I'm saying." Cress took a long breath in through her nose.

"Gramps, I'm not a little girl anymore." She crossed her arms. "I left my career for you. And one day I've got to take over this farm and run it." The bald acknowledgment crashed over Jake like a bucket of ice water.

"If you trust me enough to heal the trees, then you've got to trust me to learn the business side too, to handle situations with you. What happens when the training wheels come off and I've had no experience dealing with the tough stuff?" She looked at them, jaw working. Her eyes were shining, and there were spots of color high on her cheeks.

Earlier in the truck, he'd agreed with Bo not to tell Cress

about the deal until Bo had everything worked out and done. Now Jake looked at his boots, his stomach tied in knots. He'd wanted to protect her, not make her feel incompetent. Bo stood up and hugged her, wrapping his arms tightly around his granddaughter.

"You're right." He kissed her cheek as she hugged him back. "Of course, you're right. I should have told you everything. You're smart and talented, and I know how much you're capable of. I was just afraid of overwhelming you." He held her at arm's length. "But you are a grown woman. And it's time I let you do everything you're capable of." Jake suddenly felt like he was intruding, but he didn't want to move and disrupt the moment.

She sniffled and hugged him. "It's all right." Brushing at her face, she nodded, eyes closed. "Let's do it. Let's buy the land. I still have enough money left in my trust from Dad to use as a personal guarantee for a business loan." She swiped at her nose. "I was saving it for a rainy day, but I think this will be a much better use than some unforeseen emergency."

She smiled timidly at Jake. "Besides, this will be a good chance for Jake to help me assess the land and design an orchard from the ground up."

Warmth spread over him at her words. That she trusted him with such an undertaking, and with her dad's money... His eyes misted, and he had to look away as loneliness welled up in him. Eve would have been so proud to see him take this on.

Cress continued, "And who knows? Maybe we'll branch out and do something like peaches or heirloom apples instead." Jake made a face.

Bo threw back his head and laughed. "One thing at a time, but I like the spirit." He pulled Jake to his feet and into a group hug. Jake stood, hardly daring to breathe, as his face pressed into Cress' hair and her arm slid around his waist. It hardly mattered that Bo's shoulder was squished uncomfortably into his neck.

Releasing them, Bo patted their arms. "How about I go see if Lynn left any of the pound cake from last night? I want to celebrate you being here properly."

Cress beamed at him. "I'd like that."

In the silence that followed the screen door falling closed behind Bo, Jake didn't know what to do with his hands or his eyes. He still felt out of place, an intruder in an intimate moment where he wasn't wanted. Cress leaned against the rail lost in thought, wreathed in bougainvillea. The setting sun gently touched her face with gold and pink, like an elegant oil painting.

Deciding a moment of awkwardness was better than stretching it out for the next thirty minutes, he stood. "I think it's about time for me to head on back."

She looked at him, eyes widening in surprise. "Oh! You're not staying for cake?"

"Doesn't seem like I'm needed here." He gestured to the rocking chair. "Besides, you need a seat."

"Oh, ok." She fiddled with one flower, brows puckered, as he walked down the steps.

His heart tugged at him even as he put his foot down on the top step and turned away from her. He paused. "Cress? I'm sorry."

"For what?" She cocked her head to the side.

"Just." He shrugged and waved at the porch and orchard. "For all of this. I should have told you myself. Done better."

She sucked in her bottom lip, worrying it with her teeth, and he continued down the steps before she could confirm what he already knew; he'd messed up by stepping in and making a decision that she should have made. He'd just reached the grass when she called after him.

"Jake!"

He turned back toward her, and she smiled at him. "Stay. For some cake." She added more quietly, "I'd like it if you would."

With a grin, he climbed back up the stairs and refilled their lemonade glasses.

Chapter 10

"Is this really necessary? I have to mow and check irrigation lines…" Cress waved off Jake's complaints as they tromped through the orchard. He wouldn't learn how to monitor the orchard unless he did it himself.

And eventually, they'd need to split up to get this done more efficiently. So, she'd drug him from the barn that morning, where he'd stood discussing a sad-looking tractor with Franklin and Mac, to continue their inspection.

"C'mon. We've got to get this finished in the next week, or I'll be late putting in our order for the winter, and then where will we be?" Cress threw her arms wide, making a sweeping gesture at the surrounding trees. They had to get this rejuvenation off on the right foot. Lord knew, with the loan they were taking out for the new property, they weren't going to have the money to fix expensive mistakes.

Jake grumbled. "Great. Looking at more trees with the same stuff eating them." Cress frowned at his tone, but he kept scribbling on his clipboard, so she said nothing. A few minutes later, they swapped papers.

"Fire ants? They're a pest now?" Cress nearly laughed at the incredulous look on his face as he read over her notes.

She pointed at the drip line. An enormous fire ant bed had mounded up around it. "Pull on the hose."

From a healthy distance, Jake gave it a solid yank. The section of hose that slid free from the dirt was damp, even dripping in places.

Cress tried not to smile at his consternated face. "Ants will chew on the lines, leaving tiny little pinpricks. Eats up your water usage and makes it harder to make sure trees down the line are getting what they should."

She made a face as she swatted at her ankle and danced further away. "Plus, they're just mean sons of…"

Jake's laugh rang out as he watched her rub her feet through the grass, ridding herself of the stinging pests. Blast it. And she had been doing good this time, not doing anything stupid or klutzy. She stuck her tongue out at him and turned to the next tree.

"Oh, c'mon." He jogged over to her. "You got to admit that was kinda funny." He tapped his pencil on her head, and she glared at him. "Sometimes you just gotta' let the know-it-allness go and loosen up."

Frustration bubbled up in her like water in a spring. "I am loose!" She batted at him as he wiggled his eyebrows and laughed. "Not that way!" She took a deep breath. "I just mean that with my job, I take things seriously and when it comes to other stuff, I'm more laid back. I can afford to be." She pointed around them. "But not here. Not with this."

He cocked his head. "This really means that much to you." It wasn't a question. She could see understanding beginning to light up his eyes.

She nodded and fiddled with her ponytail. "Here, let me show you something." She grabbed his clipboard and set it down at the base of the trees they were inspecting then took his hand. She drug him along the row. Eventually, they would have come to this tree, but now felt like the right time to show him.

Around them soared enormous pecans, their trunks easily six feet across and eighty feet high. The soil here was soft and damp underfoot and covered in moss. Spotting the tree's distinctive scar from an ancient fallen branch, she placed a reverent hand on it and followed the trunk around. There, carved into the trunk, was a heart. The wood had darkened over the years, and with time the bark had grown and curled over the edges but the initials "H.M. + L.S."

Jake stood quietly beside her. "Bo told me this was the heart tree. Over a century old." He nodded at the initials. "I assume it's called that because of those."

Cress shook her head, suddenly misty-eyed. Her fingers traced the initials lovingly, feeling each bump the knife had made. "It's not the heart tree because of these." She nodded up at the canopy that soared over their heads.

"It's the heart tree because it's the heart of the orchard. The first one ever planted. The tree from which all the others in the section were grafted." She pressed a hand to the carving. "It's why my parents carved their initials here when they got married."

"Oh." Jake looked up at the leaves, rustling overhead, with interest. "It's seen a few things then."

"More than a few." With a laugh, she turned to Jake. "I remember the first time my dad showed me this. I asked him if he was as old as the tree. He just got all red, and I thought he was angry with me. Turned out he was laughing so hard he couldn't answer."

Jake shoved his hands in his pockets. "You got along with your dad, huh?" His mouth pinched down in a thoughtful look.

Nodding, Cress sat down at the base of the tree and leaned against its trunk while Jake settled in the grass. "Yeah, he taught me everything he knew. He's why I wanted to become a biologist." They sat in silence for a moment. "What about you?"

Wincing, Jake looked off into the distance. "We don't talk anymore."

Cress nodded and bit her lip, unsure how to proceed. She settled for, "Do you miss them? Your parents, I mean? I know you must miss Eve."

He nodded, a pained expression on his face. "Sometimes. It wasn't like I had a bad childhood or anything. But they… Well, things didn't go so well between us when I got older." He shrugged. "I dropped out of school, which they hated." He clasped his hands around his knees. "And then there was Eve. And I wasn't going to tolerate them talking about her like she wasn't worth dirt because of…" he trailed off.

It clicked. "Oh." Now Cress winced. "I'm sorry. Eve was lovely. I only knew her a little through Vada, but I liked her."

Jake sounded choked as he stared into the distance. "Best woman I ever met." Thrushes and whippoorwills sang in the trees around them as they sat in the reverent hush. The sunny smell of warm grass drifted up from the ground, making Cress drowsy. "Thank you." She looked at Jake in surprise.

"For what?"

He blinked back at her. "For not making me feel like I have to fake being all right with what happened. Any of it."

She murmured, "I know what it's like. To lose someone. You'll never really feel all right. You just learn how to live with it." Longing sliced through her for her dad's laugh, his bright smile, and the quiet way he talked.

Jake nodded, eyes lidded, and they sat together watching the sun gild the grass blade by blade.

* * *

Mac tapped Jake's shoulder. In the barn's office, Cress shuffled around, rearranging tools and storing away their notes from the day. He had to admit, things had become a lot tidier since she had arrived. Mac looked frustrated. "Hey, boss. Sounds like a bearing is going out on the well pump again."

Jake shoved his gloves into his back pocket and swiped at his head. That was the last thing he needed today. Standing out in the hot sun swearing over the pump casing was one of his least favorite chores. His eyes strayed to Cress. After confiding in her earlier, little as it had been, he wasn't too keen on spending more time with her. Still, it would be a good chance to show her an aspect of the farm she hadn't seen yet. And Bo would like it if he taught Cress something for a change.

He nodded at Mac. "All right. I'll take care of it." Grabbing his toolbox, he headed toward Cress. "Got a bit? Could use a hand."

She glanced up from the desk, a pencil tucked behind her ear. She looked down at the papers arranged in neat rows, then back at him. With a glance at the sunlight outside, she shuffled them to the side and stood. "Sure. Let's go."

They hopped into the Utility Terrain Vehicle and sped to the well housing. Jake reveled in the bright sky and ruffling wind. He looked at Cress and grinned to see she had turned her face to the sun and closed her eyes, drawing in deep breaths.

As he braked in front of the small, insulated hutch covering the pump, he could hear the whine of a strained motor.

He grabbed the toolbox and headed toward the pump, eager to be in his domain for once. Even if this wasn't exactly his favorite thing to do. Cress trailed after him.

Flipping the hutch off the pump, he watched as Cress goggled at the humming machine, shocked. "This baby draws the water for all the trees in the orchard. Gotta' lot of horsepower in here." He patted the storage tank affectionately. "There's a separate system for drinking water up at the house that's filtered."

Cress walked up hesitantly. "It's huge."

"That's what she said."

She blinked at him, then swatted, and he snickered and jumped out of the way.

"C'mon, jerk. Just show me what we're doing."

He opened his mouth to say *that's what she said* again, a grin already plastered on his face, and she held up a threatening finger. "Fine, here's what we're doing." He pointed out the four bolts they needed to remove underneath a large flange to get to the motor and impeller and replace the ball bearing.

Cress grimaced. "I'm going to pretend like I understand what any of that meant."

He chuckled. "Ok, do you know what a wrench is?" She nodded. "Want to hand me one?"

She turned to the toolbox and rustled around in it for several seconds longer than he thought necessary. He stared at the screwdriver she placed in his palm.

"Really?"

She quickly swapped it with a sly grin for a wrench she held hidden behind her back. "Of course, I know what a wrench is." Her fingertips left pinpricks of heat on his wrist.

"Smart aleck." He grinned as he turned back to the motor, easing it from the casing. She pressed next to him, their shoulders touching, for a better look. He was suddenly all too aware of the salty scent of her sweat mingling with the coconut drift of her shampoo. He frowned in concentration as he looked at the bearing and the abrasions on it.

Silence hung over them. Sweat trickled down his temple, and he squirmed in the quiet. Cress looked at the worn-out bearing as he dug for another. To break the silence, he asked, "So, Grant?" Dang brilliant conversation starter, that one.

Startled, she looked at him, her green eyes wavering. "What about him?"

He swallowed, feeling colossally stupid. Of all the conversation starters, he went straight for the ex. But, in for a penny in for a pound. "What's with him? Your mom was stuck on the topic the other night."

She brushed a strand of hair out of her eyes, leaving a streak of rust on her forehead. "We were together for seven years. Just before I came here, I was up for a big promotion, and he made a reservation at this romantic restaurant and said there was something he wanted to talk to me about." She sighed, the sound wispy and long. "I thought he was going to propose."

She shrugged and set the bearing down and leaned forward to watch as he set the new bearing in place. "Obviously, he didn't." Picking at a hangnail, she continued. "I got turned down for the promotion and broken up with, on the same day."

She licked her lips and rubbed her nose. "He didn't want to be with someone who wasn't 'ambitious.'"

Disgust at the faceless Grant twisted in Jake's gut. How dare he treat such a smart, incredible woman like she was as worthless? He grunted. "Scumbag."

Cress shook her head. "He's not a bad guy. We just wanted different things." He looked at her incredulously. "And we weren't right together. Our personalities just didn't mesh." She forced a laugh. "I mean, he was allergic to my plants. He sneezed all the time."

"Allergy shots," Jake said flatly. There was just no excuse. If you loved someone, you found a way to be with them.

She bobbed her head noncommittally, and he pressed. "Oh, come on. You can't be defending the guy! He broke up with you. When he should have been proposing! That's got to make you a little angry."

Throwing up her hands, Cress turned to him, "Of course it does! But I don't want to be angry all the time about it. At some point, I have to let it go. I can't let it have that much power in my life or it will make me into someone I don't want to be. A mean, bitter person who will always be alone."

He didn't have a response to that. She was right. He focused on tightening the bearing, kicking himself for bringing up the subject at all.

"You're the first person to ask, you know."

He glanced at her. "Ask what?"

"About what happened. Not even my mother has asked what happened. It's like everyone has assumed it's my fault." She clasped her hands, her knuckles turning white.

He touched her arm. "I never assumed that. I doubt Bo did either." Her skin was petal soft and comfortingly warm.

She stared into his eyes intensely, then bit her lip as she looked back at the pump. "Ok, now your turn." She laughed, and he could tell she was trying to lighten the tone. "You've heard the story of my non-engagement. So how did you pop the question to Eve? Was it a big, romantic gesture or a small, private moment?"

He smiled at the memory. "I took her camping. She'd never been and wasn't exactly enthusiastic, but I thought it would be romantic to propose by a fire under a canopy of stars." He grinned at the memory. "It rained so hard all weekend we couldn't even leave the tent and we both caught colds. But I'd never seen her smile so big when I pulled out the ring."

He coughed. "And I never took her camping again. At her request."

Cress doubled over laughing, tears pooling at the corners of her eyes. "That is magnificent."

He tightened the last bolt back into place. "God, I miss that woman." His thoughts flashed to her face that last day in the hospital. She'd try to smile, even through the pain seizing her body. She'd always worn a smile; it was one of the many things he'd loved about her. Despite all the medical bills he still had to pay from her treatments, he wouldn't trade one moment he'd had with her for anything.

Cress patted his leg, disrupting his thoughts, and he forced a smile. "It's nice to remember the good times with someone for a change."

"I'm happy to listen anytime." She smiled back at him. Pointing at the reassembled pump housing, she said, "That didn't seem so bad."

He stood, pulling her to her feet. "Just wait until we have to replace a stuffing box."

She made a face. "A stuffing box?"

He shook his head and laughed. "That's what she said!" She tried to punch his arm, then jogged after him as he took off back to the UTV.

Chapter 11

Champ whined and pawed at Cress' ankles as she spun around the room, trying to find her purse. He let out playful yips as she tried not to trip over him. Rooting between two towering monsteras, she finally found the abused leather bag and dumped her phone and wallet into it.

"I am so late," she muttered to herself as she hopped over Champ and swiped at the doorknob. She had to make it to Midnight Bluff before Vada's shift at the Co-Op was up, or she'd never hear the end. Not after the strings her friend had pulled to get them that discount on their fertilizer order.

Skittering echoed behind her as she headed down the hall toward the stairs, and she stopped, frowning. She could have sworn she'd latched the door behind her. But Champ sat at her heels, tail wagging back and forth and tongue lolling out in a gleeful grin.

Scooping him up, she jogged back to her room and gently plopped him inside the door.

"Stay!" she said, trying to make her voice sound firm even as his big brown eyes made her want to melt. He laid down on the floor with his head nestled on his fluffy paws and peered up at her. Closing the door quickly, she sprinted back down the hall.

"Oh, Cress!" Lynn's voice rang out as she dashed past the kitchen. Heaving a sigh, Cress turned back and popped her head into the kitchen.

Lynn pounded out dough on the counter, sprinkling it with flour in between hearty smacks. "Could you pick up a water filter for the fridge at the hardware store while you're in town? Herb knows what kind we need."

Cress flashed a thumbs up. "Sure thing!" Just as she was about to dash off again, she paused. "Hey, Lynn? Could you take Champ for his walk in about an hour? I'm trying to be a little more regular with his training."

"No problem, sweetie." Lynn picked up an egg timer and twisted the dial. "I'll take care of him. Now, shoo! I know you're running late already."

Checking her watch—she was only twenty minutes late—Cress flew out the door and hopped into her truck, jamming her keys into the ignition. The hum of a mower caught her attention as she flew down the driveway toward town.

She threw a hand out the window to wave at Jake where he twirled the mower up and down the long rows, wavering in the breeze. As he waved lazily back at her in her rearview mirror, she smiled to herself. At least one part of her job was going well.

* * *

Jake rolled his shoulder as he looked down the row of pecan trees, green shells just beginning to fill and weigh down the branches. As tall as the clover had gotten here, they'd have to bring in the weed eaters to clean up this row for sure. But for now, he leaned against the trunk and reveled in the cathedral stillness of the orchard as he cooled off in an afternoon breeze.

After a few minutes, he climbed back up onto the tractor and slowly turned it down the row, the mower whirring behind.

As he bumped along, he spotted a little brown and white body nosing around the trunk of a tree. With a chuckle, he throttled down the tractor and clambered off.

Champ looked up at Jake, head bent low and tail wagging slowly. Mud from the pond covered his paws and belly and splashed up his neck and plastered his cheeks. Burs and leaves tangled in his fur.

"Cress will not be happy with you," Jake said to the little guy. He whistled and patted his leg, and the puppy frolicked to his side, tossing his head and scuffling through the clover. Already covered in dust and leaves from the orchard, Jake didn't hesitate to pick up the wriggling puppy.

He looked toward the house, acres away and invisible through the thick trunks, then back at the tractor. With so much left to be finished, and Cress on a long errand, it would probably be best if he held onto Champ for a little while.

At least, that's what he told himself as he climbed back up and settled the pup in his lap. Champ startled when the engine revved, but settled down, content to be with a familiar person.

Jake eased down the row of pecans, letting the machine do its job, and scratched Champ's ear. He wasn't half bad—for a lap dog.

Chapter 11

* * *

Cress' shoulders screamed at her as she jolted over the gravel drive. When she placed the fall fertilizer order next month, she would tell Vada that she wanted her guys to deliver it. Days of staring up at trees and bending over to examine leaf shed followed by long nights hunched over books to brush up on pecan varietals had done a number on Cress' back.

And the long ride to town to pick up hundreds of pounds of fertilizer did not help. She twisted her head from side to side and swore under her breath as she hit another bump.

They had to grate this driveway before the winter rains hit.

She pulled the truck up in front of the storage barn and waved Mac and Franklin over to unload it. With a groan she headed toward the house, magenta bougainvillea cheerfully nodding around the porch railing, to check on Lynn, the water filter in hand. She'd been five minutes down the highway when she'd remembered her promise and had to turn around for it.

"Hey, Lynn!" The screen door slammed behind her. "I'm back. I've got your water filter. Herb sure is a character. Wouldn't stop talking my ear off about all the stuff the Ladies' Auxiliary is up to. Did you walk Champ?" She rounded the corner, still talking, into the kitchen and found Lynn wringing a dish towel anxiously.

Cress halted. "What's wrong?"

"Champ's escaped!" Lynn threw her arms wide. "I don't know how or when, but when I went to get him, the door to your room was open and he was just gone. I've searched the entire house and nearly hollered myself hoarse out in the yard!"

"Did you check under my bed?" Cress set down the filter on the island and pressed a hand to her stomach against the rising panic. "Sometimes he likes to crawl up under there and fall asleep. Scared me to death a couple of times."

"I did. And I checked your closet too. And the bathroom." Lynn flapped her hands, the dish towel waving like a flag. "Oh, I'm so sorry, Cress! This is all my fault."

Cress looked out the window. Late afternoon sparkled off the pond, one of Champ's favorite spots. She looked at Lynn's watering eyes and softened. "Don't worry. It's not your fault. My door hasn't been catching right lately. I should have double-checked before I left." She grabbed Champ's leash off its hook by the door. "I'm going to go look for him. Maybe he's tired of exploring by now and will come on back."

Lynn nodded, throat working. "That's a good idea. I'll keep looking around here."

With a nod, Cress shot out the door toward the pond. She jogged, wrapping the leash around her palm and trying to tell herself that such a small puppy couldn't have gotten far. She tried to ignore the fact that such a small puppy would be nearly impossible to spot among all the trees.

Tears threatened at the edge of her lashes, and she brushed at them irritatedly. She wasn't a bad dog mom just because her puppy was an escape artist, right? Everyone had to deal with this. At the edge of the water, she spotted fresh paw prints in the mud, but no other sign of Champ.

Letting out an ear-splitting whistle, she stood still, listening for a responding yip or the patter of feet through leaves. Nothing answered her but birdsong and the distant hum of Jake on the tractor. She whistled again and when no answering bark returned, headed into the orchard, not sure what to do except to search all four hundred acres on foot by herself.

The sun was sinking, and twilight was creeping in among the trees when Cress turned back toward the house, head hanging to her chest and eyes watering. Her throat was raw, and her lips chapped from calling and whistling. With the night rolling in fast, she'd need extra eyes and ears to find Champ in the dark.

Her stomach knotted as she imagined Jake's face, his dark eyes dancing sardonically when she asked him for help.

The hum of the tractor had faded, so he must have finished for the day. He'd be there soon to go over the day's doings with Bo. She sighed and ran her hands through her tousled hair and wiped at her eyes. All the day's soreness rolled over her in one enormous wave as the panic settled into a heavy knot of doom deep in her gut, an assurance that all things inevitably go wrong once she got involved.

Unable to stand the thought of dragging herself up the porch stairs, she collapsed on the bottom step to wait for Jake and watch the purple martins swoop overhead.

She didn't have long to wait. Through the gathering gloom, she could see his customary white T-shirt glowing in the evening blue, hazy from the dust and pollen kicked up by the tractor. She squinted as he got closer. He was carrying something. In the next second, she recognized the grinning little bundle of Champ.

Her eyes widened, and she jumped up and ran toward him.

"You found him!" Her voice peeled across the orchard, echoing through the trees standing sentinel. She threw her arms around Jake's neck, crushing a yelping Champ between them.

Jake let out a strangled *blat*, and she let go hastily. Unable to look at him, she scooped Champ out of his arms. "Where'd you find him?"

"More like he found me. Been hanging with me all afternoon. Figured you probably wanted the little rascal back by now." Jake scratched behind Champ's ear.

Cress looked up at him, shocked. "Wait! He's been with you all afternoon? I've been going crazy trying to find him. Why didn't you text me?"

Jake looked at the sky and took a deep breath through his nose. "And see, we were having a nice moment." He walked toward the house.

Hurrying to keep up, Cress grabbed his arm. He looked down at her, frowning. She sighed, "I'm sorry. I've just been worrying myself sick over him. You're right. Thank you."

He looked at her for a moment longer, his gaze flat, causing heat to creep into her cheeks. Then a grin split his face, revealing shockingly white teeth. "Well, if you keep thanking me with hugs like that, I don't mind so much." With that, he turned and strode to the house.

Groaning, she followed moment over. "Jerk!" she called at his back. His chuckle floated back to her on the evening breeze, and she hid her smile in Champ's fur before pulling her nose away with a grimace. He needed a bath.

Chapter 12

Early morning mist curled along the ground in wisps and waves. Grass crunched underfoot, releasing an earthy scent into the air. Despite the day's forecast of ninety-degree heat, Cress shivered comically in her long shirt sleeves as she clambered out of Jake's truck, and he looked pointedly at her.

"The day's going to be blazing. Wear anymore and we'll be dragging you out of the woods with heat stroke later," he growled at her as he checked that his Springfield .45 was loaded. He moved to unkennel the dogs whining restlessly in the truck's bed.

She crossed her arms. "So you've said about a thousand times."

"Jessayin'. You can always wait here by the truck. Like a sensible person."

She groused, "Like the city-slicker you think I am."

His exasperated sigh was drowned out by the joyful baying of the black-mouth curs as they leaped down from the truck and swarmed around his legs in a blur of yellow fur. Vada swanned up to them, decked head to toe in hunter's orange, and kissed Jake on the cheek. She winked at Cress then wound her arm around her waist.

"So glad you didn't let this sour puss talk you out of comin'." Vada elbowed Jake. "I always need another lady at these things."

Cress surveyed the testosterone-heavy participants of the hog hunt milling around their trucks in the fog and nodded. "It does seem that we're outnumbered."

Jake snorted as he waved at her old classmates, Floyd and Thomas. Even the pastor had come out for the event, although he seemed to be content chatting with Ruffin instead of gearing up. "Not many women want to go sprinting through the undergrowth following a pack of dogs that are trying to corner a steaming mad hog that would just as soon gut you as look at you." He handed Cress a pistol and a bowie knife. "Try not to shoot one of my dogs, would you?"

She flexed her fingers around the pistol's grip, testing its weight, then sited along it. "I'm an excellent shot you know."

He shook his head, dark hair flopping into his eyes before he brushed it up under a ball cap. "Won't do much good if the pack is swarming the sucker. You won't have a clear shot." He tapped the bowie knife. "That's what this is for. You've got to get in there and slit its throat before it disembowels a dog."

Cress gaped at him. "You're talking about a half-ton hog!"

Vada scowled at Jake. "You didn't give her the rundown before you got here?"

He shook his head sheepishly. She muttered curses under her breath. Thumping him on the chest with her forefinger, she warned him, "You better keep up with her! Cress is like a sister to me. And, so help me, if you let her get hurt, you're going to wish the hog had chopped off something you hold w-a-a-a-y dearer than your bowels!" She spun on her heel and stomped off.

Cress pressed her lips together, trying not to laugh at Jake's stricken look. He stared after Vada, Adam's apple working up and down. She giggled, and he scowled at her, face pale in the early morning light.

"Just stay close to me, all right?" He grumbled, "Don't need Vada busting my ass 'cuz you run off and get yourself hurt."

"Vada will cool down." Cress slid the pistol and knife onto her belt, settling them as comfortably as possible over each hip. "Besides, I'm here to hunt."

He grunted. "Ruffin's offered to let us join him on his ATV today." He strode off through the fog, the dogs frisking at his heels.

"What bee got in your bonnet?" Cress mumbled to herself. She checked the safety strap on the pistol one more time, tugged again at the knife to make sure it was secure, then trudged after him.

Ruffin sat behind the wheel of his ATV, little curls of steam rising from his Yeti mug as he sipped on some coffee. He eyed Cress but gave her a friendly enough wave. He spat into the mud and called the group to order with a military-crisp voice.

"All right, everybody! Mr. Leonard tells me he's got a passel of hogs rutting and digging up his fields." He took a sip of his coffee as he eyed them. "He reached out to me to set up this hunt." With a jerk of his chin, he nodded at the torn-up field around them.

"I sent up a drone last week to get some footage and from the extent of the damage, it looks like we've got at least a couple of breeding sows around here, which means piglets we've got to flush out as well. And probably a big ole boar or two." He cleared his throat and glanced at Cress.

"Most of you know the drill. Flush out the piglets onto open ground. Once we've got as many of them out as possible, we send the dogs in to pin down the big hogs. Keep the bulldogs on the ATVs. Don't wear 'em out running before we get to the hogs. And for goodness' sake, if you run into a hog by yourself, let it run off. I don't want to practice my field aid on you."

With that, Kevlar-vested dogs were let off leashes and went bounding into the underbrush with excited yips and bays. Cress watched fascinated as Jake sent his dogs into the thicketed growth along the edge of the field, then settled onto the front seat of the ATV next to Ruffin with a friendly pat on his shoulder. Clicking his tongue, he ordered Zeus, his American bulldog, up into the basket on the back, where he sat quivering with anxious excitement to follow his companions.

Not knowing what else to do, Cress settled onto the back seat and lightly stroked at his ears, but the hound's eyes stayed peeled on the woods. Belatedly, she wondered if Champ had been bred for this sort of thing; not hogs perhaps, but maybe birds or field rats. As she mused, dogs wove in and out of the trees and weeds, working for scents. Occasionally, one or more would take off with a bugling call into the shaded wood.

The men milled around quietly, seeming unconcerned, every once in a while driving an ATV toward a point where more barking emanated from the ringing woods. Ruffin studied a GPS monitor, grunting at the readout and occasionally showing it to Jake, who shook his head.

At last, someone pointed and with a shout, they all darted

156

toward a bevy of hoglets darting across the open ground. Men charged on foot and in ATVs in the direction of the squealing hoglets, hounds flying after them. Cress clung to the side of the ATV as they rattled over the field. As fast as they got there, it was over, hoglets quickly dispatched with knives to the heart.

Cress stared in horror as Jake tossed a hoglet into the basket. Ruffin elbowed him and pointed to her frozen face.

He sighed as he looked at her. "You knew you were coming on a hunt, not a picnic. What did you think we would do?"

With a shiver, Cress looked at him. "I thought it would be more like a deer hunt." She enjoyed the serenity of deer hunts, the long stretches of gazing through the cold fog rising from the fields. This felt wilder, more feral.

Jake shook his head. "Hogs are too smart for that. You shoot or trap them in one spot, they learn to avoid it."

"It just seems so… cruel… to kill the babies, too." Her lips curled at the thought.

Jake sat beside her. He gestured at the field, swaths ruined with muddy ruts, the knee-high corn chewed up from the roots. "You can see the destruction even a small founder can do, and they have more babies like this one at an immense rate. These aren't native animals, and there are no large predators left to keep a check on their numbers. It's up to us to control the problem we created." He patted her leg. "I promise we don't do this to be cruel."

She nodded. "I know." With a sigh, she said, "There's just a lot about nature that seems unfair."

He stood and held out a hand to her. "Now that I'll agree with." She took it reluctantly. "But we manage the best we can." They headed toward the tree line.

In the distance, the baying of dogs echoed in the trees, like the bells of a church ringing randomly. As Cress and Jake stood together at the edge of the woods, slowly, a familiar bugling converged together. Cress tilted her head.

"Is that—?"

Jake's brow furrowed. He pulled an odd-looking device out of his pocket and pressed a button. A small GPS screen flickered to life. Without warning, he charged forward with a shrill whistle. Zeus leaped from the ATV, causing Ruffin to startle and look at them.

"Four dogs are all on one point!" Jake called to him as he ran into the trees. "Get one of the bulldogs headed this way." Ruffin waved and took off on the ATV.

Leaving Cress standing by herself, alone, at the edge of the woods. Swearing, she turned and ran after Jake, wondering what in the world she had gotten herself into.

Leaves crunched underfoot, mud squelching up around her boots as she pushed through the thick brambles. In the distance, dogs howled, their howls echoing hollowly. She struggled against the thick vegetation until she burst through the thicket into the forest.

Pine needles blanketed the floor and draped themselves over vines and fallen boughs in a thick, red carpet. The morning light struggled to penetrate the thick loblolly canopy, and chilly air stirred the dangling needles of a prehistoric gloom.

Finding herself alone among the dim trees, Cress paused. Somewhere to her right and far ahead she could hear the dogs barking and snarling. Behind her stood the intimidating wall of brambles. Heart pounding, she swallowed and jogged forward to the sound of the dogs, hoping to find Jake before something popped from the mist and found her.

The sound of yapping and growling grew and with it the sound of hollering men. But she still hadn't spotted them through the trees. Spinning in circles, she looked up, trying to spot the thin sun and orient herself. The calls seemed to shift, and she dizzily moved to follow, but a crash behind her spun her around.

A huge boar stood glaring at her, tail whipping back and forth. From its shoulder dripped blood, where it looked like a dog had savaged it. An overwhelming musky stench washed over Cress and slowly she backed away, feeling her steps over the crunching pine needles. Her heel struck a branch, and she stumbled. With a snorting squeal, the boar charged at her.

She turned and sprinted through the trees, branches slapping at her. One struck her arm, and she screamed out in agony as she felt it rip through her skin. The baying of the hounds was close, but the enraged boar was closer, and in her panic, she realized she had turned away from the dogs. The pistol jolted uselessly on her hip as she hurdled over a log the boar simply ran under.

Her legs burned with the strain, and her lungs threatened to seize. Gasping, she fumbled for the pistol at her belt, knowing she couldn't go any further. Suddenly, a huge weight tackled her to the side, rolling her into the underbrush. The boar charged past and whirled, dirt spraying up around him.

Cress sat up, Jake spitting pine needles beside her as the dogs raced past, encircling the boar. With growling lunges, they latched onto its legs and throat, ensuring he wasn't going anywhere.

Jake stood, yanking Cress to her feet without a word. He walked over to the boar and hauled its hind legs out from under it. Suddenly, the animal gave a great heave, throwing most of the dogs off, and turned on him. It slashed at his arms with its tusks, squealing and thrashing.

Kicking and grunting, Jake windmilled backward away from the dangerous tusks. Just then, Zeus leaped forward, sinking his teeth into a rear leg and tugging the mud-covered boar away from his owner. The other dogs circled, trying to regain their hold.

Spinning to Cress, Jake held out his hand. "Give me your pistol!"

She slid it from her holster and tossed it to him, staring at the dogs as they fought the angry bore. Mud churned around them.

"Damn, can't get a clear shot!" Jake paced, trying to dart in and grab the boar's legs again, but at every turn, the hog lunged at him. "We've got to do something before he guts Zeus!"

The poor hound was still hanging on, winded and bloodied on one hip. The boar turned toward him again, exposing his shoulder. In a flash, Cress remembered her father wrestling down a distressed cow. She yanked the bowie knife out of the scabbard and leaped in, Jake's screech muted in her ears as she landed on the hog's shoulder with her full weight.

The boar tripped and went to a knee, but it wasn't enough. He was bucking back up underneath her, even as she scrambled to grab an ear, a leg, anything. Then, the dogs rushed in, and Jake was beside her, kneeling on the boar's side as well.

"Do it!" he shouted. Without thinking about it, Cress pressed the tip of the knife behind the hog's shoulder, then drove it in with the heel of her other hand. Slowly, the hog stopped thrashing and lay still.

Cress slid off its side and sat in the mud, panting and shaking as the adrenaline wore off. Offering her a hand, Jake helped her up, a gleam in his eye.

"That was quite the move there, cowgirl."

She eyed the hog as the dogs now milled around it, sniffing and whining. "It's one I wouldn't recommend trying."

Halloos echoed through the forest and the other men and Vada jogged up to them. They nodded at the hog appreciatively while Vada stared daggers at Jake.

"Damn, Jake! You had all the fun without us." Floyd bent to look at the hog sprawled in the mud, his curly hair plastered to his forehead with sweat.

Shaking his head, Jake pointed at Cress. "It was all her."

Mac and Franklin jumped forward from the group to high-five her. "First blood! Congrats, girl." Cress just smiled tightly at them as she cradled her elbow.

Vada hissed, "I thought I told you to look after her."

Ignoring Vada, Jake *tsked* and looked at Cress' arm, which had started to throb. "C'mon. Let's get you back to Ruffin. Don't want this getting infected." He looked around. "Guys, I'll leave this to you to drag out so Bo can get started on barbecuing it for us."

He led Cress in the opposite direction she would have guessed as the way out as the guys congratulated her again with pats on the back. Vada's scowl lingered on their backs until they were out of sight.

"What was all that about?" Cress asked.

Jake shrugged. "After Eve, Vada decided it was her job to make sure I was ok." He glanced at Cress out of the corner of his eye. "You being her friend and all has put her on even higher alert, I'd imagine."

Sighing, Cress replied, "I can take care of myself."

He looked at her, mouth quirked up in a rueful grin. "Yeah, you were sure showing that hog who's boss before I got there."

Cress sniffed but didn't reply as they pushed through the last veil of brambles into the field where Ruffin waited for them. He blessed her out for going in alone as a newbie, then dressed her arm with enough stinging alcohol, antibiotic cream, and gauze for a small army. She was not allowed to go back into the woods for the rest of the day but had to remain in the field as they flushed out the hoglets.

Jake gave the leash of his dogs to Franklin and stayed with Cress, surprising her with his willingness to chase down the small hoglets usually reserved for the kids. Faster than a jackrabbit, they sprinted after a hoglet. She laughed as he tripped over a churned up row and face-planted into the soft earth. As he stood, wiping the muck off, he took a big handful and chunked it at her. Gasping, she scooped up a wad of the sticky mud and threw it at him. Soon, they were both covered in muck and laughing like children.

Ruffin sat on his ATV, shaking his head at them.

That evening, as the honeyed sun slid down the sky, the group slowly filtered out of the woods, dogs and men tired and drooping from a long day of tracking. Quiet chatter filled the field as everyone loaded up to head to the barbecue at Mr. Leonard's. As the truck rumbled over gravel backroads, Jake and Cress sat in companionable silence while they studied the burnished copper sunset.

Cress pressed a thumb to her mouth to hide a grin that threatened to stretch across her face. For the first time in weeks, she felt uncontrollably happy. She stole a peek at Jake, then turned to look out the window, finally allowing herself to smile.

Chapter 12

***

Coals crackled in the grill, fat dripping down with hisses and pops onto the embers. Jake stood staring into the glowing mass as he waited for Bo, wrung with sweat and the smell of smoke, to render a verdict on the pork.

With a grunt, the older man sliced off a piece of the tender meat and tasted it. He nodded and grinned. Brandishing his grilling tongs above his head, he called to the crowd lounged about on hay bales. "Let's eat, boys!"

As everyone shuffled into a winding line toward the grill, Vada complained, "Finally! I can near 'bout eat this whole hog myself."

Clapping her on the shoulder, Jake laughed. "I'd pay good money to see you try."

She glared at him and went silent. With a sigh, Jake pulled his ball cap off his head and ran his hands through his hair. She still had her panties in a twist over Cress.

"It wasn't the hog, you know, that got her. I think she ran into a branch."

She crossed her arms and squared up to him as the line inched forward. "Running *from* the boar. When you shouldn't have left her alone in the first place."

He held up his hands. "You're right. And I'm sorry." He put a hand on her arm. "I am. I shouldn't have bolted like that. I know as well as you do how quick these things can turn. It was stupid." Vada nodded and uncrossed her arm. He laughed. "But you should have seen her take a flying leap at that thing not two minutes later."

Chuckling, Vada shrugged. "That's Cress for you. She's no delicate flower." She cocked her head. "Did she really kill the boar? That's mighty bold for a first hunt."

Jake nodded. "Didn't hesitate."

Vada glanced over to where Cress sat on a hay bale. Zeus sat with his head on her knee, his rump bandaged from his brawl with the hog.

"Boar was about to gut Zeus. She jumped on top of it, near about tackled it to the ground, too." Jake shook his head.

"Sounds like you owe her a thank you." Vada glanced up at him. He saw a smile lift the edge of her mouth. She nodded toward the refreshment table. "I think I saw some Southern Comfort over there. She's a big whiskey lover."

"Is she now?" Jake grinned. Now he could get along with a woman who liked her liquor. "Maybe I'll take her a glass."

Vada laughed and took a plate heaped with fragrant barbecue from Bo, who studied them suspiciously. "You do that now." With a little hop and a wink at Bo, Vada sauntered off.

"I know that look," Bo said as he piled meat on a paper plate for Jake. "That girl is up to something."

Jake grunted. Vada was always up to something. He'd stopped guessing at it long ago.

Bo lowered his head and asked in hushed tones, "She's not trying to set you up with Cress, is she now?"

Throwing up his hands, Jake *harrumphed*. "Cress and I can't be in the same room together without trying to kill each other. Why would she do that?"

Waving the tongs, Bo *shushed* him. "All right, all right. Forget I asked." He winked as he turned to the grill, and Jake groaned.

"She's probably just trying to make sure I apologize to Cress for leaving her out to dry today during the hunt." Jake pulled a strip of the barbecue off the hog, and Bo slapped at him with the sauce mop.

"How'd she do out there, anyway?" Bo handed him the plate and pointed toward his granddaughter. Jake studied Cress, who leaned back against a bale of hay studying the stars. Bo plopped a second plate in his hand. "For Cress." He grinned at Jake. "Since you got some apologizin' to do. Best way is with food."

"Well, I'm not sure she'll want to eat this considerin' she killed it. And she was none too happy about the hoglets we killed this morning."

Bo blinked at him then looked at the hog on the grill. He rubbed at his chin. "Ah. Well, still best not to go empty-handed. Just pile a bunch of fixins' around the side." He pointed to the buffet table loaded with coleslaw, baked beans, potato salad, and more. With a deep breath, Jake headed over to do as he was told.

Ruffin stood at the end of the table, swigging a beer. He smacked his lips at the sight of Jake. "Making plates for two?"

Wordlessly, Jake nodded. He was already worn out from this gauntlet and knew Ruffin's thoughts on the matter anyway.

"Now, I know one of those ain't for me." Ruffin looked slyly over at Cress. "It wouldn't happen to be for some green-eyed girl I spied you laughing and cutting up with this afternoon, would it?"

"Ruffin, cut me a break, man, would you?" Jake slapped potato salad onto the plates and straightened. "She nearly got skewered because of me. I'm just being nice." He turned and poured two slugs of whiskey into plastic cups.

The smile slipped from Ruffin's face, and he reached out and grabbed Jake's arm. "Dude, I'm just joshing ya'." He tightened his grip when Jake tried to pull away. "But, as your friend, I haven't seen you be *nice* to a woman since Eve died. I know you. You'll be in so deep, you won't know you're drowning until it's too late." Jake looked into Ruffin's steely blue eyes, his stomach clenching into a fist.

Over Ruffin's shoulder, he could see Cress turning to look at them curiously, as his friend continued, "If you want to be nice to her, be nice to her. Even get some *energy out*, if you have to." Anger lanced through Jake at the insinuation as Ruffin kept going, "But heads up, man. That's all I'm saying."

Barely parting his lips, Jake replied, "I hear ya', man." He strode away from Ruffin, his friend's words thrumming in his chest. Everyone at this blasted party thought he and Cress were… something. And they were barely friends. That thought annoyed him more than all the busybodies.

He sank onto the hay bale beside her and plunked the plate in her lap. She studied his face, worry crinkling her brow. "What's wrong? You look like someone just told you they'd lost one of your dogs or something." She stroked Zeus' shoulder and glowed up at him, the air *whooshing* out of his lungs at her look.

Jake shook his head, settling for telling her half the truth. "Everybody at this shindig seems to think we're a thing. Or trying to fix us up. Or warning us off each other." He muttered into his cup as he took a sip of his whiskey. "Can't mind their own business to save their lives."

He glanced at Cress to see her staring back at him, eyes wide and lips pressed together, cheeks flushed. "What?" he asked, and she burst out laughing.

She fanned her face and grabbed her cup. "It's just… you seem so upset." She took a sip and touched his arm, her fingers sending little sparks up and down his side. "I thought you didn't care what anyone thought."

He sighed. "I don't. I just don't like them being up in my business, is all."

"And you think I'm your business?"

He glared at her, but her teasing grin made him relax. He sank back against the hay bale. "I dunno. Do you wanna' be?" What was he doing flirting with her in front of all these people? He had lost his mind.

She choked on her whiskey and pressed a hand to her chest as he thumped her on the back. Once she quit coughing, she shot a glare at Bo, who spun back to the grill from where he had been blatantly staring at them. She groused, "Nosey people."

The dark look on her face as she scrunched her eyebrows and sucked her lips into a tight little rosebud made him throw his head back and laugh. After a second, Cress joined him and soon tears were streaming down their cheeks.

Cress crossed her feet and scooped up a big bite of barbecue. The sauce smeared across her face. Jake smirked at her. She talked, mouth full. "I mean, let's look at this objectively. I annoy you." He watched, fascinated, as she dug in, oblivious to the mess. Most women seemed so shy about eating anything messy in front of guys, but Cress just dove right in.

He leaned into her, smirking. "Oh, absolutely." Her eyes danced in the firelight, like pine trees in a windstorm.

"And you annoy me?"

He shrugged, scooching closer. "You tell me."

"And we work together. It would be disastrous if we dated." Her voice lowered, uncertain as he slid an arm around her. "Wouldn't it?"

"Of course it would. Absolute disaster." She relaxed into his side. His breath hitched at the warmth of her body pressing into him.

"I mean, we barely get along and we live too close for comfort as it is. Dating would just make things weird. Right?" Cress swiped at her face with a napkin. She missed a streak of sauce. It clung to her cheek as she gazed at the fire dancing in front of them.

Without thinking, Jake leaned forward and wiped away the sauce with his thumb. His hand lingered on her jaw as she looked at him, her eyes sparkling in the firelight. A slight smile curved her lips, and he wondered if they tasted as soft and sweet as they looked. Her breath tickled his cheek, warm in the cooling night air.

Forget what Ruffin or Vada or anyone else thought. Cress was here now, and while he didn't exactly understand what this thing was between them, he wanted to. And he knew how fleeting moments like this could be. He wouldn't let any opportunity slip away again.

As slowly as if he was trying not to spook a deer in the woods, he leaned forward and pressed his lips to hers. Gently, she kissed him back, then more deeply, taking his top lip between hers. Even though his eyes were closed, he could swear the stars spun overhead as she pressed her hands to his chest, and he cradled the small of her back.

Then, she was pulling back, her eyes large and breath shallow and fast in the cool evening air. His heart tried to fight its way out of his chest as he studied her, trying to read her expression.

She swallowed and dropped her gaze, cheeks blazing, as cheers broke out around the clearing. With a jolt, he pulled away and patted Zeus' shoulder. When he looked up, Vada was watching them from across the fire, a smirk on her face.

Chapter 12

She mouthed at him, "I told you so." Bo grinned at him from his station by the grill.

He rolled his eyes and looked down at his food, even though his stomach was careening around inside his abdomen like a jumping beetle. Lynn had been right; he was a goner.

Chapter 13

T he road rolled and bumped underneath them, gravel spitting from underneath the tires of Jake's truck. Cress held onto the door handle even though they weren't going that fast, afraid the truck would fishtail them straight into a ditch. Jake frowned at her and punched on the radio, "When Will I Be Loved" blasting out with an ear-splitting twang of guitar.

Cress slapped her hands over her ears and glared at him. They hadn't talked since last night, but if Jake's teenager-worthy antics this morning were any indication, he was feeling just as self-conscious as she was. They needed to talk—and soon.

"Can you cut it out?" she shouted.

He cupped a hand around his ear. "Sorry, what was that? I can't hear you."

She slapped the radio off. "Really? Must you be so juvenile?"

"Juvenile! There's a ten-dollar word for ya." He grinned at her, and she pressed her lips together, trying not to smile.

"Think you can spell it for me?"

"Oh, grow up!" She punched his shoulder.

He circled a finger around his face. "Being juvenile is part of my charm." He pulled the truck through an open gate and to the side of the one-track road. Beside them lay an open field, plowed under for the season. Along one side ran a small stream, badly grown over with weeds and vines. Cress stared. It seemed to stretch for acres, crisscrossed with run-off ditches and small stands of scrub.

She swung open the truck door, feet hitting sandy soil. "This it?" Bending down, she scooped up a handful and let it run through her fingers, watching how it drifted in the wind.

Jake's door creaked open, and he strolled around to join her. She could feel his eyes on her, crinkled at the corners in amusement, as she kicked at clods and rubbed some more dirt between her palms and sniffed, trying to concentrate despite his distracting presence. "Can't imagine that smells very good."

"You can tell from its color and texture a few things about the soil health of a place right off the bat." She held out a handful for him to see. "Soil in the Delta should be rich in carbon. It's dark and has a nice crumb. Unless it's been over-farmed and under-rotated. Which this has."

She threw the soil down, the clods hitting the earth with little pops, mirroring the pings of tension racing through her. "We've got a lot of work to do preparing this ground." Running her fingers through her hair, she walked out into the field trying to put some distance between them, stepping between the uneven rows.

She hadn't been able to sleep last night after their kiss, and she desperately needed to think. The soil clung thick and heavy to her boots, sticky as clay, dragging her legs down. They'd need to plant several seasons of clover and peanuts to reintroduce enough organic matter back into it then add sand so it could drain.

Her mind spun away from the field, still in problem-solving mode. As for her and Jake, she sighed. Things could never work, no matter how much chemistry there was between them. They were coworkers. She choked at the sudden knot of longing in her throat. It was doomed from the start. She needed to nip this in the bud.

Trying to soothe the sudden ache, she leapt into action. Pointing toward the stream, she drew an imaginary line along it. She called back to Jake, "The stream is good at least. Pecans love water. So, we'll need to clear that and the ditches out. Use them to our advantage."

She scanned the acreage, heart still hammering. "We're going to need a lot of water. We'll have to find out about the well situation." Her hands shook at the thought of telling him they had no future, but for now, she just had to evaluate this field. She took a deep breath.

Spinning on her heel, she headed for the truck. She just had to get through this. "I need my kit. We'll bore some soil profiles to send to the MSU extension for testing. I've got to know exactly what we're dealing with." As she passed Jake, he grabbed her arm, his hand warm at her tingling elbow.

"You're worried." He didn't ask. His brown eyes bored into hers and she dropped her gaze guiltily.

Glancing at the field stretched out around them, early morning sunlight dappling it, she bobbed her chin in a short, jerky nod. "Yes. The profile from the NCRS was old, from the 50s. And I'm not sure if Mr. Brooks followed the suggested protocols." She swallowed as she looked at his hand on her arm. "This land … this land looks worn out. I don't know if laying fallow one season is going to be enough." She pulled away from him slowly and drew her bulky kit from the truck.

"Well, what are we talking about? Two seasons? Three?" Jake's voice hitched up as she strode away. "How are we going to afford to do all this if we have to wait three seasons before we can begin planting grafts?" He followed her into the field. "Cress! Are you going to answer?"

"I don't know." She set the case down, letting the handle fall with a clatter. "If we're lucky, two and some topsoil enrichment. Maybe."

"Maybe's not good enough, Cress." Jake paced back and forth, mud flying from his boots in small chunks.

"What do you want me to say?" She threw her arms wide. "I'm trying to do my job right now so I can get you answers."

Jake stopped pacing and stared at her, his hands on his hips. "You've sunk all of your savings into this. If this doesn't go right—"

Cress cut him off, irate that he thought he was the only one who cared about Gramps. "I know how much this matters!" she shouted.

"You don't!" Suddenly, Jake was the one yelling. "I was the one who told Bo we could do this. Billy's run a great farm for decades. I didn't even think to check…" He waved at the dirt, face crumpled, and Cress realized that Jake had just as much staked on this going right as she did. "I was just thinking about labor." He trailed off shoulders slumped. "This is my fault."

Cress grabbed his hand, voice softening. "Hey! We're in this together." She tugged on his arm, drawing him into her. She lowered her voice and saw his shoulders relax. "Look, maybe I'm overreacting. That's why I'm taking a deeper sample for lab testing."

Realizing that their fingers were entwined, she released his hand and stepped back. They didn't need to get any more entangled right now. Not before...

Bending to open the case, she added, "Anyway, there will still be plenty we can do to get this place in shape."

Jake sighed. "It's going to take a lot of extra hours. We will not be able to hire extra hands until we're harvesting from the new orchard." He was always so practical. She supposed that was why Bo had made him farm manager.

"No one said farm life was easy." She fiddled with an auger. "Besides, it's about time you taught me how to use the tractor, anyway."

He eyed her, eyebrow cocked. "Really? You've been making excuses to not get on that thing for weeks."

She tossed her ponytail over her shoulder, pretending she hadn't heard him. The tractor made her nervous. "I've been doing the orchard surveys. Now it's time for me to learn from you."

He snorted. "So, the student becomes the master."

She tried to smile, her stomach twisting into knots. "And here we were getting along so well!"

His laughter peeled out over the field as he knelt in the mud to help her with the samples, his arm brushing against hers. The sparks that had rushed through her last night at his unexpected kiss lit up again, and she bit her lip at the memory of his lips on hers. Yep, they needed to talk soon.

Her shoulders clenched at the thought of it.

* * *

As they got out of the truck back at the house, Jake spotted Mac pulling the tractor with the mower attachment out of the barn. He glanced off through the trees, scrubbing his jaw. Mac needed to finish the mowing Jake had begun a couple of days ago, before the weeds got out of hand.

But this was a perfect opportunity. He called out to Cress before she disappeared into the house, arms loaded with carefully bagged soil samples.

"Cress!"

She turned to him, flipping her ponytail over her shoulder and frowning into the morning sun.

"Drop that stuff real quick, then come with me. I'll teach you how to run the tractor."

With a nod, she slid into the house. Jake turned to Mac, griping under his breath about insane ideas.

Mac bobbed his head toward the house as he hopped down from the tractor. "You sure about this? She nearly ran over Franklin last week on the Bobcat."

Jake shook his head and shrugged. "She's the boss' grand-daughter. Gotta learn sometime." He thumped the side of the tractor. "And those rows aren't going to mow themselves. Perfect opportunity."

"If you say so." Mac slapped him on the shoulder. "All the same, I'm glad it's you and not me. Good luck not getting mowed over."

Jake shoved him lightly, and the man trotted off with a laugh toward the barn. After discovering their little problem with the fire ants, they had irrigation lines to repair. Shoving his hands in his pockets, Jake leaned against the tractor and looked at the July sky, cornflower blue and so bright it hurt to stare at too long.

Why hadn't he gotten Mac or Franklin to show her how to run the tractor? Lord knows he had plenty to do, making sure the irrigation lines were all intact now that he was seeing fire ant beds everywhere.

An image flashed into his mind of that morning, out in the field, Cress kneeling in the dirt, eyebrows pinched with intent as she took sample after sample, the morning light gilding the soft curls in her hair. The way her arm had traced the arc of the stream. In those moments, all the bluster had melted away, and he'd seen the same quiet concentration, the same devotion to the soil and the land that he felt. It was almost as if…

At the sound of the screen door slapping shut, his heart thumped in his chest, and he jerked up straight before forcing himself to relax.

He shook himself. There was nothing else to it. He was just doing his job, teaching Cress how to run her farm. If it meant spending more time with her, so be it.

Cress walked up to him, tugging on her work gloves. She flexed her fingers against the grain of the leather and smiled up at him, her cheeks dimpling. His hammering heart gave away all the lies he'd just told himself, and inwardly, he cringed.

"Let's get to it." Then she looked at the looming tractor behind him and blanched. "I take it back. I want to live to see another day."

He chuckled, swallowing against the sudden lump in his throat. "C'mon. You'll be fine." He climbed up and patted the seat. "I won't let anything happen to you." He held out a hand.

She looked from him to the tractor, mouth pinching in, but

finally accepted his hand, hopping up with a little grunt. He nodded, pleased, as he stood next to her on the running board.

"Now, the first thing to understand is that if you somehow miraculously manage to fall off, the tractor will stop running. There is a safety mechanism under the seat that acts like a kill switch, so if your weight comes off it, it cuts the engine."

Cress nodded enthusiastically at this, and Jake relaxed a bit. He handed her the key.

"Already? But you haven't even shown me what all these other gears and things are."

"Part of showing you those is also showing you how to crank it. Now take the key."

She snatched the key out of his hand and jammed it in the ignition. He grabbed her hand before she could twist. "Foot on the brake." His voice was quiet but firm.

"Well, which of the three pedals is the brake?"

He pointed. "Both of those."

"Wait. There's two?"

He grinned. "So, it won't matter if you're a rightie or leftie or panic. Either one you hit will brake the whole tractor."

She bit her lip. "That's convenient."

"Thought you might like that, you racing machine."

"You bump into someone one time…" she groaned. Cress cut her eyes at him and blew out a sigh. "All right. What else do I need to know about this thing?"

"Thought you'd never ask." With a wave, he showed her the clutch and gears, watching as Cress relaxed at his explanations, the familiar smell of diesel and engine oil rising around them. Sweat beaded up along their brows as they leaned over the dash of the tractor in the sun, and Jake placed his hand on top of hers as he showed her how to work her way through the gears.

"Remember, you control this machine. You're in charge. It can only do what you tell it to." Cress nodded, eyes serious at his words as she repeated to him what each lever did.

He lingered over the instruction, the simple pleasure of feeling like the expert for once flooding over him. It helped that Cress was truly interested in learning, completely focused on what he had to say, eyebrows squinched in concentration.

After a few minutes, he let her take several excruciatingly slow practice passes up and down the driveway while he watched appraisingly, encouraging her to try different gears so she could get used to how they felt. At last, they headed, still at a snail's pace, toward the West lot to get started mowing. He was confident it would take them all day at this rate.

As Jake walked alongside the growling tractor, he glanced up at Cress. A proud smile sat on her lips and her eyes shone as she sat tall in the seat. She glanced down at Jake and grinned. A lump rose in his throat, and he swallowed, glancing off through the trees. He was just doing his job, after all. What did it matter if it meant spending more time with Cress?

* * *

Sunlight slid down Cress' back, hot and itchy, as they finally headed to the orchard. She eyed the drive ahead of them, gently tugging on the wheel to correct the tractor as it pulled toward the edge of the gravel. This wasn't so bad. Despite the deep rumbling bass of the engine and the vibrating hum of the wheels, she was in command of this behemoth of a machine. Maybe she could learn all the ins and outs of a farm after all.

The tractor ground to a halt with an ear-splitting squeal

and slapping noise. She threw up her hands. "Wasn't me!"

Jake leaped up onto the running board and hit the throttle, choking the engine down until it died. "Sounds like the timing belt slipped. That's going to be a pain to fix." He rubbed his face. "All right. Hop down." He jumped off and walked around to the front, flipping the engine cover open and peering in. Cress followed him nervously.

She leaned her elbows on the casing and studied the hunk of metal, gears, and parts seeming to meld together in front of her. "What exactly are we looking for?"

Jake reached in, his arm disappearing up to his shoulder as he fished around in the pinging and popping engine. "Yee-ouch!" He swore quietly as he grazed his shoulder. After a few seconds, he re-emerged. "Yep, looks like the timing belt gave out." He let out a groaning sigh. "That's at least an hour to town and back to get the parts from the hardware store. Then another hour to get this," he slapped another unidentifiable hunk of metal, "up where I can get it on. We're going to lose the whole afternoon."

"I can go to town." The words were out before she had even considered them. Jake eyed her skeptically. She shrugged. "I'll go get the... timing belt." His eyebrows shot up.

"Probably going to need a new camshaft, too. Do you know what you're looking for?" He twisted his mouth to the side as he studied her.

She shook her head, feeling anything but certain, but slipped her phone from her pocket and took a photo of the tractor, getting the numbers on the side. "I'll ask Herb for help. He can look it up if he doesn't know it off the top of his head."

Grinning, Jake nodded. "Knew there was a reason we kept you around."

She gave him a nonplussed stare, trying not to encourage him before she broke the bad news. "Besides, you know, saving the trees and whatnot."

He wrapped an arm around her waist. "And what not." She swallowed and put a hand on his chest.

"Jake," her voice came out low and shaky as he tightened his arm.

His eyes searched hers, a teasing smile playing on his lips. "Mmhmm?"

She pushed lightly against him. "Jake, we need to talk."

He dropped his arm and stepped back. He grabbed his ball cap from his head and ran his hands through his hair. "Don't do this, Cress."

She snapped. "And what do you think I'm doing?" Men always thought they knew better than her, what she was doing and what she should do instead. And she was so tired of it.

He set his hands on his hips, studying the ground and then her. "I think you're about to throw every excuse in the book at… this," he waved his hands at the space between them, "before it's even off the ground so you can run away." He huffed and clenched his hands. "I'm asking," he paused, his eyes shimmering in the light, "to just give us a chance before you decide whether we click."

"Jake—" she bit her lip. "You know this can't happen. We work together. We annoy each other. How would this even…"

He cut her off by taking her hands. "That's what I'm talking about." He squeezed her fingers. "Cress, c'mon. There's something here. You know there is." He took a deep breath. "And if, *if*, we don't work, I won't make it awkward for you. I promise."

She whispered, "That's a pretty big *if* you're gambling on."

180

He grinned at her. "I'm feeling pretty lucky today."

She searched his face as his hands slowly slid around her waist. "You have to be on your best behavior." She watched as the corner of his mouth quirked up.

He pulled her closer. "Mmhmm."

"No more teasing me about being a doctor." She swallowed, her heart beating mutinously fast.

He kissed her neck and hummed in her ear, "Got it."

"And no more griping about orchard inspections." He tightened his hold on her waist, and slowly she slid her arms around his neck.

He kissed her jaw, his stubble deliciously rough against her skin as he worked his way to the corner of her mouth. "I can think of something better to inspect, but sure."

She breathed against his lips, the heady scent of his cedar-wood cologne filling her senses. "I'm serious. Best behavior."

"I'll be an angel. I swear." His touch was just a whisper against her nose, sending a shiver down her spine.

She wound her fingers into his unruly hair. "Oh, just come here already."

He chuckled as he kissed her, his chest rumbling against her and sending waves of delight down into her knees. His lips met hers gently, so gently that she couldn't tell at first that he was kissing her.

Then, she was rising onto her toes, a hunger to be touched and known so powerful she didn't even recognize it as a hidden need until it was building and cresting over them like a tidal wave at the beach, deep and cool and sparkling. At the end of the kiss, she drew away breathless, gasping for air, and saw Jake panting as well.

She straightened her shirt, at a loss for what to say. What in tarnation was that? Jake leaned against the tractor and rubbed at the back of his neck as he looked at her. Her eyes fell on the timing belt, draped over the side.

She snatched it up and began backing away. "Well, I guess I'll go get this now." She turned around and power walked away her face bright red.

"Cress!" Jake called after her, and she waved over her shoulder.

"Don't worry! I've got it." Her feet carried her toward her truck of their own accord. Could she make this anymore awkward? She got in the truck and slammed the door. As she sped down the driveway, she spied Jake, still standing by the tractor, hands on his hips and laughing at the sky. Yep, that made it worse.

She rubbed her mouth, where his stubble had left a slight chafe. With a flick, she turned on her favorite smooth jazz station and grinned stupidly at the road.

Chapter 14

Cress eyed the Loveless Bakery, then her mud-caked wellies. Only a few other souls braved the heat shimmering off the brick streets, but her mouth still watered at the thought of one of Willow's sticky buns. How Jake's eyes would light up at the sight of a cup of chicory coffee and a cream cheese Danish. She glanced down at her boots one more time and hefted the sack with the new timing belt in it.

Willow worked in a farming town. She wouldn't mind a little mud. Cress hurried across the street and pushed the door open with a cheerful clatter of the bells.

Her eyes were already studying the pastry case as she called out, "Willow! Could I get a Danish and a sticky bun?" She ran right into a broad back. Hard.

As she rubbed her sore nose, the familiar scent of orange blossoms washed over her. Disbelieving, her eyes scanned the towering man in the perfectly pressed white shirt in front of her and watched in stunned silence as he turned around.

A slow grin spread across Grant's face as his hazel eyes twinkled at her. "Hey, baby. Fancy running into you here." To her horror, he tried to hug her. She ducked under his arm and backed away.

"Wha... Grant!" she sputtered, waving her hands in front of her. Her heart flip-flopped around in her chest like a fish at the bottom of a boat. "You're in Wisconsin. You're supposed to be in Wisconsin. What are you doing here?"

Willow poked her head out from the back room where she had watched the encounter, a rolling pin gripped in one hand. Concern rippled across her face as she eyed Grant, then Cress. Cress shook her head at her, and Willow took a half step back, her eyes never leaving Grant.

Grant held out his arms. "I'm here! After I got your text, I got to thinking, what if we could make this place the next Waco or Laurel? So, I convinced my company to pitch your mayor and here I am! This is perfect." He sneezed.

Groaning, Cress dropped her head into her hands. This was a disaster. This was so like him to go overboard from just one text.

He stepped forward again but didn't try to touch her. Lowering his voice so Willow, who still stood glaring at him from the back room, couldn't hear, he said, "I've... I've missed you." He looked at the floor and shoved his hands in his pockets.

Cress looked up at him, shocked tears finally shimmering in her eyes. Numbness froze her in place as she realized she hadn't missed him, at least, not since the drive here. She'd been too busy with the orchard and with helping Jake... She blinked as his face flashed through her mind.

She grimaced and wiped away the tears. "You were right.

I've had a lot of time to think since I got here," she fibbed, "and we just don't fit. Breaking up was for the best." Their sniffles echoed each other, his from allergies and hers from an overwhelm of emotion. They stood in awkward silence for a moment.

"How are things going at the farm?" he finally asked.

Cress was surprised he knew she was working there but shrugged it off. If he'd been in town for longer than a day, he could have learned that anywhere. She crossed her arms, feeling unkempt in her sweaty clothes covered in grease and mud.

"We just bought some new acreage, but finding the funds to plant it is a little tight." She forced out a strained chuckle, not sure why she'd told him anything at all. It was always hard to keep quiet when those eyes seemed to bore into her soul.

"I keep asking myself what you would do." Why could she not stop talking?

He studied her, a small smile crooking up one corner of his mouth. "Well, I'd look for a way to diversify my revenue streams. I'd take into account my skills and capabilities and see what other opportunities are in the area and try to work with other farmers and possibly artists and craftsmen."

"It sounds so simple when you put it like that." She rubbed her thumb across her elbow, possibilities already churning in her head.

He shook his head. "The trick is knowing what's a good fit for you. Just because it's an idea doesn't make it a good idea. And even a good idea can be a bad fit for you. Gotta do your homework."

She nodded, biting the inside of her cheek to keep from saying anything else, and they lapsed into silence. Finally, she burst out, "Well, I'll let you get back to it!" and darted out of the bakery with a wave to Willow. Sitting in her truck, she leaned her head against the wheel.

Around her, the buildings loomed, their hollow eyes seeming to taunt her. What was that? Of all the things she could say to him, should have said, she had to blurt her money worries about the farm? Had she completely lost her marbles? She groaned and thunked her head on the steering wheel. A soft knock on the window made her jump upright, heart skittering.

Willow stood outside, smiling. Rolling the window down, the smell of sugar, spice, and coffee wafted in. Willow passed her a fragrant white bag and two cups of coffee.

"It's on the house today." Willow winked at Cress as she peered in the bag at a cream cheese Danish and a sticky bun. Willow patted the hood of the truck. "Tell Jake I said hello."

As Cress bumped over the knobby brick streets, buildings crumbling around her, overwhelmed with gratitude at being home and among people who cared so fiercely surged through her. Somehow, she'd find a way to give back.

* * *

With Mac's help and the other tractor, Jake got the old hunk of metal to the barn. Now, he cranked the engine block out of place and onto a waiting stand just as he heard the crack and rumble of gravel. Dust rose behind Cress' truck in a billowing cloud as she halted outside.

His hand fell heavily from the wave he'd been about to give when he glimpsed her blankly staring face through her windshield. What in God's name was eating at her now?

186

Through the static of the old radio perched precariously on the workbench behind him, Etta Jones plaintively crooned "Bye Bye Blackbird." With a huff, he twisted the volume dial down.

She climbed out of the truck and slammed the door with a grimace, a white paper bag clutched in her hands. At any other time, the sight would have delighted him—a signal that she'd been thinking about him while she was gone. Now, his mouth just felt sour and dry from the heat. Still, best to play it cool until he knew what was up.

"That doesn't look like a timing belt." He pointed at the bag as he wiped his hands clean of grease on a red rag.

Cress plunked it in his outstretched palms as she walked around to the other side of her truck and opened the door. "Willow says hello." He heard a rustle, and she emerged with another bag and two cups of coffee.

He dug into the bag in his hands and pulled out a danish. "My hero." She grinned mechanically at him as she walked over, then leaned against the tractor. Staring vacantly into the trees, she sipped the coffee. The silence stretched.

He didn't like this kind of quiet. Cress wasn't exactly chatty, but she wasn't one for silent musing much either. She was focused, directed. Not distracted and moody. Had she changed her mind about them again, already?

Clearing his throat, he began, "So… you all right?"

She looked up at him, startled. "Yeah?"

Thoroughly confused, he asked, "About earlier? Us…" He gestured between them. Her lips worked up and down as she tried not to laugh. It would have been adorable if it didn't leave him completely in the dark.

"Yes, we're fine." She sighed and handed him the other cup

of coffee, then dug into the bag. "I'm just thinking, is all."

"Thinking?" he repeated stupidly. Getting any information out of her was like trying to get blood out of a turnip. It just wasn't happening. "About what, exactly?"

"How we can fund the new orchard. I ran into Grant in town, and it got me thinking about a bunch of different ways…"

He cut her off. "Hold on." He set the coffee down on the running board of the tractor and crossed his arms. "You ran into Grant? And you didn't lead with that." He gritted his teeth as alarm bubbled up. Somehow, that rat had clawed his way back into Cress' life, just like he'd feared. "What is he doing here? I thought he was in Minnesota?"

She frowned. "Wisconsin. And he just showed up." She raised a hand and dropped it helplessly. "The company he works for specializes in revitalizing towns and small cities. They thought Midnight Bluff was promising, pitched Patty, and sent him." She chewed while talking. "I'm not sure if he's here just for research or the duration." Swallowing, she added, "He's been itching for a higher position, and being the lead on a major project like this would be huge for him. So…" She shrugged and trailed off.

Jake groaned and thumped the side of his fist against the tractor. Just what he needed. A jealous ex getting in the middle of things just as they were getting started.

Cress continued, oblivious as she waved her sticky bun, "But it's not all bad. He gave me an idea about how we can keep this place afloat while we get the new orchard established."

Jake shoved his hands in his pockets, trying to be calm. "You mean besides the massive loan we've already taken out?"

She made a shooing motion with her hand. "We have so

much downtime in the off-season. And a lot of the other farmers do, too. What if we teamed up with them to offer something unique to the area? We could do tours, cooking and barbecuing classes, woodworking. We're about to have so much extra wood to cure, we'll be set for years. And things like this will be a huge draw to the folks in Cleveland."

Cress was speaking so fast, he wasn't sure if she was breathing. "And it will be an opportunity to show off all the different things you can do with pecan wood and get some of the local craftsmen involved. Maybe even the university." Her eyes sparkled. "Just think of being able to pull the community together on this!" Grabbing his arm, she bounced a bit.

He sighed. "Cress, these are great ideas." He took a deep breath, wondering just how to pour this bucket of cold water on her without completely dousing the fire. "But 'off-season' doesn't mean we have that time *off*. We've got to process the harvest and there's a ton of equipment maintenance." He shrugged.

"I don't know how we'd coordinate something that massive and…" As her face fell, he hastened to continue. "I don't know how many other farmers and craftsmen could take us up on it either. They're in the same spot seasonally speaking. Plus, we're talking about splitting the profit with a lot of people. We need to do the math before we jump into something this huge."

"The split would only be on the activities they're involved in, and we could charge a coordinator fee to minimize our loss." She crossed her arms. Her jaw worked back and forth as she stared at the ground. He ground his teeth, not wanting to get into a big fight this soon. He decided to take the easy way out, hating himself a little for doing it.

He spread his hands. "Look, I'm not the one you have to convince. Ultimately, it's Bo's decision. If you can talk him into it, I'll go for it. I just think we have enough to do right now without splitting up our focus with a… a… circus." He grimaced as soon as the word left his lips.

She scowled at him. "Fine. Then I'll talk to Gramps. He'll love my idea. When, ironically, my boyfriend doesn't." She slapped a package into his hand, turned on her heel, and stomped into the barn's office.

He blinked down at the timing belt. He grinned. "At least she called me her boyfriend." He flicked the volume on the radio up and turned back to the engine, whistling along to "Fools Rush In."

Chapter 15

W hen the phone rang in the quiet of the barn's office, Cress nearly jumped out of her skin. She placed a hand on her hammering heart and pulled her cell phone out of her pocket. From the floor of the barn, she could still hear Jake whistling along to the radio as she closed the office door.

"Hey, Mom. What's up?"

"I just ran into your darling Grant at the courthouse. Why didn't you tell me he was in town?" Leora's voice was high and breathy. Cress could just imagine her power walking down the sidewalk in town, flushed with excitement after an unexpected encounter with Cress' hulking ex-boyfriend.

"I didn't tell you because I didn't know." She glanced at her watch. "I just ran into him myself a little over an hour ago." Gossip sure traveled fast in this town.

"Surely you knew he was coming!" Her mother's protest pinged up at the end. "He's here at the mayor's special request."

Cress dropped her arm onto the messy desk. The mayor

had requested him? Crap, that didn't bode well for getting rid of him quickly. "We don't keep in touch, Mom."

Her mother clicked her tongue like a tutting hen. "That's not what he told me. Said he wouldn't be here if it weren't for you."

Staring at the water-spotted ceiling, Cress groaned. "I don't know what to tell you. I sent him the lead on the town. I didn't expect him to show up here himself."

Out in the barns, she could hear the rev of an engine suddenly drown out the low strains of jazz. Good thing she'd closed the door when she did.

Her mother gushed. "Well, I think this is just wonderful. Everybody back together."

Stirrings of panic bubbled up in Cress' throat. "No, Mom!"

Her mother kept chattering, "I invited him to dinner Friday night and assured him we were *all* excited to have him here." Her tone dropped lower. "And Cress, try to do something a little classier than a beef pot roast this time." Her voice sweetened. "You'll never be able to keep a man if you don't at least try to feed him well."

Cress groaned. "Mom, it's not like that. Grant and I—"

"Oh, I'm so glad to see you have a second shot at happiness. I've got to go tell the ladies about this. Talk to you later!" The line clicked dead.

Cress dropped her head onto the desk with a bang. She clutched at her hair, mind spinning. How would she navigate an entire dinner with her mother trying to set her and Grant back up? And why was her mother trying to set them up? She thought Leora didn't like Grant. Her head shot up as she leaned back in the chair and put her hands over her face. And what would she do about Jake? She screamed quietly into her cupped hands.

"You ok there, kiddo?" Gramps stood in the doorway looking at her with big, concerned eyes. He crossed the small room and sat on a corner of the desk, pushing aside some papers.

"I'm fine." She crossed her arms and bit her lip.

"Looks like you were having a bit of a meltdown." He patted her knee. "Want to tell me about it?"

She wiggled her nose as she thought. Maybe Gramps could help—run interference or something. "Mom just invited Grant to dinner on Friday night. She seems to think we are getting back together."

His eyebrows shot up, but he took the news in stride. "And are you?"

"Oh God, no!" She slouched in the chair. "I've got too much going on here." Her thoughts flitted to Jake outside, working on the tractor. "And besides, we were never right together." She knit her fingers together, searching for words, but Gramps held up a hand.

"You don't have to explain it to me." His teeth twinkled in the dim office light. "When you know, you know." They sat for a moment. "So, it sounds like you need some help with this dinner then?"

Cress leaned her head against the back of the chair. "Mom said something about pot roast not being classy enough."

He laughed. "I think Lynn can help us out with that. God, that woman can cook just about anything." He patted her knee again. "Leave the rest to me. We'll get you through this, don't you worry about it."

She squeezed his hand as he stood. "Thanks, Gramps. You're a lifesaver." As he turned to go, she took a deep breath.

It was now or never. With the way Jake had reacted, she'd lose her nerve to bring up her idea again if she didn't do it now. "Hey, Gramps!"

He turned back around, and she launched into her spiel about teaming up with other farmers and local craftsmen to create an off-season destination. She watched his face pucker in thought, and he put a hand over his mouth as he considered.

After listing some of her original ideas for ways to highlight the orchard's natural charms, she finished with her strongest point. "I think it could be fantastic for the town's morale, to see everyone working together, and it could get some revenue flowing in our slowest season."

Gramps *hmmed* in the back of his throat as he looked at the ceiling. He crossed his arms. "It's a lot to think over." She sagged in her chair. She'd expected him to be more excited about this. He held up his hands. "I like getting more people involved, but it complicates our off-season. And there's the expense of it, too."

She opened her mouth to protest, but he cut in. "I know what you're going to say, and I like where your heart is at. But this is a big undertaking. If it's not done right, it will quickly turn into charity marketing for the town instead of driving business for us. It could bankrupt us." He bobbed his head as he rubbed his lips together. "Lots to think over."

She stared at her lap, dejected. Jake not liking her idea she could live with, but Gramps … that stung. He patted her shoulder, smiling. "Have I told you lately how proud I am of you?" He nodded. "You're so much like your father. All these big dreams."

Covering his hand with hers, she smiled up at him. "It sounds like something he would come up with, doesn't it?"

The thought made her chuckle. He had been forever driving Mom crazy with his wild ideas. She glanced back up at him. "Thank you for helping with dinner."

"Don't worry about it." He winked. "Now, I'm off to do some scheming."

* * *

The goblets sparkled on the table and the blue willow plates shone impeccably on their silver chargers. Fragrant magnolia blossoms floated in a crystal bowl in the center of the mahogany. Cress lit the last taper and stood back. The effect was understated but elegant. A perfect Southern dinner. If Mama found fault with this, well, she was determined to be a sourpuss.

Cress took a deep breath and shook out the match impatiently as it nipped at her fingertips. She jumped as the doorbell rang through the house with a heavy gong. How odd. Mama usually just breezed on in, carried along by a cloud of Chanel No. 5 and chit-chat. At a second, longer ring, Cress leaped toward the front hall, her heels echoing on the hardwood.

Her mother's voice rang through the door as Cress reached it. Was she talking to herself? Was she breaking one of her own rules and on the phone in front of other people? Perturbed, Cress yanked the door open. Heart sputtering, she froze.

Towering over and slightly behind Leora, stood Grant, a slight smirk on his face and a loaf of bread tucked under his arm. Their eyes locked. Cress could feel her mouth part slightly as she struggled for words.

Her mother prattled on about... something, oblivious to

the awkward silence between them as Cress' mind spun for words and for an explanation why her mother would arrive with her ex, never mind that she had invited him much to her daughter's open discomfort. Finally, a flicker of motion on the drive behind them made her blink.

Jake strode toward them in a fresh, white linen shirt. She blinked again as she looked closer. His face was smooth. He'd shaved. She'd never seen him without the permanent ring of stubble. His mouth was pressed into a tight line as his eyes flashed over Grant, who stood a good two inches taller than him.

Leora cleared her throat, scowling at her daughter as she glanced between her and Jake. "Cress, dear. Are you going to stand there blocking the door or are you going to invite your guests in?"

With a shuffle, Cress slid to the side and waved them forward. Grant placed a hand on her arm, his fingers encircling her forearm. He leaned in, the familiar smell of his orange blossom cologne washing over her. "It's good to see you again so soon, Cress." White noise flared through her brain. Numbly, she accepted the loaf of bread he placed in her hands as he stepped inside behind her mother, toward Bo's cheerful greeting.

Jake's boots thudded on the porch. He stopped a few feet away, wavering between her and the door. She stared down at the brown paper wrapping the loaf, Willow's logo twinkling up at her. He took a step closer and again stopped. "That the ex?"

She swallowed, her head feeling heavy with everything running through it, and forced out, "Grant." She couldn't look Jake in the eye.

He whistled. "I didn't expect him to look like a male model." The words came out clipped. "What's he doing here?"

She shrugged, tightening her grip on the bread. "Mama invited him." Risking it, she looked up. Jake studied her, hands in pockets, but he didn't look upset. She let out a heavy breath, her lungs aching.

"Are you all right?" His words wrapped around her, reassuring.

She pressed her lips together and nodded. "I'm not thrilled he's here, but it'll be fine. I think. I'm more worried about Mama behaving herself than him." She grimaced and shrugged.

Jake reached for the door behind her to hold it open for her. "Well then, let's get one heck of an awkward dinner for you out of the way, shall we?" As she brushed past him, he placed his hand on the small of her back and followed her in. She glanced up at him as her stomach fluttered.

In the living room, Gramps stood pumping Grant's hand up and down, a pained smile plastered across his face. Seeing Cress and Jake enter together, Jake's hand still on her back, he dropped Grant's hand like a hot potato and smiled for real, the gleam of his teeth dashing across his face.

Leora settled into an armchair, watching the scene unfold, a bemused expression on her face as she rested her cheek against a poised pointer finger. With a squeak of his heel on the wood floor, Grant turned.

His glance swept over Cress and Jake. His eyes, which had been wide with confidence, narrowed as he studied Jake's hand on Cress. Jake wrapped his arm around Cress' waist and gave her a squeeze. Nervously, she giggled, then pressed her lips together. Her heart thudded in her chest at Grant's glowering face, and she watched in horror as a flush worked its way up his neck. Her mind spun for a way to prevent the inevitable blowup.

She tensed as Grant took a breath, and Jake rubbed his thumb back and forth against her ribs. Willing herself to breathe, she glanced at him, and he quirked an eyebrow at her. With a sigh, she leaned into him slightly. They were in this together despite her mother's machinations.

Suddenly, Grant's face contorted and puckered, his hand flying up to cover his mouth as he let out a deafening string of sneezes.

Calmly, Leora held a tissue box toward him. "Bless you, dear."

Grant choked out a thank you as he took a tissue and wiped his face, still sneezing. Consternated, Cress looked at him. She hadn't worn perfume, and he had seemed fine when he walked in with her mother despite her perfume. She couldn't think of anything that would set off his allergies… The magnolia blossoms.

She spun away and sprinted into the dining room, snatching the bowl of flowers from the table and hustling to chuck the offending blooms out the front door.

When she returned, Grant eyed her. "Trying to kill me already, Cress?"

She sniffed at his bad joke as she sat beside Jake on the settee, the loaf of bread between them. "If I wanted to do that, I'd just go roll in the grass and be done with it. For the final time, Clar-i-tin."

Her mother tutted, but Grant's lips turned up tersely, and he turned to Leora instead, asking about the Ladies' Auxiliary efforts to revitalize Midnight Bluff before he arrived. Cress relaxed, thanking God for small miracles. Not wanting to crush it, she cradled the bread on her lap as she leaned into Jake.

Her mother arched a brow at her. "Darling, you're being rather rude to your guests, don't you think?" She waved at the coffee table vaguely.

Confused, Cress shook her head. "What?"

"Drinks, dear?" Leora wrinkled her brow in the universal look of motherly disapproval. "They will not float in here by themselves." She put a finger to her chin. "And why don't you slice that lovely loaf Grant brought you and put it on your grandmother's silver platter? You know the one. With the grape filigree."

Resisting the urge to roll her eyes, Cress stood silently and slipped into the kitchen. Lynn winked at her as she entered.

"The ole bat at it again?" she asked.

"That ole bat is my mother, thank you." Cress plunked the bread down on the island and crossed her arms. "And yes, she is."

Lynn nodded matter-of-factly. "I thought so the moment I saw that stud walk in behind her. That the ex?"

Cress groaned and leaned her elbows on the countertop, plunking her head into her hands. "Yes. This night is going to be a disaster. Jake and I barely even 'Jake and I.'" She air-quoted. "And Mother is already trying to scare him off. It's going to work, too. Who wouldn't run with this kind of drama?"

Reaching over, Lynn patted her shoulder. "Sugar, when people get tricky, you get trickier. You need that platter, right?" She pointed to the plate shelf that ran around the top of the room. Grandma Elena's platter sat in a spot of honor above the cabinet that held the glasses. Cress looked at it, then at

Lynn.

"What's that got to do with anything?"

With another wink, Lynn pulled the step ladder from its hidey-hole in the pantry, opened the back door, and chucked it into the yard. She grinned. "I can't seem to find the ladder. Going to take a tall, strong, young fella' to fetch that down."

Cress smiled and stepped over to the door to call Jake.

* * *

"I can't imagine where the step stool got off to." Jake couldn't keep the chagrin from his voice. But he was still thankful for the slight break in the kitchen, instead of sitting on Bo's settee with *Grant* staring daggers at him.

This evening's dinner was already shaping up to be even more awkward than the last. Jake had been expecting Leora, but the addition of Grant's hulking form had completely taken him by surprise. That dude had to be at least two or three inches taller than him.

He supposed he had Bo to thank for the surprise. As he stretched up for the platter on the high plate shelf, his glance flashed to Cress, who stood beside him. In the last few days, she'd opened up and relaxed. But tonight, the guarded, worried expression was back, eyes hooded and eyebrows drawn together. She fidgeted with her navy-blue dress and kept tucking strands of hair behind her ears.

It irked him to see how anxious Grant's presence made her. With Leora, she was withdrawn and petulant. But Grant brought out an entirely different side of her.

He grasped the weighty platter, his wrist burning and cramping from working on the tractor more that afternoon.

The repairs had taken longer than he'd expected and left him sore and strained.

Before he could drop the heavy platter, he set it down with a *thunk* and leaned against the counter, rubbing at his wrist and studying Cress' still-pinched face. She glanced up at him and tried to smooth away the unhappy wrinkle between her brows, but the twist of her mouth and squinch of her eyes betrayed her.

Her mother's voice echoed to them from the other room. Cress' eyes darted to the door at the sound then dropped to the floor as she gripped her elbows and hunched her shoulders. He hadn't seen her this tense in weeks.

With a sigh, he leaned into her and tilted her chin up. "You shouldn't let one jerk get to you like this. He's not worth it."

Her shoulders crept further upwards to her ears. "Not according to my mother. I've thrown my last chance for marriage and a career away if you listen to her."

He grinned. "What was that you said? I seemed to have developed a sudden case of deafness. Most unusual. Only happens when your mom's around."

Cress pressed her lips together, but he saw a small smile tweak up the corner of her mouth. "Come on. Be serious."

Jake placed his hands on her shoulders and pressed down, easing the tension away. "I am. You're working your butt off here. Doing things I can't even wrap my head around. And if your mom can't see that, well... maybe she has a case of selective blindness instead."

Cress' eyes shimmered, and she swallowed. He hesitated, not wanting to overwhelm her, but another look at her flushed face and he pulled her toward him and wrapped his arms around her. He heard her inhale, soft and surprised, and for a moment her spine stayed rigid under his hands. Had he misread the moment?

Then he felt her melting into him, her soft arms encircling his waist and her warm breath on his neck as she stretched up onto her toes to rest her chin on his shoulder. With a chuckle, he kissed her cheek and squeezed her as she sniffled. They stood there for a moment longer, basking in the closeness.

As he leaned his cheek against her silky hair, his mouth went dry, his tongue clinging to the roof of his palate. The crisp ocean water of her shampoo tickled his nose, but underneath that was salt and sun and the musk of a hard day's work.

Suddenly, every nerve ending in his body was on fire, aware of her curves pressed to his chest, the way he could feel the rise and fall of her breaths. His heart hammered. Not wanting to get swept up in this heady reaction, he cleared his throat and pulled away. At her startled look, he chuckled and rubbed at his wrist again.

"Confounded thing won't quit aching." It was true. His wrist was burning. And his hand. But not in the way she thought.

Her fingers encircled his wrist, and she pulled his arm toward her. He tried to tug it back.

"I'm not going to bite. Just relax!" She smiled at him, her teeth pearly and glowing from the light above the sink. Gently but firmly, she pressed her thumb into the flesh of his forearm and his hand went limp, tingling with pins and needles. He groaned as she slid her warm palm down his, the tension seeming to melt away under her hand and with it the bone-deep ache in his wrist.

"You'll want to put some ice on this for about ten minutes tonight before you go to bed, but it should feel a lot better tomorrow." She bit her lip as she continued to massage away the stress in his wrist. He nodded mutely as he stared at her lip.

"Well, this looks cozy!" Bo boomed into the quiet of the kitchen. He smirked at them from across the island, his eyes sparkling with mischief.

"I hurt my wrist working on the tractor this afternoon. Cress was just helping," Jake stuttered out the explanation, his voice sounding high and thin, even to him.

"Sure, she was." Bo put his hands on his hips and broke out into a full grin.

"Grandpa!" Cress' voice came out in a squeak and a glance revealed she was flushed right up to her hairline. Jake's mouth twitched at the adorable sight and Bo's eyes darted between them, missing nothing. Jake wiped the smile off his face right quickly.

"Leora sent me to see what was taking so long about getting one platter. Now I know."

Jake crossed his arms and huffed at Bo while Cress fluttered her hands in distress. As Bo crossed the kitchen, he made shushing noises. "Oh, calm down. I'm not going to say anything. Your secret is safe with me."

"Secret! What secret?" Cress trotted after him, whispering at his back, and Jake hung his head, laughing. This night had just gotten even weirder.

* * *

Cress' back ached from sitting ramrod straight through dinner, but as she gathered up the last coffee cups from the side tables, she exhaled in relief. The evening was almost over.

And Grant had only been minorly insufferable, talking about the incredible manufacturing opportunities in Vermont. He always monologued when he was nervous. And Jake's little staring contest with him over the soup hadn't helped.

Fortunately, Jake's eyes had glassed over an hour ago and he'd begun making the polite *hmms* and *ohs* of the deeply disinterested. And now they were all having to suffer through Grant's stream of consciousness as he talked about everything Vermont.

As Grant blathered on about microbrewing and ice cream, Cress beat a hasty retreat to the kitchen to dump the coffee cups. She grabbed some bourbon and took a shot straight from the bottle. A footfall behind her made her spin around guiltily.

Jake grinned at her. "You weren't going to share?" He took the bottle and chugged back a swig. "Need something to numb the pain." He took another swig.

"He is pretty awful when he gets going, isn't he?" She brushed at her mouth with her fingertips, then drank a sip of water straight from the tap to hide the smell. Her mother had the senses of a bloodhound, and she didn't think Leora would approve of taking shots in the kitchen to escape boredom.

"That's no way to speak about your guest, honey."

Cress and Jake both jumped at the sound of Leora's voice. How in the world she had sneaked down the hall in stilettos was beyond Cress, but there she was, silhouetted in the kitchen door. She raised one immaculately shaped brow at them, her eyes traveling to the bottle.

In the silence, Cress could hear the tap drip behind her.

"Well, aren't you going to offer me any?"

Cress' mouth fell open at her mother's question, but Jake

was already handing the bottle to her. She watched in stunned silence as her prim and proper mother slugged back enough bourbon for a grown man. Leora winced in satisfaction as she lowered the bottle.

"Good Lord, he is full of himself." Leora set the bottle down and glanced at her watch. "We'll have to rescue Bo in a minute." She looked at Cress, who stared back, utterly confused. "Why in the world did you date that bore for seven years?"

"Don't you have to drive back?" Cress sputtered, her mind skipping a track.

Her mother waved off the question. "I made him drive. And since he's hogging the conversation, he just voted himself DD." She took another pull from the bottle, color already high in her cheeks. "Now, why, Cress, did you stay with him?"

Cress threw up her hands, looking to Jake for help.

He shrugged. "I want to know, too."

"Because he's not always this way." They stared at her. She waved her hands back and forth. "Ok, I don't know. When we met, he was witty and charming, and we had a great time together." She shrugged as she looked at the counter, not wanting to explain it. There had been so much more between them. "At the time, I didn't need more than that."

"After a while, I dunno. We just didn't fit the way we used to, but we thought if we stuck it out, it would get better." She looked up, trying to appear calmer than she felt. "Obviously, it didn't."

They all stared at each other. Finally, her mother offered her the bottle of bourbon.

"Thanks." This was probably the closest she'd get to an apology from her mother for all the catty comments about her dating life. She started to take a swig from it, then set it down. She didn't want to try drinking her troubles away anymore.

Jake wrapped an arm around her shoulder, and she leaned into him. Leora studied them, deep green eyes always assessing. Before she could say anything, a cheerful voice boomed in the doorway behind them.

"So, here's where the party moved!" Grant stood behind them, eyeing the tableau. A smile that didn't quite reach his eyes was firmly fixed on his lips. Bo hovered nervously behind him in the hall.

"Leora, I hate to rush, but I have a meeting with the aldermen in the morning that I need to prepare for." Ever the gentleman, Jake strode into the living room to retrieve her mother's purse and in a matter of moments, the entire group was saying their goodbyes.

Buzzed, Leora patted cheeks and wove her way, as steadily as possible, toward the front door. She turned and winked at Jake and Cress as she let herself out.

"Tata, y'all!" She giggled and lurched down the steps.

Grant watched her with a bemused expression. He turned to Cress and stepped forward. "I'll make sure she gets home all right." He bent and kissed her on the cheek. Cress froze. Beside her, she saw Jake stiffen. Grant straightened and said to both of them. "I'll see *y'all* later."

Trying to brush off Grant's forwardness, Cress laughed and asked, "Since when does my mother say 'tata'?"

Jake rolled his shoulders as he headed toward the back door. Disappointed, she watched him go. "Are you not staying for a bit?"

He looked at her, his face strained. "We've got an early morning, too. Good night, Cress." The door shut with a *clack* behind him.

Chapter 16

Hefting the weed eater onto his shoulder, Jake headed out of the barn into the already hot morning sunshine. After last night's surreal encounter, he needed an early start at some old-fashioned physical labor to clear his head. He hated drama, yet drama always seemed to find him like he had a bullseye painted on his back. He shook his head as he headed toward the edge of the orchard.

Movement by the pond caught his attention, and he glanced in that direction. Cress stood in a rumpled shirt and shorts, haloed in a shaft of early morning light, as she watched Champ frolic around the water. The excited puppy snapped at a dragonfly then tumbled into a panting heap. Throwing her head back in laughter, Cress bent to rub his belly. As if sensing Jake's eyes on her, she glanced up, a tentative smile on her face. She waved at him as she straightened up, tucking her tousled hair behind her ears.

He walked over to her and gave Champ a hearty scratch between his ears. "You're up early." He grinned as he surveyed her pajamas.

She crossed her arms over her chest. "I could say the same about you." She coughed. "Usually no one is out here."

Jake shrugged as he watched Champ scamper off after another dragonfly. "Wanted to get a jump on the day."

Nodding wordlessly, Cress stared across the pond, shoulders hunched, obviously on edge. They had left things on a weird note last night. He scratched his jaw, trying to think of a way to put her at ease.

"I like the new look." He smiled. "Is this the new fashion in Minnesota?"

She faked a glare at him. "Yes, bedhead is all the rage in Wisconsin."

He grinned at her, tilting his head. "Hey, bedhead is always ok with me."

She swatted at his arm, and he danced away a step before coming back closer. "Jerk," she complained, "You promised to behave."

He held up a finger. "I promised not to tease you about your doctorate." He set one end of the weed eater down and rested an arm on it. "And I have kept that promise. I did not, however, say anything about other forms of teasing."

Cress stuck out her tongue at him, and he pulled her into a hug against her protests. "I have morning breath!"

"Darling, we work on a farm. I have smelled far worse."

She grumbled but relaxed against him. After a moment, she asked, "Are we good?"

He looked down at the top of her head. "Why wouldn't we be?" He could feel her shoulders shift nervously.

"I mean… we've been 'together' less than a week and we've already had our first fight, and last night my mother sprang my ex on you. I wasn't sure after how you left."

He swallowed against the knot in his throat. He'd been a heel. "I'm sorry about that. It was a long day, and he'd been getting on my nerves all night. I shouldn't have let it get to me." He chuckled and squeezed her. "It's going to take a lot more than one fight and an ex popping up to scare me off."

She sniffed. "It's still not a great start."

He gently held her out at arm's length. "Hey, remember what I said? Don't go borrowing trouble before it gets here. We're giving this thing a real chance."

She nodded slowly, rubbing her lips. "In that case, I'd like to make last night up to you."

He shook his head. "You don't have to—"

She cut him off, grabbing his arms. "I want to. Besides, it's time we do a proper date. Let me cook for you tonight. Just you and me. You haven't seen what I can do yet." She smiled. "I'm sure Lynn will enjoy having a night off. We'll make Gramps go out."

He studied her face, lit up with excitement, and a knot formed in his throat. Time together sounded nice, homey. He hadn't had that in so long. He nodded, a wide smile breaking out. "It's a date."

She patted his cheek. "Don't worry about shaving." Inching up onto her tiptoes, she snuck a kiss and whispered, "I like the stubble." She spun away and whistled for Champ as she headed for the house.

He chuckled as he watched her butt sashay away in the cutoff sweat shorts. Now he needed some physical exertion for a whole other reason.

The sun was just sliding below the horizon as Jake leaped into the shower. He scrubbed the sweat of the day off as quickly as he could. Cress had disappeared into the house about an hour ago, and he didn't want to keep her waiting. He toweled off and drug a shirt over his head, splashing on some cologne. Despite how sparingly he used it, the green glass bottle was getting perilously low. He held it in his hand for a second, staring at one of the last gifts Eve had ever given him. With a shake of his head, he carefully put it in the mirrored cabinet and strode from the cabin.

The dogs' braying caught his attention as he hurried past. He needed to feed them; tomorrow he would have to spend some time loving on them and working with them. He glanced at his shirt and grimaced, yanking it off over his head. Grabbing the sack of dog food from its crate, he wiggled through the gate as the dogs leaped around his legs, begging for attention as much as dinner.

He doled out their kibble as quickly as he could, scratching heads and patting shoulders as he went. Hoping the musky smell of hounds wouldn't cling to him too strongly, he leaped for the gate and swung it closed behind him, hearing it clang shut.

He tossed the sack toward his cabin and swiped the shirt back over his head as he strode to the house, brushing dirt and hair from his jeans as best as he could. Glancing at his watch, he smiled. Right on time.

* * *

Cress surveyed the beef tenderloin with satisfaction. Its roasted perfection gleamed, surrounded by stewed carrots and potatoes. The fragrance of thyme and bay leaves filled the kitchen, signaling the perfect meal after a long day out in the fields. She uncorked a bottle of red wine and set it out to breathe next to the roast, along with a freshly tossed salad just as the oven *dinged*. The rolls were ready, a classic yeasted recipe of her Gran's.

She brushed butter generously over the rolls, her mouth watering. She might be a homey cook, foregoing all the fancy pasta and pastry making that Grant had always urged her to try, but dang, if she couldn't put on a good spread.

The back screen door creaked open, and Jake poked his head in. "Knock, knock." He smiled at her, and then his eyes widened. "Man, it smells like heaven in here."

She hastened to pile the rolls onto a serving plate. "Sorry, it isn't fancier. This is just what I could whip up on short notice."

He came over and wrapped his hands around her waist. "Nonsense. This is fantastic." He kissed her forehead, then looked her up and down with a cheeky grin. "You look good in flour."

Embarrassed, Cress backed away, swiping at her messy apron. "I haven't cleaned up yet."

He leaned against the island, plucking a cherry tomato out of the salad as she swatted at him. "You don't hear me complaining." He chuckled. "Next time, let me help you. I like cooking, too."

Her eyebrows shot up. A man that liked helping in the kitchen? Maybe this could work after all. "I might take you up on that." She peeled off the apron. "I figured we'd forgo the dining room table and have a picnic in the living room. Gramps has got one of those fancy fireplaces that doesn't put out heat unless you want it to." She stepped toward the living room. "I'll be right back."

Jake nodded. "I'll be right here. Admiring your handiwork." His hand was already hovering over the rolls. She smiled as she slipped into the living room. Earlier, she'd laid out a bunch of old quilts in front of the fireplace and lit candles around the room. Now she fiddled with the remote, trying to figure out the settings to get the fireplace to turn on. It remained stubbornly dark.

Pinpricks of frustration licked up and down her arms. She dropped her hands and forced herself to take a breath. The night wouldn't be ruined if she couldn't figure this out. Her hands trembled. She'd wanted everything to be perfect.

"You ok?" Jake stood in the doorway behind.

She hadn't even heard him. Shocked, she realized tears were brimming in her eyes. She wasn't a crier, but the last few weeks had left her worn out and tender in a way she hadn't ever been before. She tried to laugh the tears away. "It's fine."

He walked over to her. "It doesn't look fine." He put a hand under her chin. "It looks like you're crying. What's going on?"

She wiped her nose. "It's silly but… I can't get the fireplace to turn on."

"Oh." He looked at the dark hearth and back at her. Gently, he took the remote from her hand and sat down on the stone in front of the grate. He patted the stone beside him, and she sank down. He flipped down a gilt grating, pointed at a knob, and spun it to the *On* position. "You have to turn the gas line on first." He handed her the remote. "Now it should work."

She clicked the button, and the fire roared to life. With a few more clicks, she turned it down so that it wasn't heating the room. She sighed as she let the remote drop to her lap. "I can't seem to do anything right." She gestured to the room. "This was all supposed to be a surprise for you. A chance to relax after last night. Not put you to work some more."

He shook his head. "I don't think that's quite fair." Taking her hand, he scooched closer. "You've put together an amazing evening. So what about flipping on a fireplace?"

She looked up at him, confused by his laid-back attitude. A misstep like this with Grant would have... Taking a deep breath, she released it slowly. She wasn't with Grant anymore. Tension seeped from her shoulders. She wondered how much anxiety she'd kept pent up all these years?

Nodding, she tried to smile. "You're right. It's fine. Let's enjoy ourselves." She swallowed, her eyes locking onto his.

He squeezed her hands. "I'm just glad to be here with you." Stroking her cheek, his fingers sent shivers down into her belly. It had been a long time since someone had said anything like that to her. She placed a hand on his thigh, leaning toward him, wanting to be closer. His nose brushed her cheek as he leaned in.

A crash echoed from the kitchen and the sound of scrabbling feet and growling dogs filled the house. Cress shot to her feet, panic filling her. "The roast!" She sprinted into the kitchen to find a disaster.

She skidded to a halt, staring in disbelief as Jake's hounds rocketed around the room. The silver platter lay empty on the floor. The rolls were gone, and the plate they had lain on shattered on the floor. The salad lay trampled and muddied as the hounds bound about snuffling and looking for more. Zeus sat looking up at her, mouth smeared with grease and tail wagging.

Behind her, Jake let out a piercing whistle, and the dogs froze. In unison, they sat, eyes expectantly on him. Heat filled Cress' face as the extent of the damage finally hit her. In the quiet, she could hear the drip of wine splashing onto the tile floor from the overturned bottle sitting precariously close to the edge of the counter. Dazedly, she reached over and set it upright.

She placed trembling hands on her cheeks as Jake touched her elbow. "I'm so sorry about this." He snapped his fingers at the dogs and pointed at the backdoor. "Kennel!" As one, they turned and nosed their way out the screen door, Jake following them, leaving her alone in the sudden silence. Cress stood for a second amidst the shambles, gulping deep, calming breaths. Hand still trembling, she reached for the broom and dustpan.

So much for their date.

She sniffled as she picked up the platter, then swept up the shattered china. At least now she knew. Things were over between them before they started. She sobbed over the broom at the thought, the missed moment hitting her harder than she had imagined.

She'd wanted it to be real, for his words to mean something. But all it took was her forgetting to latch a door for things to fall apart. A hand touched her back, and she nearly jumped out of her skin, the dustpan falling out of her hand and into the trashcan where she stood weeping.

Jake looked at her, his eyes scrunched with concern. "Hey, don't worry about it. Everything is fine." A pair of keys dangled from his hand.

She blinked at him, uncomprehending. "You came back." The words trembled on her lips, and she hated how pathetic and hopeful she sounded.

His eyebrows shot up. "We're not done with our date." He shoved his hands in his pockets. "Besides, it's my fault the dogs got in here. Must not have latched their kennel all the way."

He dropped his eyes to the grease and wine-streaked floor. "I feel awful that your dinner was wasted on a bunch of mutts."

Jake thought this was his fault? She studied his face for a moment, realizing he'd told the truth unprompted and when it might cost him a fight with her. His admission released some part of her that felt she was the one who always had to keep things together, keep her relationships working smoothly. A weight lifted from her shoulders.

As she leaned the broom against the fridge, hope twisted painfully in her stomach. "I guess I could find us something else."

Jake grabbed her hand. "You've cooked enough tonight. I've got a better idea." He held up the keys. "C'mon."

She eyed the keys, then him dubiously. It was a little late to head out for dinner; everywhere around them would be packed.

He grinned. "I know a place. Just trust me."

She weighed his words, wondering if it was worth a second shot. She glanced at the back door and realized that he had come back when he didn't have to, when the night looked ruined. Finally, she smiled at him. "All right. But only if there's dessert involved."

He threw his head back, laughter booming. "Oh, there's dessert all right." He squeezed her hand. "Let's go."

As they drove into Midnight Bluff, Cress looked around at the boarded-up storefronts, nostalgia for the town she had known gnawing at her. Down buckling and cracking Main Street, she could see Al's Diner lit up, bustling with activity, one of the few places open at this time of night outside of Cleveland. Jake parked in front of Loveless Bakery and hurried around the front of the truck to open her door.

"Such a gentleman." She hopped out. Looking at the cheerily lit bakery, she raised an eyebrow at him, smirking. "I thought we were headed to dinner."

He chuckled. "I told you. I know a place. C'mon."

The bells rang out as they entered, and Willow popped her head out from the back. A toothy smile spread over her face as she spotted their joined hands.

Jake held up two fingers. "Two specials, please, Willow. And we'll start with dessert."

Her smile widened. "You've got it." She disappeared into the back and a moment later the dreamy tones of Nina Simone floated over a crackling sound system.

"You have the inside scoop, don't you?" Cress settled into a rush-bottomed chair in front of one of the red-checkered tables. She watched as Jake eased into a chair on the other side. He reached for her hand, and she let him have it. He stroked his thumb over her knuckles.

"I might know a thing or two."

They sat in silence for a moment as Willow bustled out. With a flourish, she set a slice of seven-layer fudge cake on the table along with two glasses of port. With a wink, she lit a taper and then bustled back into the kitchen.

"Oh, my God. This looks heavenly." Cress could practically feel the sugar zinging through her veins already as she picked up her fork. Digging in, she was already down three bites when she realized Jake was watching her with an amused expression. She set down her fork and wiped her mouth. "Did I get chocolate all over my face?"

He reached over and gently brushed the corner of her mouth.

"Just here." His hand lingered on her jaw as his eyes burned into hers, capturing her breath. Her skin felt flushed as if one more touch would either set her on fire or melt her completely. As if in a dream, she blinked and looked down, breaking the spell, and his fingers dropped away. Nina Simone wailed away on the stereo, pleading with her lost love.

Cress' hand shook as she reached for her fork again. They needed an icebreaker, but Jake beat her to it before she could blurt out something embarrassing.

"So, why did you become a biologist?" He waved his fork before he plunged it into the cake. "Why not a doctor or a lawyer or something like that?"

Cress tapped her fingers on the table. "Well, I am a doctor. Just not the kind with a stethoscope." He inclined his head, and she continued. "And I dunno. I guess a lot of it has to do with my dad. He taught me everything he knew about trees. And I just sort of fell in love with them. How they're so solid and steady, yet alive and growing at the same time. They never seem bothered by the weather or what's going on around them. They just accept things as they come."

"Dependable."

"Yes." Cress slowly slid her fork through the velvety layers of the cake and lifted the heavenly bite to her mouth. "Dependable. I look at them and I see how my dad used to watch me climb through the branches, urging me to go higher. They've just always felt like home." She put down her fork. "What about you? Why do you stay at the orchard? Good help is scarce around here. Surely you've got options."

He chuckled darkly, and Cress studied him. "It's tough for a high school dropout." He shoved a bite of cake in his mouth. "If I wanted to do anything other than grunt work on a farm,

I'd have to get my GED and I'm a little old and stupid for that."

Cress took his hand, her heart clenching at his words. She felt like such a heel now for waving her degree in his face. "You're not stupid."

He grunted. "Maybe not." Looking at her, his face softened. "But I do like it at the orchard. Bo is one of the best guys I've ever met, and it's peaceful. Like my own sanctuary. And I feel like I'm part of something that's going to last, you know?"

"Part of a legacy?" she asked, intrigued. She'd seen how Bo treated Jake like part of the family, but she hadn't realized Jake felt the same way.

"Yeah. That." He nodded as he released her hand and rubbed his fingers through his hair, his dark eyes sparkling in the candlelight.

She beamed at him and leaned forward. "Well, as long as I'm around, you will be. You've got nothing to worry about."

Grinning, he put his hand on her wrist, brushing his fingers against her veins. "I'll hold you to that promise." She sucked in a breath as he traced light strokes up her arms. She could swear even her blood was fizzing from his touch.

After a few seconds, he squeezed her hand. "Let's finish our cake before Willow gets out here with those patty melts. You want to eat them while they're hot or they get nasty."

"I heard that!" Willow shouted from the back.

"Quit eavesdropping!" they hollered in unison, then dissolved into a fit of giggles.

"What is in this port?" Cress gasped as she wiped her eyes.

"I don't think it's the port." Jake shook his head as he stared into her eyes. "It's the company."

Warmth spread through Cress' chest as she looked at him. The candle flickered between them, making his smile waver from incandescently happy to dark and dreamy. A little brooding even.

She bumped his knee with hers under the table. "You're kinda cute, you know."

He flashed a lop-sided grin at her. "Oh, am I now?"

Trying not to giggle, she smiled back at him. "What can I say? The whole, gruff farm boy thing really does it for me." She waved at the line of his farmer's tan standing out starkly on his arm where his shirt sleeve had inched up.

He winked. "You're going to l-o-o-o-o-ve my pasty white chest then."

"Been there, done that," Cress deadpanned, willing herself not to crack a smile as Jake choked on his bite of cake.

They broke down in a fit of laughter as Willow brought their patty melts to the table with another round of port and a fond roll of her eyes.

Chapter 17

As they finished up their patty melts, Jake studied Cress. After the disaster in the kitchen, he had no idea how to recover the evening. In desperation, he'd thought of Willow's late-night wine and dessert bar at the bakery and had called and begged for a favor despite his reluctance to rely on anyone else. Seeing Cress so relaxed and happy now made it worth it.

He flipped a few bills onto the table to cover their dinner and waved to Willow as they stood. She waved cheerily from the back as the clang of the bells ushered them out into the night. Cress reached for the door handle on the truck, but Jake stopped her.

Being together off of the farm was a moment to savor.

"Why don't we walk around for a minute? Let dinner settle." He wrapped an arm around her shoulder as they strolled down the sidewalk in silence. The quiet stretched out companionably as they navigated the buckled walkway, giggling as they each tripped and clung to one another in the dark. He was just about to admit defeat and suggest they head back when they rounded a corner and drew close to Al's Diner, one of the few sections that were fairly smooth and well-lit.

The door flew open, and a boisterous group of people spilled out onto the sidewalk in front of them, chatting and laughing. Mayor Patty spotted them immediately. She put a hand to her bosom, her eyes widening at the sight of them together.

"Oh, Jake, honey, we were just about to head to Willow's for some dessert. Do you two want to join us?" Her eyes cut between them and their joined hands.

He shook his head, already resigned to being tomorrow's gossip. "We just came from there. Out for a stroll." Taking a step to maneuver around the group, he gently tugged Cress along, but pulled up short when he felt her stiffen. Grant had just emerged from the diner into the center of the group with a loud laugh. He quieted when he spotted Jake and Cress, a scowl settling over his face.

A dust devil of emotion whirled through Jake as he watched Grant and Cress stare at each other, one looking thunderous, the other wide-eyed and mutinous.

Finally, Grant turned back to Jake and stuck out his hand. Around them, the group had gone silent, watching gleefully as moviegoers at the miniature drama in front of them. "Nice to see you again, Jake." He smiled, showing teeth. "Good to see Cress getting along so well with her co-workers for once."

Beside him, Cress huffed.

Jake took his hand and bore down, keeping his face relaxed. He hated this guy already. "Pleasure working with her. Shame Minnesota let her get away."

The wince was small, but Jake watched in satisfaction as Grant's eye twitched. "Wisconsin." Mayor Patty's entourage stirred in a collective inhale. Grant's smile was back in place, eyes cold and tone flat. "You should visit sometime. Great place to get close to nature."

"Might do." He shrugged. "But I got lots of nature to take care of right here." He released Grant's hand and wrapped his arm around Cress' waist. She looked nonplussed and subtly elbowed him in the ribs.

Mayor Patty spoke up, not one to be left out of the action. "Grant is helping us create a plan to revitalize our beautiful town." She placed a hand on Cress' shoulder. "It wouldn't have happened if Cress hadn't referred our little corner of the world to him. Thank you, sugar."

Jake looked at Cress, surprise smothering all the other feelings. She hadn't told him that. Her guilty look confirmed what Patty said, and Grant looked at them smugly, his lips twitching in a half-formed smile. Patty's hands fluttered as she realized her misstep. She tapped Grant's arm.

"Well, best if we let these two get back to their walk. No use dithering." With a round of overly chipper goodbyes and awkward waves, everyone shuffled past each other. Grant lingered, casting one last look as Jake and Cress hurried down the walk.

Jake waited until they were out of earshot before he dropped his arm and asked the obvious question. "So, did you want him to come here?"

Cress looked up at him, hurt etching her face. "What? No! I'd just gotten here, and I was shocked at seeing the town. I didn't think... I didn't think their company would pitch it, much less send him." She bit her lip.

"Sometimes, when he's assigned research on a potential subject, even if the company decides not to go with it, he'll send along his case notes and a few recommendations." Jake gave her an incredulous look, and she held up her hands. "That's it. That's all I was hoping for. I never expected him to just show up out of the blue."

"Why would he send info for free?" He shook his head, disbelieving.

Cress crossed her arms and gave him a scathing look. "Despite what you may believe, he's not the devil. He's a decent guy when he's not toggled to jerk mode." Her nostrils flared. "And I don't need you getting in a 'who can be a bigger jerk' contest with him, either."

Jake scratched the back of his neck and frowned at the ground. He probably had just given the gossip mill even more fodder. Lord knows what they'd come up with from the little dick-measuring display they'd just given them. He sighed.

"I'm sorry." Waving a hand toward the diner, he tried to explain. "I was taken aback seeing him so suddenly. And he was staring at you like..." He searched for the right words. "Like you were a misbehaving kid." He shoved his hands in his pockets. "It got me riled up."

Her mouth twitched to the side. "That's a pretty good way to put it." She exhaled. "I guess I've been on edge ever since I saw him, too." He watched as her shoulders sank in the moonlight. "It's got me reverting to all sorts of bad habits. Like assuming the worst."

He wrapped an arm around her shoulder and kissed her temple. "Hey, between the two of us, we can handle anything. And if we can't, we've got enough dogs to run him out of town if we need to."

She snorted, then laughed, her shoulders shaking as they continued around the square, just like he'd done so many times with Eve. As the night wind blew a cloud over the moon, Jake shivered and wondered just what she'd make of all of this. He stared at the lit windows of Loveless Bakery, so far away across the square, and frowned at the sight of the shadows flickering back and forth inside.

* * *

The air shuddered, lightning cracking with a threatening snap right outside of Cress' window. With an excruciating burst, the room lit up in a blue-white blaze of light, shadows thrown against the wall in grotesque shapes. She knew it was just the trees outside, but the effect was still eerie enough to make her shiver.

Champ whimpered and burrowed his cold little nose under her back, hiding his eyes from the storm as thunder rolled over them with a menacing growl. Cress sighed and rubbed her eyes. Her alarm clock read 4 AM, and with so much racket going on outside, she knew she'd never get back to sleep now.

Not that she'd been sleeping that well, anyway, with Jake's laughing brown eyes dancing around in her dreams. With a sharp kick, she flailed her way out of bed, only stopping to pick up her unhappy puppy before trudging downstairs. A light already glowed from the kitchen, the tell-tale sign Gramps was awake as well.

A steaming cup sat at his elbow as he stared out the window, fingers tapping on the butcher block island. Outside, trees thrashed in the distant rows.

Without turning his head, he said, "Lots to clean up today."

Cress set down Champ, and the puppy skittered over to huddle between Gramps' feet. "I reckon we'll have plenty of limbs to pick up. Maybe even an old tree or two will split from this one."

Gramps sighed, the sound long and shuddering in the sudden quiet between lightning strikes. "Just what we need. More work to do."

It wasn't like Gramps to be morose. Normally, he'd relish a good day's work. Disquieted, she picked up the teapot and opened the lid, sniffing. "Peach?"

Rubbing a swollen joint, he nodded. "Peach rooibos."

"Gran's favorite." Cress grabbed a cup from the cupboard and poured herself a serving of the delicately sweet liquid. She took a careful sip and set it down. "I didn't know you liked it."

He glanced at her and then back out the window. "I loved everything about your grandmother."

Cress clasped her hands around the scalding cup. "She loved wild weather like this. Said it made her feel alive."

With a sad smile, Gramps replied, "That she did. For being so peaceful herself, she had a wild streak." He brushed a hand over his mouth. "Wonder what she'd say now, seeing me start up a new orchard when I should be retiring." Blinking, Cress studied him as he stared out the window, flashes and pings of lightning highlighting the crags of his weathered face.

Cress took a deep breath. "She'd probably say that we're both damn fools."

Gramps looked at her, a twinkle in his eye. "And that she was proud of us."

Without thinking about why she picked up her cup and the teapot. "C'mon."

Silently, Gramps followed her, opening the back door, then holding the screen door aside as she stepped out on the porch.

The wind whipped her hair into her face and plastered her pajamas to her, but she didn't care. Without a word, they settled into the rocking chairs, the pot of tea on the little wicker table between them.

With a whine, Champ hopped up into her lap and hid his head under her arm. Pulling her legs up to her chest, she stroked his silky fur and leaned her head back, deep contentment settling over her. With a storm howling around her, this was the most at ease Cress had felt since she'd turned in her application for project lead back in Wisconsin. Then, she hadn't been sure of what she wanted from her career. Urged on by Grant, she thought she was doing the right thing in "climbing the ladder."

Now, she wanted more than anything to make this orchard something to be admired again. Sure, it wouldn't get her name in any big journals, but it was a legacy all the same. Something to be proud of. Funny how things could turn out.

In the distance, a light clicked on in Jake's cabin and she watched, pulse quickening, as his shadow wavered across it. Fiddling with her necklace, she rubbed the cold, silver cross against her lips as she stared at the light from his windows. He was as unfussy as a man could get; nothing like Grant. She banished the thought. She was already toying with disaster dating a coworker. It was just inviting trouble to compare him to an ex.

Still, she was unable to shake away every thought of Jake. "Have you given any more thought to my idea?" She breathed the words out, not sure Gramps had even heard them over the wind. Jake's reaction to her profit-sharing idea still bothered her. Her heart clenched at the thought of her grandfather's decision.

After a few minutes, she saw him shift in the rocking chair. "I have." He turned to her, blinking slowly behind his glasses, and took her hand. "Your heart is in the right place." She inhaled at the words, knowing what would follow. "But we must focus on just our farm and what we can do. If we waver in that right now, we'll fail and we'll lose everything. We wouldn't be much good to anyone then."

She swallowed against the sudden lump in her throat as disappointment pressed her back into the rocking chair. Gramps squeezed her hand. "It is such a lovely idea."

"Just not good enough." She bit the words out.

"That's not what I'm saying." He shook his head. "I'm saying we've got more urgent things to focus on." He released her hand and waved at the orchard. "In time, we might do some of what you've imagined, but right now, we just have to get steady."

"How are we going to get steady if we run out of money?"

He winked at her. "Have a little faith in yourself, darling." He looked at the trees as they swirled in the wind. "You're just like your dad—you know what to do. You just have to step out and do it."

"He always seemed so sure of himself." She buried her nose in Champ's fur.

Gramps smiled into his tea. "Did you ever realize he never went to college?" She looked at him, startled. He continued, "He got himself some books from Lord knows where and pored over them. We started getting all these pecan magazine subscriptions." He took a sip. "And before I know it, he's got us doing all this fancy 'modern' stuff, just like you're doing."

He shook his head. "That boy was terrified the whole time, too. Worried he was going to ruin the orchard. But he'd read upside down and backward just about everything on pecans. Sure enough, we started getting better-filled pecans and we were the first the wholesalers came to." He grinned at her. "Within a few years, we could afford the shelling equipment."

He patted her knee. "It's thanks to him we are where we are today. And you're just like him. So, when I tell you to trust your instincts, it's because I already do."

Cress blinked against the tears in her eyes and squeezed his hand as she nodded. Wordlessly, they turned back to watch the storm play out in front of them.

Lightning cracked the sky into shards of purple and blue, striking deep into the old orchard. Somewhere, the distinct sound of a tree splitting and falling, the crack of timber and the wet rip of earth, echoed back to them. The thunder was immediate and deafening, shaking the ground. Tomorrow, they'd have a mess to deal with, but now they had the love of family to get them through the storm.

"That was a good one," Gramps remarked.

"A real heart-stopper," Cress agreed, her hair frizzing in the humid air. Grinning, they sat watching the trees dash and whirl about in a crazed dance through bursts of lightning, sipping their cooling tea until Lynn found them at sunrise as the storm eased into a gentle mist.

She stood before them on the porch tapping her rainboot. "Y'all are such a pair." Behind her, the last drizzle of rain caressed the bruised earth as the birds joyfully trilled at the blushing sun.

"You know me," Gramps stood and stretched, his joints cracking and popping, "I'll never pass up a good show."

Lynn rolled her eyes. The slam of the screen door echoed her protest, and Gramps chuckled as he shuffled to follow her.

"You comin'?" he called over his shoulder.

"In a minute," Cress answered. "The best part is just coming up." She gestured to the pinkening line sliding through the trees. He smiled at her, fondness crinkling the corners of his eyes, and eased the door shut.

Champ lay exhausted and snoring in her arms as Cress watched the sun ease its way up the sky, touching each leaf and limb with a gentle glow. Soon, everything was bathed in a rosy light, revealing leaves and branches plastered across the fields. She knew out in the heart of the orchard lay a fallen giant they'd have to take care of as well. They'd have a full day of it, cleaning this mess up, that was for sure. Still, she sat, contemplating the orchard and worrying at her bottom lip with her teeth.

She watched as Jake hurried from his cabin to the barn, his dogs howling at his retreating back. He was right. With three seasons, two at least before the new orchards could be planted, they needed some sort of plan for handling the tightening they were about to feel. Her mind spun, empty of ideas. Irritated with herself, she stood. Grant would have had half a dozen plans ready to spin out already.

Hand on the screen door, she paused. Grant. He would have ideas. She twisted her hair behind her ear. She'd already texted him once, and it hadn't gone terribly. Being friends with an ex wasn't out of the realm of possibility. She rubbed her thumb over the handle of the door, considering. Innovative business ideas were his area of expertise.

But she didn't want him to think she couldn't do this on her own. And then there was Jake to consider—what would he think if she went to Grant for help? She blew out a puff of air. Then again, why not get help when she knew she was out of her depth, especially on the business side? Rocking herself back and forth, Cress let out an exasperated *argh* and snatched the door open.

Any decisions on calling Grant could wait. Right now, she just needed some breakfast and to get this day started.

Still feeling unsettled, Cress strode into the barn, dust motes swirling around her legs. Jake hung precariously from a ladder as he worked to rivet two enormous machines together. One hand on his hip and one on the ladder, Mac stared up at him, eyeing his progress. In another corner, Franklin gathered rakers and lop-jaws to load into the utility terrain vehicle's trailer that waited outside.

"All right, let's test it!" Jake leaned back from the machine and Mac flipped the cover on a nearby switch and pounded it. Brow furrowed, Jake watched the rumbling machine before motioning to cut it.

He climbed down the ladder and jumped to the floor with a *whisht.*

Mac handed him a bottle of water. "How's it look?"

"'Bout as good as we're going to get it until we run a load of pecans through. We'll have to adjust the tension manually from here." Jake wiped his face, the barn already growing stifling as the July sun crept up the sky.

Cress strode up to Jake. "You ready to get started on clean up?"

He looked at her wide-eyed, dark circles ringing his eyes. "Clean up? I've got a dozen more connections like this I've got to test today." With a wave toward Franklin, he said, "Franklin will handle raking up the little stuff today. Anything big we'll just have to get to later."

"If we have downed trees out there, the sooner we get to them, the better."

Jake raised his hands and dropped them. "What do you want me to do? I've got to get these machines reconfigured. They chewed up a good five percent of our harvest last year and we can't afford that this year. It will just have to wait."

"Wait how long?" They needed to clear away debris before it attracted termites and mildew. She didn't want next year's crop to take a hit because they had procrastinated this year. But Jake just shrugged. Already reaching out to grab the ladder, he turned back toward Mac.

Frustration bubbled up in her. "For someone who says they love this orchard so dang much, you sure don't seem very interested in taking care of it!" Cress bit her tongue as soon as the words flew out of her mouth.

He pivoted back to her, his boots scraping on the concrete the only sound to be heard in the now silent barn. Franklin stood frozen in the door, watching them, and Mac pretended to be fascinated with a scuff on the side of the machine. Jake stared down at her, brown eyes blazing and lips pale with anger.

"Jake, I didn't mean—"

"Just because I don't think that your opinion is law doesn't mean that I don't care." He spat the words out. "And if you haven't noticed," he stretched his arms wide, "it's just four of us running this operation. I'm doing the best I can." He snatched the ladder down, forcing her to step aside.

"Why don't you go with Franklin." The words weren't a question as he nodded at the door.

Face stinging with embarrassment, Cress hustled out of the barn. She stood, arms crossed, beside the UTV, waiting for

Franklin.

He finally emerged from the barn and set some equipment down in the trailer. "Everything look good?" He avoided her eyes as he gestured at the four-wheeler. Another wave of heat swept up her face as she quickly scanned their load. She'd really stepped in it this time.

"Let's grab a hacksaw, hatchet, and chainsaw just to be on the safe side." She ignored his eyebrows steadily rising up his forehead before he scurried back into the barn. Re-emerging with full arms, Jake shadowed him in the door, watching as they strapped everything down.

"He doesn't look happy," Cress murmured.

"He's been in a perpetually bad mood since Eve died. It's not you." Franklin waved at the UTV. "Shall we?"

"Might as well get me out of here before I do anything else to tick him off."

Franklin chuckled, finally glancing up at her, and revved the engine.

After the tension in the barn, working in the orchard was soothing. Cress' muscles soon burned as they hauled limbs and branches into small brush heaps and raked the worst of the fallen leaves away from the base of the trees.

As they turned down one row, Cress let out a long whistle. Lightning had struck a tree the night before, just like she'd thought. A charred streak marked the pale inner wood, and the trunk was split down to the ground. One side was still standing with several branches snapped off at horrendous angles. The other half had fallen over, tearing up a good chunk of earth and toppling into the empty center of the row, a small blessing.

She hopped off the four-wheeler and studied it, hands on

hips. Franklin walked up beside her, kicking at stray sticks on the ground.

"Looks like we lost a good tree." He clicked his teeth. "Just how it goes sometimes." He turned back to the UTV, ready to head on.

A fierce determination warmed Cress' belly. "I'm staying."

He blinked at her. "What?"

She turned back to the trailer, tightening her ponytail. "I'm cleaning this up."

"Sweetheart, the trunk has split." Irritation boiled in her as he gestured at the tree as if she hadn't seen it. "We're going to need some chains… It's a full day's work—"

"Only if you don't know what you're doing." She pulled the chainsaw out of the trailer. "And I know what I'm doing."

Franklin eyed her skeptically, head tilted to the side. "If you say so." He grabbed the hacksaw. "I'll get this stuff cleared out of the way."

She headed toward the tree. This was just what she needed to work out some aggravation with the men in her life after the last couple of days.

* * *

Jake tossed the can of WD-40 to Mac, then slid down the ladder, exhaustion washing over him. He stretched an arm across his chest, trying to ease the ache out of his shoulder that had been building ever since Cress had left. Why had he snapped at her like that? Even if she was being pigheaded, she was just doing the best she could. They all were. He leaned against the ladder and plucked his sweaty shirt away from his skin.

Chapter 17

The storm the night before wasn't the only thing that had kept him awake. He'd lain staring at the ceiling, replaying the encounter with Grant for hours, picking at it like a hangnail. The way he'd looked at Cress like they shared a secret.

When the first crack of thunder hit, Jake had given up and sat looking at the picture of him and Eve, noses red, soaked to the bone in front of their tent from over a decade ago when he'd proposed. He'd promised to be her one and only, and here he was dating another woman. An incredibly smart, infuriating woman. He rubbed his face, trying to shake off the weariness weighing down his limbs.

A shadow passed over the barn's side door, and Jake looked up, his chest tightening with hope and dread. Franklin entered alone and headed for the tack wall.

Puzzled, Jake followed him as he began selecting chains and ropes. "What are you doing?"

A guilty look flashed across Franklin's face before he answered with forced nonchalance, "Got a tree to pick up. Grabbing the Caterpillar and some chains."

Panic flared through Jake. Cress could barely handle the tractor, much less a Caterpillar. And Franklin had gone and left her with power tools?

"Where is she?"

Reluctantly, Franklin answered, "East lot, but boss—"

Jake was already out the door and hopping on a four-wheeler. Panic flooded him as he revved the throttle, barely aware of Mac and Franklin both standing in the door staring after him. Vaguely, he wondered if Dr. Alldread still did rounds in the ER at the Bolivar Medical Center and cursed himself for deleting all the doctors, medical offices, and caregivers on his phone after Eve died. Except for the bill collectors, he'd tried not to think of them in years.

Rounding into the East lot, he raced past the deep green rows, searching through the branches and swearing under his breath at each empty aisle. Finally, the whine of a chainsaw caught his ear over the engine's hum, and he turned that direction, skidding around the row only to come to a halt, the short grass flying up in little puffs around him.

Cress stood with her back to him, chainsaw wailing as she deftly cut through limb after limb of the downed tree. Even as a line of sweat worked its way down her back, she looked completely at ease, touching the blade to the limbs almost reverentially as they fell away around her, landing with resounding thuds he could feel from yards away. Golden sawdust drifted around her feet and flaked the legs of her jeans in bright splashes.

Tension oozed out of him as he watched her confidently move among the few remaining limbs. She had this. The orchard was her realm, and she knew how to handle herself in it. He chuckled and walked over. She must have caught a flash of movement out of her eye.

Turning toward him, she let the chainsaw drop, the blade falling silent. Swiping at her forehead, she peeled the safety glasses off and studied him, face carefully blank.

He stopped a foot or so away, at a loss for words. She rubbed a welt on her arm, where a branch had undoubtedly slapped her.

Looking around at the piles of limbs, he shrugged and tried to smile. "Want a break?"

She looked at him and then back at the tree trunk, three massive limbs still rising from it. "I got this." With a jerk of her chin, she pointed at the mess of smaller branches around them. "But clear these away?"

He saluted her with a grin and turned, glad to not be entirely dismissed.

"And Jake?"

"Yep."

She stood, biting her lip. "I'm sorry. For what I said. I know you care."

In two strides, he had her in his arms. "I'm sorry, too." He inhaled as her arms wrapped around his waist. "I shouldn't have reacted the way I did."

"We're ok?" He could feel her chin resting on his shoulder.

"We're ok. Just figuring this out one day at a time." His thoughts flicked to Eve. That sentence was so much truer than Cress knew. He slid a hand up to the back of her head and drew back enough to kiss her, softly at first, then with more passion, her teeth nibbling at his lower lip, and his tongue tracing circles on hers. Firmly, she pushed him away, hand lingering on his chest.

"Time to get back to work." Her green eyes sparkled playfully, and he groaned.

"But it was just getting good!"

She swatted at him. "Remember! You promised to behave."

He turned back to the UTV to retrieve an axe. "Still only applies to your doctorate, Dr. McBride."

A stick pinged off his back, and he laughed as the chainsaw revved back up. He smirked as she cut into the tree, sawdust flying. He knew one thing. He was always in for a surprise with Cress.

Chapter 18

P apers covered the dining room table in neat rows, a mixture of both laser-printed and hand-drawn notes and charts scrawled across them. The printer in Gramps' office whirred with even more. Cress stood to one side, twirling and yanking a strand of hair as she stared at the sheaves, willing them to reveal a fact she didn't already know.

What it boiled down to, she was looking at how much she wanted to gamble on being able to pay off the loan and how soon. Planting the new orchard drastically affected those odds. It was looking more and more like their best bet would be to let the land lay fallow while they rejuvenated the original orchard and then plant it in stages.

And all of that depended on being able to find the money to do some of the more drastic things their orchard needed. She hunched her shoulders at the thought of having to tell Jake that maybe they should have let the land go to Van after all.

She flexed her hands nervously and winced at the blisters rising from this morning's labor in the orchard. Chewing on a stubborn splinter still embedded in one knuckle, she glared at the papers again. Footsteps resounded in the hallway behind her, and she glanced over her shoulder as Jake walked into the room.

Sweat plastered his shirt to his chest, and streaks of dirt and bark scraped up his arms. He wrapped her in a hug from behind as she wrinkled her nose.

"You're all gross." She wasn't in much better shape, having skipped the shower and come straight here to work on their newest problem after her rage had worn off.

"Look who's talking." He turned her around, his hands gliding around her waist and traveling up to her shoulders. He glanced over her shoulders at the reams of pages. "You never take a break, do you?"

"We can't afford for me to." She sighed as she swiped a speck of sawdust off his cheek. "All done out there?"

"Worst of it's taken care of." He nodded toward the stacks behind her. "We've got the logs put away to be planed and cured. We can chip smaller limbs for smoking. What's all this?"

She leaned away from him slightly and rested a hand behind her on the table, suddenly wishing she could hide all the papers. She wasn't anywhere near ready for this conversation. "Just projections I'm running."

"A lot of projections." He looked levelly at her and gently put his thumb on the crease between her eyebrows. "Let me guess." He deadpanned. "We're a little bit screwed."

Cress sputtered. "A little bit?" She waved an arm over the table. "We might get our orchard where it needs to be. Might. By some miracle. If we can find a pot of gold somewhere. I have no idea how we'll do the new one. Maybe in ten years, when we're finally making steady payments on the loan, we can look at it." She wound her fingers into her hair and tugged, mind spinning.

"But I have no idea how we're going to do it all." She released her hair and put her hands on his hips. "I just… Getting the other farmers involved would be a way to get more revenue going, but without that… I have no idea how to fund all this."

Jake stepped around her and picked up one sheet, then another, letting them drift back down. "What are our biggest pain points?"

He was surprisingly calm about this. Cress studied him as she pointed at a couple of line items. "We don't have a budget or equipment for tree trimming or aerial spraying. And we'll need a lot over the next two to three years to give this place the best chance." She let her hand drop. "Unless you've got a grapple saw and a crop duster tucked away somewhere that I don't know about."

Jake laughed, the sound low and rumbly. "No, but I know the guys who do." He glanced at her. The corner of his mouth quirked up. "Being a volunteer with the fire department has some perks." Pulling his phone from his back pocket, he scrolled through his contacts. "Let me give the guys a call, and see what we can work out."

He strode out the door and Cress could hear him pacing on the front porch, his steps thudding on the boards as he talked on the phone. She plunked heavily into a chair. If they could work this out, they had a fighting chance at making it. Her mind spun through the math, coming up with the same depressingly low numbers each time. But they technically were in the black. It would have to do. A spark of hope flared to life.

Jake came back in, a wide grin on his face. "It's done. Floyd Kelly will help us with the trimming if we'll harvest his dad's old grove. I offered the same deal to Thomas Pipkin for the crop dusting, provided we buy the sprays."

"That's incredible!" Cress sprang to her feet and hugged him. "We'll have to work out how to pay labor—"

He waved a hand. "Already did that." His smile broadened. "We'll sort and shell the nuts for them and market them. 80/20 split. The twenty percent we keep should cover our expenses."

Warmth washed over Cress. "Have I told you how incredible you are?"

Jake flushed up to his ragged hairline. "I wouldn't go that far. It just seemed sensible to me."

"Well, good sense is more than most people have." She kissed him on the cheek then grimaced. "Hygiene, too. I think it's high time both of us got showers."

He swatted her behind as she turned for the stairs and she danced away, sticking out her tongue. There wasn't anything they couldn't do when they worked together. She skipped up the stairs, feeling lighter than she had in days. But she paused at the top, peering through the gap to where Jake stood, still beside the table. He stared down at the spread of paper, a sheet clutched in one hand and the other pressed over his mouth as he studied it. His brow was creased in an unfamiliar expression that was hard to identify from her perch.

She searched his face for a moment, trying to put her finger on it before it came to her. Panic. Jake looked panicked. Her elation of a moment before faded into unease as she turned and tiptoed to her room.

* * *

Jake strolled into the barn the next morning and stretched, reaching as far as he could toward the lofted ceiling. He didn't bother to cover the yawn that nearly unhinged his jaw as he studied the tractor, not looking forward to another long day in the sun. He was just yawning again and debating heading to the house for a cup of Lynn's stout coffee, and a chance to say hello to Cress, when Bo entered the barn.

"Gonna' swallow a fly if you keep that up."

Jake snapped his mouth shut, and Bo chuckled. "You been looking mighty tired the last couple o' days. Everything all right?"

Jake would never admit that he'd been losing sleep worrying over Cress and the state of the farm, so he just shrugged and said, "The usual." It wasn't exactly a lie, but it wasn't fully true either. He had bills piling up again, but that didn't have him worried as much as it usually did. If the farm went under, he was well and truly screwed, bills or not.

Bo shot him a sharp look. "Bill collector didn't come after you again, did they? I can front you some money if you need it."

Jake shook his head. He didn't want to put any more stress on Bo. "No, no. Nothing like that. I'm on a payment plan I can mostly manage." Bo gave him a skeptical look, so he added, "With everything going on... it dredges up a lot of memories, ya' know?"

The old man nodded knowingly and clapped him on the shoulder. They stood for a moment, remembering. Bo said, his voice falsely hearty, "Nothing like a good day's work to chase away your troubles." He pointed at the tractor. "Fortunately, I have a task right up your alley. The millet stand needs a good spraying of insecticide. Checked it this morning and looks like the chinch bugs are trying to move in."

Jake scratched the back of his neck. He didn't particularly relish having to spray the field from the open-cab tractor, but it was a rare occurrence and beat just about everything else that was on his to-do list. "All right. Let me go grab a cup of coffee, then I'll head out."

Bo flashed him a thumbs up and ducked into the barn's office while Jake headed to the house. Cress was just setting her plate in the sink when he walked in the door. She turned to smile at him.

"Morning, handsome." She was already dressed but still barefoot, her boots sitting by the back door.

He pulled her to him as he buried his face in the nape of her neck, relishing the ocean smell of her shampoo. "I like the sound of that." Before he could stop it, he yawned again.

"All right, mister. Time to get you some coffee." She pushed away from him with a laugh and turned to the fragrant pot on the counter.

"Thank sweet baby Jesus." He inhaled the steam from the mug she handed him.

"Are you all right?" She eyed him, concern pinching her eyes.

"Everyone keeps asking me that this morning. I'm fine." He took another sip of the scalding coffee and tried to laugh off her concern. He didn't want a repeat conversation at that moment, and they weren't at the stage for him to confide in her about the leftover medical bills from Eve yet. "Nothing a little caffeine won't fix."

"You look like you haven't slept in days." She stood by the island where some croissants and fruit were laid out. "Let me make you a plate."

He snapped, "I said I'm fine." As the words flew from his mouth, he was already regretting them. They were much too sharp. Cress' hand dropped and her face fell. She crossed her arms and leaned against the island silently.

He finished his coffee in one big, burning gulp. In a softer tone, he said, "I'm about to head out, anyway."

She eyed him, lips in a flat line, and he saw a flash of her mother, poised and commanding. "Don't let me keep you."

"C'mon, Cress. Don't be like that. I didn't mean it. I'm just tired. A good night's sleep will put me to rights." He walked over and kissed her on the forehead, and she relaxed a little.

"See you in the orchard?" she asked, eyes hopeful.

He shook his head. "Bo's got me spraying the millet field today."

Confusion swept over her face, and he instantly realized his mistake. They had planted the millet a few days before she arrived. Bo must not have told her about it, and Jake certainly hadn't gone over it because it didn't have anything to do with the orchard.

He groaned and explained. "We're hosting the big dove hunt this year. It's our turn after the Conroys hosted last year. The millet is for the birds."

Incredulity spread over her face. "So, you mean, while I'm scraping and sweating over every last penny, praying that we can keep it together, that big line item labeled 'Entertaining' is for a party for the *whole town*?" Her voice ticked up. "I thought that was a marketing expense, like taking wholesalers out to eat or something in Cleveland!"

Now it was Jake's turn to look at her, confused. "At that amount, that would be considered a kickback, Cress! It's illegal... or unethical... or something!"

"I didn't know!"

He sputtered. "But you didn't ask what it was for?"

She waved her hands, her face reddening. "Why would I think we would throw a party for the whole town when Gramps just nixed my idea of working with the town?"

He quieted, not having a suitable response for that one. "I... I don't know."

She huffed, crossing her arms again. If looks could light fires, he'd have been a roaring bonfire right then, with the stare she was giving him.

"I didn't realize that field was even on our property." She bit the words out and pinched the bridge of her nose. "It's got a power line on it for Chrissake."

His stomach dropped. Coughing, he muttered, "It's a dummy line."

She dropped her hands. "I don't even want to know what that is."

Stupidly, he explained anyway, the words pouring out even as her eyes snapped sparks at him, "We built a fake power line so the doves would have better roosting spots. Make it easier to spot them."

He could hear her teeth grinding. "I've got work to do finding the money that's going to pay for all this." She turned and clunked his mug into the sink. "Don't you have somewhere to be?"

He had never bolted from the house so fast before in his life. One thing he had forgotten was just how scary it was to be on a woman's bad side. As he hightailed it back toward the barn, a plume of dust worked its way down the driveway from the highway. In the back of his mind, it clicked that today was

Vada's day to deliver fertilizer. She'd finally convinced Cress to let her deliver after the last time.

Glancing back at the house, he laughed mirthlessly to himself. He sure hoped she knew how to handle Cress' temper because it scared the stuffing out of him.

* * *

Cress gripped the edge of the sink and took slow, deep breaths. Of all the foolish things, throwing a dove hunt the year they start a rejuvenation project *and* a new orchard. And they didn't even bother to tell her about it. Typical.

She could wring both their necks. What were they thinking? Slapping the hot water on, she scrubbed dishes and plunked them into the drying rack, almost daring them to break from her vigor.

The rumble of tires on gravel outside made her pause. Was it already Thursday? She glanced out the window and saw Vada's truck, trailer in tow. She took one more deep breath and dashed the water off, reaching for a kitchen towel. Before she had finished drying her hands, Vada had bounded up the stairs and slammed the screen door open, a warm smile spread across her face and clipboard tucked under her arm.

"Your favorite delivery person is here!" Vada chattered as she swept into the kitchen and poured herself a cup of coffee. "You ought to love me because I insisted on making this trip myself instead of leaving it to Dewayne to do." She hopped up to sit on the island counter. "Told him I know just how you like everything done. Should have seen how he rolled his eyes at me. Dis-re-spectful."

A snort escaped Cress as she leaned against the sink. Vada

eyed her over her mug. "All right. What is with this storm cloud that's sitting on your face?" She wagged her finger in a circle. "Something's up? Has Jake done something royally stupid already?"

Sighing, Cress rubbed her forehead. Vada would understand; she always had. "There's just so much going on. We're trying to rejuvenate the orchard. And Bo and Jake went and bought a completely new plot of land... Lord knows how we're going to make that work! And this morning I find out that we're hosting a dove hunt? I should have known that tidbit weeks ago."

She dropped her hands. "How are we supposed to pay for all this? It's not like we're made of money." Shaking her head, frustration at all her careful planning being thrown off swelled up, and she burst out, "We're just going to cancel the hunt. That's what we'll do. It's the only thing that makes sense."

Vada choked on her coffee. "Hold on!" She set the mug down as Cress looked at her wide-eyed. "I get where you're coming from. I do. Money worries... well, it's enough to drive anyone up a wall."

She slid off the counter and faced Cress. "But remember your debutante ball? How you and your mother planned and prepped for that months in advance? Most of the money was spent well before the event. Etiquette lessons. Custom tailoring. Non-refundable deposits. The whole nine."

Vada crossed over to her and rubbed Cress' arms. "What I'm saying is, I got the invite for the dove hunt two months ago. I'm sure everyone else did as well. And I'm sure Bo has paid some deposits he can't get back." She bit her lip. "Look before you leap with canceling the biggest social event of the season. You'll rile up a lot of folks."

Cress' shoulders slumped, the fight gone out of her. Vada was right, of course. If she canceled the dove hunt, she'd make them social pariahs until someone else screwed up worse. And with the orchard in the state it was, they would need all the help they could get at some point. They couldn't risk being shunned right now; it would put them at Van's mercy. And she had fussed at Jake because he was just doing what Bo had asked.

"I'm such an idiot." She blew air out through her nose, frustrated with herself.

"You're doing the best you can. Anyone would be stressed out in these circumstances." Vada tried to reassure her, not understanding what she was talking about.

"No, I... I yelled at Jake this morning about the millet field."

Blinking, Vada asked, "The one with the sunflowers?"

Cress closed her eyes for a second, willing down the blip of irritation. She'd forgotten about the sunflowers. "Yeah, that one." She rolled her shoulders back. "I didn't know it was ours, much less for the hunt. It... took me by surprise."

"Ahh." That one syllable told Cress all she needed to know.

"I owe him an apology, don't I?" The words weighed down her tongue with guilt.

"Sooner the better." Vada patted her arm. "Best not to let him stew about it."

Cress winced and turned for the door. "Thanks."

Vada called after her, "So, should I just forge your name or—?"

Cress called over her shoulder, "Bo's in the barn. I'll catch up with you in a bit." She needed to find Jake now.

The wide, bright blades of the millet rose from the field, their small stalky blooms fully open and buzzing with clumsy bees as Cress surveyed the field, glazed in the morning light. The cheerful faces of sunflowers bobbed around the edge as a light breeze kicked up. At the field, the tractor growled down a row, Jake scowling atop it as a fine mist spewed from the trailer sprayer.

Cress waved at him, and he gave her a flip of the hand in acknowledgment. Slowly, the tractor drew to the end of the row, and he clambered down, face stoic as he looked at her. She rubbed her nose, not sure where to start.

"You going to stand there and stare at me, or can I get back to work?" He held his arms up and let them drop. Maybe he'd already had too long to stew about it. Her heart squeezed painfully at the thought that she might have already sabotaged their nascent relationship.

Nodding at the tractor, she asked, "Should you be doing that without a filtered cab?"

He eyed her, lips pressed into a thin line. "You didn't come out here to ask me about safety regs, did you? I'll be fine." Crossing his arms, he waited, fingers tapping on his elbow.

It occurred to her that the words she was struggling with were simple but stung her pride. She dropped her eyes to the crushed grass. "I'm sorry."

His fingers stilled. She repeated herself. "I'm sorry. I shouldn't have gotten mad at you. Being stressed is no excuse for going off on you."

"It's not." His voice was low, and he sighed. "Cress, we have got to stop taking things out on each other. We can't get into this pattern." He dropped his arms. "It's not healthy."

"I get that." She looked up at him and reached for his hand. "You know what else isn't healthy?"

"Hmm?" He looked at her with amusement as she wound

her fingers through his.

"Willow's cream cheese danishes." She pressed a hand to his chest as she crept up onto her toes to whisper into his ear. "Want to play hooky with me?"

He chuckled and looked over his shoulder at the field. "Only if you cover for me with Bo."

"I think I can manage that." She smiled at him then stole a quick kiss, flutters rippling through her. Tugging on his hand, she pulled him away from the field as they laughed like truant schoolchildren.

Chapter 19

The truck bumped against the curb as they pulled to
a stop in front of the Co-Op. Jake chuckled at Cress'
questioning look.

"Uhh... This doesn't look like the bakery."

He laughed. "It's not. I figured while we were here, I would
run in and grab a part I need for the harvester." He kissed her
cheek. "Why don't you go on over to Willow's and grab those
danishes for us?" He waggled his eyebrows at her. "If you
hurry, I know a good spot to park along Jones Bayou where
we can enjoy the... scenery."

She swatted his arm. "I'd best hurry then." The door creaked
as she swung it open with a giggle. He clambered out with
a laugh and headed toward the Co-Op. The real reason he
wanted to go to the Co-Op was to get a surprise for her, but he
couldn't very well do that if she was with him. He strolled in
and waved to Dewayne, covering the counter for Vada while
she was out, as he peeled right for the Garden Center.

Hidden in the back behind a chain-link fence overhung

with a green mesh to shield off the worst of the sun, the Garden Center was tiny and stiflingly humid. But it held an amazing variety of plant starters for home garden vegetables and herbs—and a few local varieties of wildflowers that Vada saved from the edges of the fields whenever farmers called her about widening rows or draining off swampy patches.

Gently moving aside pots and trenches, he spotted the perfect present for Cress: a beautifully blooming native passionflower, twining up a small trellis and complete with some swelling maypops already on the vine. As he picked it up with a grin, he glanced through the fence at the bakery to be sure Cress hadn't already headed this way and spotted him.

He froze, hands clutching the pot. Cress and Grant stood on the sidewalk in front of the bakery, locked in what seemed to be a serious talk. Cress' arms were crossed as she looked up at Grant. From this distance, it was impossible to read their faces.

Bright July sunlight streamed down on their shoulders as they exchanged words, Grant's hands moving in lazy circles. Finally, Cress nodded and stretched up on her tiptoes to hug him. She turned and disappeared into the bakery without a backward glance as Grant moved on down the sidewalk toward the courthouse.

Jake blinked and swallowed, unsure of what he'd seen. He glanced down at the flower in his hands, then, mechanically, walked back into the dim interior of the Co-Op. Dewayne was nowhere to be seen, probably stocking some distant shelf. As he stood in the entranceway debating what to do, with the frigid blast of the A/C washing over him, a thought struck him.

Why was he buying a plant for Cress when her ex was trying

to weasel his way back into her life? When she was clearly falling for it?

Feeling like an idiot, he set the plant down on the counter and turned toward the parts aisle only to draw up short at the sight of Van smirking at him.

"Interesting purchase you have there. Starting a garden?" Van fiddled with a leaf, and it was all Jake could do to keep from growling at him.

"Something like that."

Van studied him with a calculating eye. "How's it going on the farm?"

Suspicion instantly lurched into Jake's mind. "What's it to you?"

Holding up his hands, Van chuckled. "Just being neighborly. Making sure Bo is doing right by you is all."

Bo had kept Jake off the streets and out of the poorhouse more times than he could count, but Jake pressed his lips together. Van was playing some sort of angle, and the best way to find out what it was would be to make him come right out with it. He crossed his arms and waited.

Van chewed on the inside of his cheek as he looked at Jake, clearly displeased with his silence. Finally, he said, "I hear you've got a bit of a cash crunch going on."

Jake waved a hand, playing at nonchalance. "Nothing we can't handle. Cress is doing a great job getting the orchard back to prime condition."

Smiling so that his eye teeth gleamed in the dim light, Van replied, "I didn't mean the orchard." Jake's stomach flopped. "I meant you." Van clasped his hands on the countertop and leaned on his elbows. "Little birdy over at Bolivar Medical told me you had quite the outstanding balance."

Jake gritted his teeth. "That information is confidential."

"Not in this town, it's not." Van rubbed one thumb over the other. "You know how word gets around. And any idiot with eyes could have guessed that Eve's treatment cost a fortune."

Resisting the urge to add a new crook to Van's nose, Jake clenched his fists until the knuckles cracked. "What's your point?"

"We can help each other." The words were so smooth, Jake was sure he had misunderstood.

"Excuse me?"

"I need a good farm manager to take the reins at one of my new properties. You need a higher salary. Much higher than what Bo can offer on that piddly excuse for an orchard." He held out a business card. Stunned, Jake just stared at it. "Offer's on the back. You've got two days to think about it before I find someone else, but you're my first choice."

Jake owed Bo so much more than money; Van would never understand that. He pressed his lips together and refused to take the card. Without a shrug, Van strode past him, slipping the card into Jake's shirt pocket with a little pat.

He called over his shoulder as he walked on down the aisle and out the door, "Call me when you decide. Tell Cress I said hello." The bells rang hollowly as he shoved his way out.

Feeling numb, Jake pulled the card from his pocket and looked at it. The number on the back was triple what he was making. He closed his eyes and slid it back into his pocket, inhaling. The money didn't matter, and neither did the ever-growing pile of bills. He couldn't work for a man like Van or betray Bo like that. When he opened his eyes, Vada stood in front of him, arms crossed, and a ferocious scowl etched into her face. He knew without asking that she'd heard everything.

* * *

Cress hurried across the street, mouth-watering at the thought of Willow's danishes and coffee from the Loveless Bakery. Maybe she'd even branch out today and try something different. The petit fours always looked so tempting. Her mind was so fixated on thoughts of sugary treats that she barely registered the door of the bakery swinging open until Grant was standing in front of her, blinking in the blazing sunlight and blocking her way to the door.

She skidded to a halt, unsure of what to do. "Excuse me," she mumbled and reached to open the door behind him, but he grabbed her arm, fingers wrapped gently around her wrist. She pulled away and took a couple of steps back on the sidewalk.

"Cress…" His eyes pleaded with her, pinching at the corners.

"What do you want, Grant?" The words snapped out of her, the frustration of the last few days spilling over. "Why are you even here?"

He jammed his hands into his pockets. "I'm here working on a revitalization plan for the town. You know that."

She huffed. "But why are *you* here? Anyone else in your entire company could have come. Why you?"

Sighing, he closed his eyes for a second. "For a chance to make things right between us." He pulled his hands out of his pockets and waved them in the air in small circles. "I… didn't handle things right. Didn't appreciate you."

She held up a hand to cut him off, not in any mood to put up his lectures. "Save your speech."

He nodded. "I know. I've seen… Well, you two seem great together." He swallowed. "Look, I know things are over between us. And I know I was a royal asshole. But can we talk?" He waved his hands again as she screwed up her mouth for a stinging retort. "Just so we can do things properly this time. Try to part as friends?"

The offer hit her harder than she could have imagined. They'd been together for seven years, and she'd never thought that there'd be a day when Grant wouldn't be in her life. Until he'd dumped her. She struggled to breathe for a moment, her anger warring with her desire for the tension to ease between them. For some glimmer of a way forward.

"I'd like that. I'd like… to be your friend." Her vision blurred as she blinked away tears.

"All right. Let's meet here tomorrow night, then. We'll talk. And we'll see if we can't do better this time." His smile wavered in her eyes.

She nodded and tried to smile. "See you then." She reached up to hug him. The smell of his orange blossom and sandalwood cologne washed over her, stirring so many memories. She pulled away before they could grow and darted into the bakery, the bells jingling brightly overhead.

Willow stood behind her, arms crossed and a worried expression on her face. "You ok, hon?"

"I'm fine." She brushed her eyes. "The usual."

Willow gave her a tight nod as her glance darted behind her, following Grant down the walk. Cress swallowed, a guilty feeling creeping around her shoulders with little pinpricks. "It's nothing. He just wants to talk, is all."

"Uh-huh. You don't owe *me* any explanation." The emphasis was unmistakable. Willow busied herself snapping open paper bags and pouring cups of coffee from the carafes.

"Really. He just feels bad about the way we broke up." The

words sounded forced even to Cress.

Willow dropped the bags on the counter and gave Cress a level look. "My sweet, summer chile'. No man moves his butt to a backwater Mississippi town in the heat of July unless he's trying to get his ex back." She punched numbers forcefully into the cash register. "And you're a big ninny if you think otherwise."

Cress handed her the cash in stunned silence. She turned back to Willow as she reached the door. "Thank you," she said, her words wafting through the quiet bakery, "For telling me the truth."

Willow's face softened, and she gave one sharp jerk of her chin. Cress pushed her back against the door and ducked out into the screaming light of another scorchingly hot July day.

* * *

Vada poked Jake in the chest with enough force to rock him back on his heels. "Just what was that?" She spat the words.

"Nothing! It was nothing."

She slammed up the door of the counter as she stomped over to the computer. "I can't believe you. Why were you even talking to him?"

Jake groaned. "It's not like I sought him out. He was just there!"

She leveled a soul-scorching gaze at him. "And you should have put an end to that nonsense right then and there."

"I'm not going to take it!" She looked at him in disbelief, so he repeated himself. "There's no way I'd ever take it!"

She extended a hand and waggled her fingers. "Give me the card, then."

He stared at her, outraged by her doubt. "Vada! You've known me for years."

"And I've also seen men just as good as you do stupider things for money." She kept her hand held out. "So, why don't you give me the card? Put an end to this right now. Cress will never have to know."

"I'll never have to know what?"

Jake spun at the whispered words. Somehow, they'd missed the tinkling of the bells amid their argument. Cress stood in the middle of the aisle behind him, eyes wide with confusion. Her face paled as they fell silent.

"What don't I know?" The white paper bags in her hand crinkled as she tightened her grip, looking first at Jake then at Vada. His heart hammered in his chest, beating painfully against his ribs as he looked at her pinched face.

Vada groaned, the sound loud and wheezing. She rubbed the bridge of her nose. "Oh, Lord. Worst way possible."

Hands shaking, Jake pulled the card from his pocket. "Van offered me a job."

Cress' shoulders relaxed and she laughed. "Oh. That's no big deal." Jake glanced at Vada, catching her scowl. She motioned for him to continue. Cress' brow wrinkled as she watched them, and he took a deep breath.

"It's a lot of money." He handed her the card as she moved to set the fragrant bags down on the counter. "Way more than what Bo pays. And it would take care of some things for me."

Disbelief swept Cress' face smooth as she studied the card, turning it over to look at the back. "But why would he offer you this much? It doesn't make sense."

Jake clenched his fists, trying to keep his voice steady. They'd only been dating for a couple of weeks and there'd been no reason to discuss money. This was going to hit her like a ton of bricks. "Because I have a lot of debt," he stuttered. "Bo helps me out from time to time. Keeps me afloat. But with the loan... well, Van must have found out somehow and put two and two together that my buffer is gone."

The sound of Cress' inhale was the only thing he could hear. She handed the card back to him as if it were a live coal and scrubbed her hands on her pants.

"I... I need some time to think about this." She turned and hurried down the aisle, back toward the door outlined in sunshine.

"Cress, wait!" He shot Vada an irate look, but she just shrugged, a worried expression twisting her mouth. He snatched up the pastries and hurried after her. "Cress!"

By the time he caught up with her, she was already in the truck, seat belt buckled. She pressed a fist to her mouth.

He slammed the door shut behind him. "Cress."

She held up a hand. "Please, I just need to think."

Panic settled low and thrashed in his stomach. "Cress, I wasn't going to take it."

She pressed her hands to her flushed cheeks. "Please, Jake. I just... need to process some things. Can we just go home?"

Feeling like he was going to jump out of his skin, he put the truck in reverse. As they rattled out of town, he glanced at her as she stared out the window. In the window, he could see her reflection, faint and wavering, there one second and gone the next.

Chapter 20

T he ride home was unbearable. Cress sat hunched in the passenger seat, trying not to notice as Jake first flipped the radio on, then as Nina Simone's smooth voice poured out, slapped it right back off.

She didn't know which was worse, the crooning of love songs or the humid silence. Fields flew by on either side of them, drenched in sunlight, cotton and corn bobbing cheerfully on this bright day. Nausea roiled in her stomach, hot and anxious.

Jake cleared his throat, shooting a nervous glance at her. "Look, I wasn't going to take the job. And I'm sorry you found out the way you did. That was awful."

Hurt curdled her kindness into sour words. "It was."

"I should have thrown the card in the trash right away." She nodded and bit her lip, trying not to snap at him while he was apologizing.

"But of all people, why Van? I mean…" she rubbed her dry lips. "If you're looking for another job because you need to make more money, that's one thing. But Van? There's only one reason he would offer you a job, and that's screwing over Bo."

Jake pressed his lips together and drummed his thumbs on the wheel. Another uneasy thought reared up in Cress' mind. What debt? And why would a smart guy like Jake be stuck on a farm in the first place? A list of unsavory possibilities ran through her head from gambling to addiction to run-ins with the law. It could be as simple as bankruptcy, but that complicated things, too. She rubbed her forehead.

Did she want to be involved with someone she knew so little about? Maybe her first instinct was right and getting involved with a co-worker was the disaster she knew it to be.

Jake sighed. In a quiet tone, he said, "I haven't been looking for another job. Van somehow knows about my medical debts from Eve. That's why he made me the offer."

Relief washed over Cress, along with guilt, as they pulled onto the long gravel drive to the house with a jolt big enough to rattle her teeth. This was something she could handle, something she could fix.

"Why didn't you just tell me?"

Jake remained quiet as they pulled up to the house, his face thunderous. He stopped the truck with a jerk and spun to her. "Cress, we just started dating, and I didn't want to lay all that on you." He made a sweeping gesture with his arm. "I wasn't exactly expecting this situation. Being a widower is complicated enough without someone using it to manipulate me."

She took a deep breath. "All I meant was that if I had known, maybe I could have helped. Maybe I can still help." She touched his arm. "We don't have to plant the second orchard.

We can sell the land and use that to pay off the debt."

He recoiled from her, and she let her hand drop, confused and hurt. "I don't need you to rescue me, Cress. You don't need to fix this situation. I just need you to trust me," growled, "But you don't, do you?"

"What? Of course, I do." Somehow, this moment was spinning away from them. Jake leaned against the door of the truck, anger etched into the lines of his face. She had no idea what she'd done. "I'm just trying to help… "

"I don't need your help. Or Grant's help. Or anybody's help."

"Grant's help?" Her heartbeat sped up. She couldn't get away from Grant's cloying presence, even here. From the glint in Jake's eye, he felt the same way. "What are you saying?"

"I saw y'all earlier. And the way you ask him for ideas. Obviously, you two are still tangled up somehow." He crossed his arms.

Outrage flared through her, even as the truth of his observation hit. "He can take a hike for all I care. I didn't ask him here." She sat back in her seat with a huff. "I've already told you that." She clenched her fists. "As for 'seeing us,' he was just asking me if we could meet up to talk. He feels bad about the way he broke up with me and wants to make up for it."

She saw Jake's nostrils flare. "Sounds a lot like he's trying to weasel his way back into your life."

"Weasel!" Groaning, she raised her hands, palms up. "It's not like I was trying to keep it from you! I was coming into the Co-Op to tell you when everything blew up." She shook her head. "You're the one who was planning on keeping something from me."

He swung his door open and stomped from the barn. "I

don't know what you want from me."

"I want you to talk to me!" She clambered out of the truck after him, feeling flushed and panicked.

He spun on his heel to face her. "We are talking, Cress, and it's not getting us anywhere. I've already told you everything I have to say. It's a lot of money. What do you want me to do about it?" He spun back toward the barn.

"Maybe it's a good thing for us to have a little space from each other right now, then." She threw the words at his back. He waved over his shoulder and kept walking.

A primal rage at being ignored and dismissed by men at uncomfortable and inconvenient moments boiled up in Cress, coursing like lightning through her core and zinging down to her fingertips. "Fine! If that's how you feel, just leave then!" She screamed the words at him. With a swish of her wind-frizzed ponytail, she turned to the house, sprang over the steps, and slammed the screen door behind her.

* * *

Mac and Franklin stared openly at Jake as he stomped into the barn and laced his fingers behind his head, staring up at the rafters.

"You all right, man?" Mac scratched at his patchy red beard. Franklin shoved his hands into his pockets and looked nervously out the door. "That sounded like one heck of a fight."

Jake shook his head and let out a breath. "Shit." He slapped the side of a tractor. "Shit. I think I just got myself fired."

"Cress wouldn't fire you!" Franklin looked at him, stricken. "Would she?"

"You heard her! She told me to leave." He spread his arms wide then let them drop, his mind spinning. There weren't a lot of options as far as places for him to go.

"Are you sure that's what she meant?" Mac continued scratching his beard, a nervous habit.

Sarcastically, Jake drawled, "I dunno, bro. Her scream sounded pretty convincing to me."

Franklin shook his head. "This don't sit right. I think it was more of a lover's quarrel than a firing." His eyes shot toward the door again when Jake rounded on him.

"Lover's quarrel? What are we, in a romance novel? You weren't there. You couldn't see her. She meant it." He paced back and forth, trying to get some of the nervous energy out of his system before he exploded.

Mac leaned against the side of the separator and studied him. "This ain't right. Cress gets aggravated, sure. But she usually doesn't fly off the handle. Why don't you go straighten things out with her? At least get clear on what happened?"

Jake ground his teeth. "I know what happened. My girlfriend fired me. And I don't need two idiots getting in the middle of it." Not wanting to deal with their misplaced "help" any longer, he strode out of the barn and to his cabin. He had some packing to do.

* * *

After her... unsettling... moment with Jake, Cress had finally decided she couldn't hide in the house all day. She'd emerged and retreated to the East section to check for pecan nut casebearers. Checking the green nuts for the minuscule eggs was tedious work, but it took her attention and gave her time to cool off. And while she was at it, she could mark the spots to plant pheromone traps next season to make their spraying schedule for the little buggers more accurate.

It was late afternoon, and she'd worked her way through most of the section and back toward the barn when the rumble of tires on the driveway drew her attention. She glanced up to see Jake's truck headed down the drive. The sound of braying hounds echoed in the quiet afternoon air, and she stood in shock as she saw all his dogs loaded into the back of the truck.

Desperately, she hoped he was taking them on a vet check even as her legs set off on a dead sprint for his cabin. When she reached it, she twisted the knob and stepped inside. Even before she flicked on the light, she could tell it was vacant.

Gone were the picture frames on the side tables and the books piled haphazardly on the coffee table. The bed stood stripped, and the closet hung open and empty. Even the usually cluttered sink was spotless.

A hollow pit opened inside of her, threatening to swallow her whole. She squeezed her eyes closed, refusing to tip into the darkness inside of herself as she clutched at the doorknob, shaking with silent sobs. Pressing a fist to her mouth, she turned out the light and closed the door. Not knowing where else to go, she headed for the barn.

Around her, the world flattened out. The thrum of cicadas and crickets quieted to a gentle whoosh, and she passed unseeing by the aisles of whispering trees. If a fallen branch had lain in her path, she would have tripped over it in her state.

Her footsteps fell heavily, their drum echoing through her with a shock as she entered the barn. Serene afternoon light spilled through the barn door. Crickets chirped against the dim thrum of cicadas. Inside the barn, Mac and Franklin turned to her from putting away their tools for the day, faces grim. Cress would have given anything to be elsewhere, but she couldn't let her nerves show. Jake could run away, but she couldn't.

Gramps strode out of the barn's office and joined them, and for all the world they looked like a country version of the Three Musketeers in plaid shirts and cowboy work boots. And all three of them looked... weirdly sympathetic and irate at the same time.

"So, Jake's gone?" At least her voice didn't shake. She didn't need to look like a scared little girl in front of Mac and Franklin. Although, she probably did anyway. She was sure they thought it was her fault, and she couldn't blame them. She thought it was her fault as well.

Gramps crossed his arms and looked at her. "He left to help Vada."

She swallowed and shoved a sweaty lock of hair out of her face that had worked its way out of her ponytail.

Mac shifted nervously. "Did you fire him?"

Gramps narrowed his eyes at her, daring her to try lying to him. She didn't know if her grandfather would fire her, but she didn't want to find out.

"Van offered him a job and... and I found out. I lost my temper, and we got into a fight. I... told him to leave." She held up her hands. "I thought it was just *us* arguing. And he was already walking away from me." She darted a look at Gramps, nerves skittering through her. "I meant it like we needed some time apart to cool off. I didn't even think I *could* fire anybody."

Franklin slapped the wall and stormed out of the barn. Mac

shot her a wounded look and followed. Gramps studied her. "It's going to take a long time to make things right with them, you know that?"

She nodded, crossing her arms. "I'll do whatever it takes."

He sighed and came to lean beside her against the tractor. "That may not be enough."

Sudden tears blurred her vision. "I know." She blinked, clearing her eyes. "I'm sorry."

"I know." He pulled her into a lopsided hug. "All right. Now tell me the rest of it."

She laughed, the sound coming out strangled. "How'd you know?"

"You two fuss at each other all the time. I figured it had to be more than the usual for him to go storming off."

She closed her eyes, letting out a long breath. "It was bad. I walked in on Vada fussing at Jake about Van. Then Jake saw me hugging Grant. We'd agreed to meet up and talk things over, get some closure. So, when I confronted him about Van, he blew up. Then, I blew up. And soon, I didn't even know what we were arguing about. Next thing I know, I hear myself telling him maybe it's better if we had some space from each other. And now..." she waved her hand at the barn, sitting quiet and still. Despite its ever-dusty clutter of equipment, it felt empty without Jake's cheerful clatter and off-key whistling. "He's gone."

She leaned her head on Gramps' shoulder, heartsick at the thought of having to go through the day without seeing Jake's smile. "I can't do this by myself."

He squeezed her knee. "Why don't you go apologize? Patch things up."

She shook her head. Jake didn't want to see her; she was

sure of it. "It wouldn't matter."

Gramps straightened, muttering, "Boneheaded." He waved at her to stand up. "Fine. Have it your way. But you'll see. Sometimes, all it takes is an apology."

She walked toward the barn door, shaking her head. It would take more than an apology to make things right with Jake. She knew that. She'd wounded him too deeply. But maybe she could start by making things right with Mac and Franklin.

She took a deep breath and stepped outside to try to repair the damage.

Chapter 21

C ress dodged around one last pothole and pulled into a parking spot a few spaces down from the Loveless Bakery. She was already late, but she just needed a moment to gather herself. Resting her head on the steering wheel, she closed her eyes, exhausted. Why hadn't she called off meeting up with Grant tonight? It was silly to do this when she was already so drained.

With a sigh, she sat up and climbed out, slamming the door behind her. She was here now; she might as well get this over with. Tucking a wayward strand of hair behind her ear, she glanced down at herself. Her jeans were spattered with mud, but at least her shirt was clean. Rumpled, but clean. It would have to do. She was here to patch things up, not impress, anyway.

She took a breath and walked into the bakery, the bell jangling cheerfully overhead. Willow waved from behind the counter, her face oddly expressionless, and Grant, dressed impeccably in a button-down and navy slacks, smiled at her from a table. Where one slice of cake and two glasses of wine already waited. With a candle twinkling beside them.

Cress frowned at the sight. It looked suspiciously like a date. As Grant rose and ushered her to her chair with a flourish, Jake's warning rang in the back of her head. She tried to shake off her sudden misgivings about the evening. Grant was always well-dressed. And he knew the kinds of things she liked. He was just being nice. Probably.

"Sorry, I'm late. It's been a long day." She kept her words light, but Grant leaned toward her, folding his hands under his jaw.

"I'm just glad we could get together at all. But why don't you tell me about it?" His eyes bored into hers, intense and smoldering in the candle's glow. That intensity used to feel flattering to her. Now, it just felt off-putting. Like he was prying where he wasn't wanted. Behind the counter, Willow shot her a worried look as she polished a wine glass and slid it carefully onto a rack.

Cress chose her words carefully. "Oh. Just the strain of working in an old orchard. Getting things going and trying to decide the best place to start. Everyone's got their opinion."

He smiled, his teeth wolfish. "Everyone?" She decided right then to steer the conversation away from Jake. If Grant got ahold of that juicy tidbit, he'd never let her live it down.

Cress pushed the cake to his side of the table. "Yep. I'm sure you run into that, though, on your revitalization projects."

He frowned down at the slice of red velvet now situated squarely in front of him. "Uhh. Yeah, but there's a pecking order. Project manager always gets the last say." He cocked his head at her. "And you're the project manager in this case, aren't you?"

She nodded slightly. "But it's never been my style to run roughshod over people. I'd rather have their buy-in." Taking a small sip of the overly sweet wine, she winced. "Takes more time and finesse," she lingered over the word, "But creates less friction that way."

"You always were a little different." He glossed over her statement, his hand sliding toward hers, and she reached for her wineglass again. She was not letting this evening turn into another... situation.

"To being friends," she said as she raised it. "It's rare to find exes who can let go of the past and truly transform their relationship."

Slowly, he picked up his glass and touched it to hers, holding her gaze. "To new beginnings."

They sat in silence for a moment, sipping their wine. Cress stared into her glass, debating exactly how long she needed to stay to avoid being rude, but to make it clear that she had no interest in renewing their romantic attachment. Was fifteen minutes too short? Or did it need to be thirty?

She didn't want to reminisce, and she didn't know if her small talk skills could withstand more than fifteen minutes of blathering about the weather and the who's who of the town. She was just about to ask him about his revitalization project for Midnight Bluff, the only topic they both would be truly interested in, when he cleared his throat.

"So, I have to admit. Inviting you here was a bit of a pretext." She groaned silently as he continued. "I felt so bad about how we broke up..."

She interrupted him. "To be clear, how you *dumped* me. When I thought you were going to propose." She was pleased to see his eyes nearly pop out of his head as he choked on his wine.

Behind his back, Willow pressed a hand to her mouth, trying not to laugh out loud.

"Ok, I deserved that." He patted a napkin at his mouth while he continued to sputter. She waited for him to recover. "So, after I…" he waved a hand, "…dumped you. I felt so bad. I wanted to do something to apologize."

He pulled two plane tickets out of his pocket. "Look. There's a biologist in Texas. He specializes in Southern pecan growing. I booked us a flight and a time to meet with him." Cress had frozen, staring at the tickets he'd laid on the table. She jumped when he touched her hand. His eyes sparkled as he spoke. "This could be your chance to start over. Just think: You could publish a paper on how you rejuvenate the orchard. We could use it to reestablish you in the academic community or as a launchpad to be a consultant." The *we* scalded through Cress like dunking her hand in a pot of boiling water.

Cress snatched her hand back. The knowledge that Jake had been right seared through her, and with it, a fresh wave of grief. She gripped the edge of the table, trying to not burst at the seams. "I don't need to start over! That's what I already came here to do! To get away from you and to get a fresh start." She continued, gathering steam, as her anger at Grant's presumptuousness built.

"I didn't ask you to follow me and try to direct my life. Again." She stood and tossed her napkin onto the table. "Sometimes, I mess up." Her mind flashed to an image of Jake's stricken face from that morning and her voice wavered, but she continued, knowing what she had to say. "And sometimes, I just choose differently than you would. But I'm perfectly capable of making my own decisions." She bit her tongue to keep from adding more, fearing she'd just turn cruel.

With a croaked *goodbye*, she turned around and shoved her way through the door. The roar of her engine as she floored it out of town and back to the orchard washed over her. The moon gleamed like a polished silver platter, and she rolled the windows down, pulled out her ponytail, and let the night breezes run through her curls until they stood nearly on end, ecstatic and wild in the humidity. For once, she breathed a little easier, feeling like she'd said the right thing.

* * *

Ruffin waved the guys together and tossed coils of rope at their feet. Jake groaned as he picked one up. He hated blind knot-tying drills. In the humid air of the fire station's garage, the other men looked just as bummed as they bent to pick up the ropes.

Ruffin swore by these drills for team building, but to Jake, they were just hours of pure torture. He could never get his partner to do what he was saying. And of course, his partner could never just *tell* him what to do. They had to be needlessly descriptive and confuse the whole thing.

As the men began milling around to partner up, he snatched up a coil of rope and tried to wave down Floyd. Before he could get Floyd's attention, Ruffin's voice cut in. "Jake, you're with me."

Jake slid over to Ruffin reluctantly. Ruffin tossed him a blindfold, then clacked two metal chairs open for them to sit in. "You first."

"How come you always seem to get out of doing this?" Jake slid the blindfold over his eyes and tightened the knot at the back. Ruffin would know if he cheated.

"Because I'm not a hardhead who doesn't listen." Jake felt the rope being placed in his hands. "Besides, it's funny to watch."

"Thanks a lot," Jake muttered. He tightened his grip on the rope. "All right. What knot are we tying today?"

"Nope. Not telling you." He heard Ruffin shuffle his feet over to his right. "You'd just tie the knot by feel without listening to my directions."

"I know all the knots. I don't need directions." Jake grumbled as he fidgeted with the rope. Ruffin slapped the back of his head.

"That's not the point of the exercise." He felt Ruffin turn the rope in his hands until he could feel the working end of it. "Now hush up and listen to me."

By the time they'd worked through a clove hitch and a sheet bend knot, Jake's teeth were aching from how much he'd clenched them out of frustration. Around them, the other guys laughed and joked around. He could hear Floyd and Thomas cutting up beside them.

"What are they so tickled about?" he growled.

"Oh, they're just laughing at you." Ruffin's voice was smug.

"What?" Outrage flooded through Jake, but Ruffin just punched his knee.

"Get real." He heard his captain chuckle. "They're not even paying attention to what's going on around them. They're just being knuckleheads, same as usual." He placed the rope back in Jake's hands. "What's gotten into you, anyway? You're not usually one to be this... tense."

Jake gripped the rope, yanking it into a figure eight, then working it loose over and over. "Cress and I broke up."

Beside him, Ruffin went still. He remained silent so long that Jake finally jerked the blindfold up. Ruffin sat with his hands folded in front of him, face pinched and serious. He glanced at Jake then back at the smooth concrete floor of the station.

He finally shrugged. "Sorry, man. That sucks."

Jake stared at him in disbelief. "That sucks? That's all you have to say?"

Ruffin stood, taking the blindfold from him. "What do you want me to say?" An eerie echo of Jake's own words to Cress flashed through his head. "But I warned you. So yeah, it sucks. But it's not like you couldn't see this coming from a mile away. Women are always going to stab you in the back."

Jake stood and stalked into the squad room, boiling with anger. He paced back and forth, fuming. Anger lanced through every part of his body, wrapping protectively around his throbbing heart. He paced faster, the faded posters on the wall whooshing past.

In the middle of a step, his back twinged from sleeping on Vada's couch. Suddenly locked into an awkward angle, he carefully lowered himself into one of the squad room's broken-down loungers. He needed to ice it after this morning's drills or he'd be completely stove up by tonight.

Jake closed his eyes as his back spasmed for real this time and swore to himself that he wouldn't end up a cynical loner like Ruffin. Even if it meant getting serious therapy that he had no idea how to afford.

The door swung open, and Ruffin entered, hands in pockets. "Look, man. I shouldn't have been so down on you. You needed an ear and instead, I gave you an earful." He held out a hand. "Peace?"

Jake grimaced, unable to sit up. "You're going to have to come over here for that."

Ruffin eyed him. "You been sleeping on Vada's couch again?"

Jake wheezed. "Yep."

"I'll get the ice and the ibuprofen."

Jake swore to sweet baby Jesus to think better of his friends in the future as his back spasmed again.

Chapter 22

Blearily, Cress followed her mother into the church. It has been three weeks since Jake had left and still no word from him. Not a call, not a text, not a sighting at church or the Co-Op, though Vada had assured Cress he was staying with her and helping at the equestrian school. Secretly, she'd thought that they'd have worked this out by now.

Early this morning, the first bite of fall had nipped the air, but now as they neared eleven a.m. it was already feeling like any other summer day. In Mississippi, it would be months before it turned truly cold, but she knew the time would fly by, and all too soon they would rake up the orchard and roll out the harvester. Tasks she had looked forward to performing with Jake. Her thoughts were so wrapped up in to-do lists she didn't even realize that a small crowd had formed around her mother.

The whispers finally reached her. "Paint the side of the old cotton gin with some garish sign." "Fix up the facades of the stores." "Bring in outside investors." "It's all the Yankee's doing." The women shot disgruntled looks at Mayor Patty, where she held court with Grant and a few of the aldermen across the sanctuary. Of course, he was the one who had everyone in a tizzy. Mayor Patty grasped Grant's arm and nodded at something he said.

Any other day, Cress would have been thrilled to hear about plans to put Midnight Bluff back on the map, but today Cress rolled her eyes and turned back to the group of tutting women. He could go suck an egg for all she cared.

Her mother asked her in a whisper, "You wouldn't happen to know exactly what Grant's revitalization plan entails, would you, dear?" She huffed. "Patty won't breathe a word of it to us." She shot her old friend a disgruntled look.

Suddenly, a dozen pairs of eyes were fixed on Cress. She shook her head, nonplussed by the assumption. "We haven't talked in weeks. I have no idea."

"That's a pity," piped up Emma Jean Hicks, the President of the Ladies' Auxiliary and Leora's best friend. "We could have used some insider knowledge."

Her mother elbowed Emma Jean. "What?" Emma Jean protested. "It's true. The whole town is talking about this plan Grant's got going, but no one seems to know anything about it."

Cress rubbed her face. As much as she hated Grant's guts right now, the town came first. "If you're worried, why don't you ask Patty to hold a town hall meeting to lay out the basics and answer questions?"

She looked at their stunned faces. "It's pretty standard with things like this. I'm sure you would have one, eventually. Might as well have it sooner rather than later." She sighed and stared off into the distance, already over this topic and thinking about the orchard and her never-ending to-do lists again. Anything to take her mind off the one person she looked for every time she came into town, for a peek of his white T-shirt disappearing around a corner.

Leora rubbed at her chin. "That's not a bad idea. I'll have to put a bug in Patty's ear about it." She looked at Cress. "What are you so spaced out over?"

"Hmm?" Cress snapped her attention back to her mother. "Oh, nothing."

The ladies looked at her, and then at the empty spot in their pew next to Bo at the front of the church, and she scowled at them. Her mother raised her eyebrows, determined to stand there in awkward silence until she spoke.

"Fine!" She raised and dropped her hands in mock surrender. "I'm worrying over the orchard, is all. There's so much to do with the harvest coming up and we've got a lot of expenses to offset the next few years."

Why was she blabbing their business again? And this time to half the ladies of the church. She was losing it. She crossed her arms. "Jake had worked out a few deals with Mr. Pipkin and Mr. Kelly before he left," she nodded to the wives of the respective men and then continued, "But it won't quite take care of everything." She pinched the bridge of her nose. "I'm stressed, is all."

Jackie Allen-Glower patted her arm. "It will be all right, dear. Give your worries to God and he'll take care of everything. You'll see." Her husband, Van, might be a regular old troll, but his wife had always been sweet as pecan pie to her since her arrival, making room for her in Sunday School and saving the best sweets for her at church socials. It was as if she was determined to single-handedly make up for all her husband's shortcomings.

Cress squeezed her hand. Reassurances echoed around the circle. Cress had never been comfortable accepting encouragement, but the women murmured their agreements sincerely. Even Lou Ellen. Cress nodded and smiled weakly.

"God's going to have to hurry up then, because I don't see how we'll save the orchard otherwise." She tried to laugh and pass it off as a joke, but as she uttered the words, she watched wistful looks flit across the faces of several ladies.

With a sigh, Mrs. Dottie Goings hefted her handbag. "That would be a shame. Y'all have such a beautiful orchard. So well-kept. I wish Ronnie would do something with ours. It's been in the family so long, but he says it costs more for the equipment than we would make off the nuts." A few other ladies nodded and murmured agreement.

Cress looked around. "Wait. Y'all have pecan orchards too?"

Leora gave her a bewildered look. "Of course, child. It was common to plant orchards of all kinds back in the day. Had to be practically self-sustaining out here. You'll find a lot of old pecan orchards in the Delta that have been left to go to seed."

Excitement whirled in Cress' chest as she thought of how Jake had bartered for the tree cutting and aerial spraying. "Mrs. Dottie, do y'all keep the orchard mowed?" She couldn't keep the blip of exhilaration from her voice. This could be her way of helping the orchard and the town, without starting a "circus." She clasped her hands together, hope bubbling up.

"Of course. Don't want snakes and all that getting up in there." Mrs. Dottie cocked her head at Cress like an inquisitive bird.

Cress twisted her hands tighter together and leaned toward the ladies, fighting to keep her voice from squeaking in excitement. "I might have an idea that will work for everyone, but I need to check a few things first." She motioned them closer and explained her plan. Quiet exclamations rang out around the circle, and heads bobbed.

Pastor Riser strode out onto the stage and up to the pulpit, motioning for everyone to take a seat and scattering them in various directions around the sanctuary to join their families. As Cress and Leora scurried into their pew, Bo leaned over to them, winked, and whispered, "What are you girls scheming up now?" Van turned around and stared at them, a sly grin on his face. His wife, Jackie, tugged at his sleeve for him to turn around. She shot an apologetic smile to Cress.

Leora settled her shoulders with a sniff as she stared down Van and stage-whispered. "Just some friendly competition." Cress' stomach flipped as Van's smile vanished, and he glared poison at her instead. Jackie jabbed him in the ribs, and he finally spun back around as everyone rose in a rustle of linen, silk, and paper to flip open hymnals and began singing "In Christ Alone."

Beside Cress, her mother belted out the next verse about the powers of hell and schemes of men, not even trying to hide her smirk. Cress resisted the urge to roll her eyes, instead flipping open her hymnal. Leora loved drama, but today Cress would let her have her moment.

* * *

Leora invited herself to dinner that night. Of course.

She insisted it was to lend Cress "moral support" when

she asked Gramps about her new idea. But what it meant to Cress was an entire afternoon spent laboring over dinner preparations because it was Lynn's day off, and her mother would still expect a four-course meal.

The doorbell rang just as she slid a perfectly done beef wellington out of the oven. As she ferried the lava hot dish to the table with a carving knife balanced across it, she heard Gramps open the door.

"Hello, Bo!" Her mother swanned into the dining room. She looked at the simple table arrangement, complete with hot pads and shot Cress a disparaging look.

Cress shrugged innocently. "What? I thought you were here to visit, not to yell pleasantries at me from another room while I played waitress all night."

Her mother's look turned chastising. Bo snorted as he popped open a bottle of wine. "Let's eat before it gets cold! We don't often get to enjoy Cress' cooking, and she learned from the best." He meant her grandmother, of course. Cress' mom was doing good to heat soup.

After a few minutes of passing plates and the usual chitchat about who was and wasn't at church that day, Cress caught Leora sending her a pointed look. Bo did as well. He set his soup spoon down with a clink.

"Now, I was just kidding earlier about you two scheming!"

Cress jumped in before her mother could. If Leora took over, Bo would say *no* out of principle. "We were only scheming a little! And it's completely your call, Gramps. I won't do a thing without your approval."

He picked his spoon up and motioned for her to continue. "I take it this is about the orchard, then. Don't think I missed that little storm brewing between you and Van today. I know when something's up." He blew on his soup noisily. Her mother looked on with distaste.

Cress drug her spoon through her soup in circles, tension bunching up her shoulders. There was nothing for it but to lay all her cards on the table. "What would you say to harvesting orchards other than ours?"

Gramps froze, staring at her. He sat his spoon down again and folded his hands under his chin. "Worth thinking about."

Cress sagged. He might still refuse, but the idea itself had enough merit to grab his attention. She rushed ahead. "A lot of neighbors have old pecan orchards that are sitting fallow. Most of them are small, but mostly, they keep them mowed and there's interest in letting us harvest on a favorable profit share." She took a breath as Bo rubbed at his chin. "Or we could trade for labor or materials depending on the person."

Leora tapped her coral-painted fingernails on the polished mahogany tabletop as she looked back and forth between them but blessedly remained silent.

At last, Gramps asked, "What kind of profit split?"

"80/20." The answer came out as more of a question, but Gramps was already half nodding, half bobbling his head. "We keep eighty, they'd keep twenty as rent."

"*If* we did it, that would be the split I'd want. Lots to think over though, what with the labor and all it would take."

Fireworks and party crackers went off in Cress' head. Gramps would come around to the idea. It would take a little while, but she was sure she could talk him into it. She nodded, ready to drop the subject and not push her luck for the evening.

"*If?*" Her mother's voice cut through her thoughts. The fireworks inside of Cress fizzled.

Leora sat back in her chair, staring at Bo. Cress wished she could take a napkin and stuff it down her throat to keep her from messing this up. Already, she could see her chances going up in smoke. *"If?"* Leora repeated. "Bo, don't be an idiot. You know this is a brilliant plan. For the first couple of years, you can harvest extra orchards with minimal costs to you." She waved a hand. "Then, as you want to scale, you can worry about irrigation and pest management to up your profits."

Bo sighed heavily. He tossed his napkin onto the table and stared down at Leora. "Of course, it's a wonderful idea, Leora. But if you haven't noticed, I'm down a farm manager. And with harvest coming up, it's going to be awfully hard to find someone with the experience to step in and coordinate the process since they've already been snatched up." He looked at Cress. "It's a wonderful idea, honey, really. But I just don't know if it's feasible this year with us shorthanded."

Leora rolled her eyes. "I don't know why you're getting so upset over one farmhand leaving, Bo." Cress' fingers clenched around her knife at the derogatory tone, but her mother continued unperturbed as she spoke to Bo. "There are plenty of more qualified men looking for work out there. I'd look at this as an opportunity to get more skilled help." Leora took a dainty bite of the beef wellington, rolling the rare steak and pastry over in her mouth, unaware of her daughter's flushed face.

Unable to take it anymore, Cress shouted, "He's not just a farmhand!" She slammed her knife down and bolted up from the table, the legs of the chair screeching against the hardwood. Her mother and Bo sat motionless, staring at her. Cress stomped into the kitchen before they could see the tears brimming in her eyes.

Jake was gone, and it was all her fault. If only she hadn't been so stubborn. Not only had she run off the man she loved, but now she'd ruined the orchard's best chance as well.

She'd been so focused on doing things her way, she hadn't stopped to consider Jake's feelings and opinions. And now it was too late for her to beg for forgiveness; he'd never forgive her.

She breathed slowly into her palms, trying to get herself under control. It wasn't like her to get so emotional. But a sob welled up in her throat, hot and uncontrollable. He was never coming back. She'd driven him away with her foolish ideas and wounded ego.

Her mind spun. She'd treated him like he was Grant, acting like everything he did was an attack. But he'd been supporting her all along, even when it meant pointing out that her plan wouldn't work and that she was making poor decisions.

A soft click of heels echoed on the tile behind her. Cress swiped at her face, trying to hide her smudged mascara. "Not now, Mother. I don't feel like talking about it."

Her mom's hand rested on her shoulder and gently turned her, pulling her into an unexpected hug. "Oh, honey. I didn't realize you were in love with him."

Taken off balance by her mother's softness, Cress melted into her, sniffling. Where had this version of her mom been all these years? Even in heels, her mother was three inches shorter than Cress, making her hunch and crick her neck. But despite the awkward posture, Cress wanted to hang on when Leora pulled away.

Her mother wiped her own eyes. "Loving a farmer is hard. You always come second to the land." Leora pushed a lock of hair behind Cress' ear. "But they are good, solid men.

285

Dependable. I shouldn't be surprised this happened." She laughed, the sound low and husky. "We're more alike than you like to think. You get your stubbornness from me after all."

Surprised, Cress looked at her mother. She'd always assumed she was like her dad. Hank was the strong, quiet type. Indulgent with his daughter, but he kept a tight ship on his farm. Lines snuck their way around Leora's eyes and the corners of her mouth as she stared forlornly out the window. As Cress looked more closely, she could see the faintest hint of coverup blended underneath her eyes.

"Have you not been sleeping again?" Concern gnawed at her stomach. "You know Dr. Washburn can give you sleeping pills that won't leave you feeling groggy."

Her mother waved her off. "I haven't slept well since your father… well. I just don't sleep well. But it's nothing a glass of wine can't fix. I don't need more pills."

"Mother, you have to take care of yourself." Cress chided, knowing her mother's tendency to fuss over everybody but herself. Leora might be brusque, but Cress knew deep down her mother cared.

"I'm fit as a fiddle. Stop your worrying." Leora pressed her lips together and crossed her arms. "Besides, you're changing the subject."

Leora leveled a cool stare at Cress. "Now, are you going to go get your man back or not?"

"Mom!"

She threw her head back and laughed as heat flared in Cress' face. Cress pressed her palms to her cheeks. Her mother reached out and rubbed her arm. "I don't think I've embarrassed you that much since your debutante ball. The look on your face." She sobered. "But darling, if you love him, you will regret it the rest of your life if you don't at least try."

Tears welled in Cress' eyes. "But how would I get him back? We were barely together."

Leora's eyes wandered to the window again. "We've just got to get y'all in the same place." She grinned triumphantly at Cress. "I've got just the thing!"

Chapter 23

J ake hefted a shovel full of manure and tossed it into the wheelbarrow. A trickle of sweat worked its way determinedly down into his eyes, but he didn't dare swipe at it with the muck on his hands. Not until he'd had a shower... or three. He scowled at the stall he was shoveling out and jabbed the shovel down again.

"Finally making progress, I see." He turned to see Vada standing behind him, a saddle slung over one shoulder and an ironic twist to her lips. She held a gelding called General who was dark with sweat by the bridle. "I was hoping you'd have the stalls finished by the time I got done exercising the horses."

Biting off a snappy retort, he waved an arm with exaggerated gentility toward the three newly cleaned stalls next to him. "You can put 'em there." Shoveling horse crap and scrubbing down stalls in this humidity was worse than a day mowing in the orchard. He'd only been here a few weeks and he was already champing at the bit to be anywhere else. Preferably somewhere with trees. His thoughts wandered to the orchard, with its long, breezy aisles and cool shadows. He snapped back to the moment.

Vada hadn't hesitated to take him in. With a sigh, he resigned himself to a couple of months of uncomplaining grunt work.

He scowled at the filthy stall. Even if it meant shoveling piles of crap daily. Without a word, Vada took General into the next stall. Her voice floated over. "Have you pulled down the new hay yet?"

Glancing at the dwindling stack of bales at the end of the barn, he winced. "Not yet. Gonna' do it right after this." He still hadn't gotten used to how things ran here at Vada's equestrian school. Poking reluctantly at the next pile, he stared out at the soft green paddock beyond the riding ring.

A steady stream of chores followed one another here. Horses weren't like tractors. You couldn't just fix one part and be done. They needed constant food, water, exercise, and cleaning. And they didn't like the racket his dogs made. That had been the biggest change—trying to get his hounds acclimated so they didn't bay at every little noise.

Rustling and the sound of pouring water followed as Vada got General settled in and cleaned up. She popped her head around the corner. "Hand me that curry brush, will you?" As he tossed her the brush, she eyed the slow progress on the stall. Vada would have had this stall cleaned and scrubbed in five minutes flat. It felt like he'd been in there for hours.

"Jake." He blinked against the solemn tone. Turning, he took in her worried face. "Jake," she repeated, "You're not happy."

He laughed, the sound sharp and brittle. "Why would you think that?"

She tilted her head, eyes serious. "We've known each

other for nearly fifteen years. I know when you're moping." Pointing at the stall, she continued, "I know you can do better than that. And I've seen you staring off into space way too many times to count."

"I have not been moping," he groused. He glanced out the door at the sunlight glinting off the sandy arena outside.

She set her hands on her hips. "I know Bo's been calling you."

He crossed his arms, refusing to answer. There was no point in arguing. She'd never understand. He'd do anything for Bo. Cress was the one who didn't want him there. And as long as she felt that way, he'd stay away.

Vada raised her hands, palms up. "Just go kiss her and apologize already, you idiot!"

He scowled at her. "I have nothing to apologize for!" Turning his back on her, he stabbed at the smelly pile of manure. "I'm not the one who kicked me out." Slapping it into the wheelbarrow, he added, "I'm not the one who wanted space or the one who went running back to their ex the first time he showed a flake of remorse." He set aside the shovel and grabbed the handles of the wheelbarrow. "She didn't trust me. So, there's nothing to go back for."

He half-stumbled past Vada, trying to maneuver the stinking load out of the stall and to the dump pile outside. Just as he was moving past her, she murmured, "But she didn't."

Pausing, he asked, "What are you going on about now?"

Vada looked up at him, her brown eyes soft and sad. "She didn't get back together with him. She was angry that he even suggested it." His grip tightened painfully on the wheelbarrow handles. She stepped back toward General's stall. "Just thought you should know."

Dazed, he wheeled the pile out into the sunlit yard and dumped it onto the pile. As he stood there, staring across the exercise yard and into the green pasture, his cell phone rang. Without thinking, he pulled it out of his back pocket and glanced at the screen. He hesitated for a moment, but he desperately wanted to hear another friendly voice. For the first time in weeks, he clicked the green icon.

"Hey Bo," he said, "Sorry, I haven't picked up before."

* * *

Jake shut the door of his truck with a raspy slam and paused, staring down the hill at the house. If he turned around now, he could get out of here before anyone saw him and escape with his dignity.

Trucks and SUVs already lined the McBride's driveway for the first dove hunt of the season. Children thundered up and down the porch and hollered by the pond, Champ yipping joyfully at their heels. Adults with rifles slung over their shoulders chatted around long tables covered in white cloths with streamers of wheat, sunflowers, and English ivy running down the center. But having parked at the far end of the line, no one had spotted him. Yet. He drummed his fingers on his side mirror, debating.

The screen door slammed, and Vada strode out with Cress right behind her, both holding pitchers of tea. Vada glanced down the driveway and grinned at him. He winced as he saw her arm come up in a big, flashy wave.

"Jake! We're over here!" Her voice carried across the open space and echoed through the trees. Everyone turned and stared at him, smiles spreading slowly across their faces as they glanced from him to Cress.

Cress stood frozen on the back steps, face beet red. Her eyes were locked on his. Then, with a shake of her ponytail, she hefted the pitcher of tea and continued toward the tables, breaking the spell. Chatter filled the yard again, and Jake found his feet carrying him to Vada, who stood grinning at him like a cat that's caught a canary.

"Proud of yourself?" he asked when he got close enough.

Her eyes twinkled up at him. "Every darn day."

Bo sauntered over, a sappy grin on his face and a hand outstretched. "Glad you're back."

Jake took his hand, pulling him in for a hug. "Now let's not go getting ahead of ourselves." He stepped back. "It's good to see you, Bo. How are things going, getting ready for harvest?" Looking toward the deep green rows of trees, he shaded his eyes against the early afternoon sun. The cool shade under their branches looked inviting. He could just imagine the gentle breeze wafting through the limbs and making the leaves rustle, Cress' hand in his... His chest squeezed at the thought.

Waving a hand, Bo retorted, "Let's not talk business today." He winked at Jake. "There's a certain young lady that I know is just dying to see you."

"Just dying to give me another piece of her mind, more like." Jake rolled his eyes even as his heart pounded. Cress had studiously kept her back to him, fluffing and fussing over the centerpiece on the table.

Her mother stood beside her, whispering to her and darting furtive looks at him. He turned to Bo. "Besides, I'm here to help you, remember?"

Bo guffawed. "If you think I asked you here because I need help, you're about as thick as the Yazoo clay we're standing

292

on. I can run one of these shindigs in my sleep." He poked Jake's shoulder. "Now, do what I say and get over there before I lock both of y'all in the barn together."

Rubbing his shoulder, Jake turned toward Cress. She glanced up at him from her station, now by the punch bowl, her big green eyes wide and … hopeful? She glanced back down so quickly that he blinked, unsure of what he'd seen. Where he'd expected anger and hostility, had he just seen an opening? She tucked a strand of curls behind her ear and said something to her mother.

Leora nodded and picked up an empty pitcher, stepping around the end of the table and coming toward him. As she brushed past him, she touched his arm, the smell of Chanel No. 5 enveloping him. "Go talk to her." The words were barely a murmur, and then Leora was gone, hallooing chipperly to the Glowers behind him as she wound her way into the house.

Cress wanted to talk to him. Disbelief melted into joy, sweet as tea, at the thought. It took all his control not to run over to the table and grab her up in a bone-crushing hug. He slowed his steps as he approached the punch bowl.

Neighbors glanced at them, then shuffled a few steps further away. A knot of women tittered close by, Lou Ellen staring at him like she wanted to pluck his plum. That woman had made a pass at him at Eve's wedding. He shot her an irritated look and watched in satisfaction as her shadows, Missy and Janie, pulled her on down the table.

Cress studied him as he stopped in front of her, lips pressed tight and fingers wound together. He shuffled his feet and scratched the back of his neck, then resettled his ball cap. What the dickens do you say to a woman weeks after a fight?

"Sure is hot today." Lamest way to start a conversation ever, but he was going to die on this hill now. "You'd think it would cool off in September."

She quirked an eyebrow at him. "That's Mississippi for you."

Man, she was going to make him work for it. "Could I get a cup of that tea?"

With a nod, she ladled up a red plastic cup of the cold, sweet beverage for him, nudging aside the ring of ice. As she handed him the cup, he placed his hand over hers, capturing her. "Cress, I…" He stammered, the little voice in the back of his head yammering at him to just apologize for being a jerk already. As he coughed and spluttered, an arm wrapped around Cress' shoulder, making both of them jump.

"Cress, I need to talk to you." The pointed look Grant shot at Jake could have run him through it was so sharp.

Vada was wrong. Humiliation washed over Jake at the sight of Grant's arm around Cress' shoulder. He shoved the cup back at Cress. "Forget about it." He turned and strode off toward the barn. He'd promised Bo he'd help drive the little kids back and forth to the millet field today on a hayride, and that's all he was here to do. He should have just stuck with that.

A muffled *oof* sounded behind him, and he heard Cress holler, "Jake, wait!" Nope, no way was he going to get tied up in the middle of anything else with her. He couldn't take any more yanking around. A hand jerked on his arm, pulling him to a stop.

Cress clung to his arm, red-faced and huffing. "Would you just wait for one second, you mule-headed idiot?" Behind her, Grant sprawled on his butt in the grass, looking stunned.

"You're not together?" Jake looked between her and Grant, who was struggling to his feet, looking more embarrassed than hurt.

Confusion crinkled her brow. "What? No." She laughed and shook her head. "I mean, he's been trying. But no, ain't happening." She took a deep breath. "I just... Jake, can we talk?"

Before he could respond, the rattle of gravel and a plume of dust in the driveway from several vehicles grabbed Cress' attention.

"That's weird. Everybody is already here." Cress surveyed the crowd.

Three black SUVs pulled up dangerously close to the tables, and a group of six men and women in dark suits and sunglasses climbed out. Out of the corner of his eye, Jake noticed Van edging away from the group of curious onlookers. Curiosity spiked into suspicion as he watched Van mosey inconspicuously down a row of pecans.

"What is this, NCIS Miami?" Jake muttered, keeping an eye on Van's progress into the orchard.

Bo walked up to a woman with red hair who stepped forward and flashed a badge. After a couple seconds of consultation, Bo surveyed the crowd, looking tired. "Anybody seen Van?"

Vada called, "He was here just a minute ago." Jake caught the agent's eye and jerked a thumb to Van's now hastening backside. She barked orders at two of her agents who took off through the trees while a distressed Jackie clutched her arm, begging to know what was going on. The red-headed agent gently led her away, with Pastor Riser following close. The other agents shooed the crowd back.

Shaking his head, Bo walked over to Jake and Cress. "Poor Jackie." They huddled together as he explained what was going on. "A warrant has been issued for Van's arrest. Tax evasion." He sighed, the sound whistling out through his nose. "I thought better of him than that. To put his wife in that situation…" He shook his head again.

The crowd had now formed a tight knot, whispers floating wildly back and forth. As the two agents returned with a pale and sweaty Van handcuffed between them, a few brave souls shouted questions at him. He just pressed his lips together and shook his head. Jackie emerged from the house with the red-headed agent patting her back. Vada hurried over to Jackie, who handed her a set of keys and hugged her before the agents loaded the husband and wife into separate SUVs.

Pastor Riser stood, hands shoved into his pockets, watching the dust settle back onto the driveway as his parishioners were driven away. Jake could only imagine how anguished and helpless he felt as his church went through this.

Cress asked, horror in her voice, "They're not arresting Jackie too, are they?"

Bo shrugged, every line on his face showing worry. "At least taking her in for questioning. I'm sure her name would have been on some of the paperwork."

Jake stood watching everything, appalled. How a man could put his wife in such a situation revolted him. "We've got to do something for her."

Rubbing his hands together slowly, Bo said, "The best thing we can do now is get the dove hunt going and try to take some of the focus off them. Jackie would be mortified to be the gossip of the year." He pointed at the barn. "Jake, get the hayride going, would you? Cress, would you lead the adults to the field and show them the blinds?"

Cress turned and dashed toward the group, now milling

296

around and gesticulating. Jake gazed after her, cursing his luck. As he hurried to the barn, the grass swishing underfoot, he just hoped that he hadn't missed his chance.

* * *

Cress plunked down next to Vada in her blind and pulled her earplugs out. Hay bales were stacked up around them to form low walls they could see over and into the field of millet and bobbing sunflowers. Vada rested the barrel of her rifle atop the hay and looked at Cress sprawled next to her on the grass, back against the wall of hay. Sweat plastered strings of Cress' hair to her forehead and heat crawled down her back like an annoying string of fire ants.

All afternoon she'd ferried groups back and forth to different blinds, making sure everyone got a turn in the best spots, while Jake zipped around on the UTV, hauling giggling kids in the trailer for a hayride. They hadn't gotten to exchange more than brief waves and head bobs. And now, she looked worse than a melted ice cream cone.

"You look spent." Vada's dry observation did nothing to help douse Cress' temper. Her friend shoved an icy water bottle at her. Pouring it over her face, Cress sputtered against the cold. "I meant for you to drink that, but ok, go ahead and ruin your makeup."

Cress swiped a hand over her face. "My makeup was already done for. And I'm not going to get to talk to Jake today, anyway."

Vada just shook her head. "No, now you'll just look like a drowned rat when you do talk to him."

Cress chunked the empty bottle at her. "It's not going to

happen. With the way things are going, another disaster will just pop up."

"You underestimate my stubbornness—and your mother's—if you think this day is ending before y'all talk."

Brushing away some grass clinging to her jeans, Cress shrugged. "There are no guarantees, even if we manage to slow down long enough to get a word in."

"Lord, chile'. Will you quit thinkin' every cloud is a thunderstorm and focus on the clear sky instead?" Cress looked up at Vada's annoyed tone; she only drawled when she was irritated. "Jake is here. You're here. There's a whole evenin' ahead of us once the shootin' is over. I'm sure you two can find a moment alone to canoodle."

Cress stuck her tongue out at her and looked over the field. A flight of doves took off, fluttering one way, and then another, before landing on the false power line. Belatedly, she reached for her earplugs, but a volley of shots was already ringing out even as Vada 'whipped up her rifle and fired off a round. Annoyed at her own carelessness, Cress sat there staring at the grass and working her jaw, trying to pop some sound back into her ears as a hollow, marshmallow buzzing dimmed the world.

A pair of boots appeared in her line of sight, and Vada glanced over her shoulder, then at Cress. As Cress' eyes traveled up the denim-clad legs, she registered with a little shock Jake towering over her, his rifle slung over one shoulder. She watched his lips move and Vada nod. She patted Cress' shoulder, then stood, gathered up her rifle and bag, and trudged off. Jake settled in beside her, looking at her intensely.

His lips moved, and she nodded with a shrug, hoping she could fake it. He quirked an eyebrow at her, clearly confused.

298

She tapped her ears and shouted, "I can't hear!" His mouth made a little *oh* as understanding lit up his features. He leaned his gun across the stack of hay and slid closer to her, pointing from the gun to her, then to the field.

She shouted again, "I've never shot doves before." He threw his head back, shaking with laughter she couldn't hear. He pointed to her earplugs, indicating for her to put them in, as he slid a pair of noise-canceling headphones over his ears.

He gently handed her the rifle, and she snugged it into the crook of her shoulder. She could feel him scooch up behind her. Slowly, he reached forward and wrapped his arms around her, resting his hands over hers and guiding the barrel of the rifle up. A flutter at the edge of the field and a clutch of doves took flight. She followed their arc, and with just a touch of pressure, he nudged the nose of the gun ahead of their arc, his cheek brushing hers as he nodded. She squeezed the trigger. Three doves fell.

As dogs bounded out into the field to retrieve the catch, she turned to him with a grin, lowering the gun so it rested safely pointed away on the hay. She pulled her earplugs out and the music of the dogs' braying flooded into her ears. He traced a finger down her jaw.

"I've missed you." She trembled as she said the words, knowing that they opened a door into her heart that he could slam shut. But he gathered her into his lap and held her tight, arms wrapping around her waist and shoulders. Sinking into his chest, she breathed in the heady musk of him and the lingering trace of his evergreen cologne.

"I'm so sorry," he whispered the words against her neck. "I blew it. I learned with Eve that we don't always get more time with the people we love, so we should make the most of it. Even our arguments. And I forgot that." He took a deep breath. "I'm sorry for not trusting you. For not telling you everything. For not throwing that stupid card back in Van's face."

He looked down at the grass. "And I'm sorry for walking away when I should have run after you and told you how much I loved you."

Cress' cheeks heated at the memory of what she'd said. "I'm sorry too—I should have trusted you. And God, I can't believe I said what I did. I can't even imagine how hurtful it was." She had to get a handle on her temper. "I was constantly comparing you to Grant in my mind instead of seeing you for who you are. It made me jump to conclusions, and that's not fair."

She slid her hand into his palm. "But I love you because of how independent you are, and how much you love the orchard, and how you support me just being me. You make the work lighter. And make me laugh. You give your all to the things you care about. And I nearly ruined that."

He shook his head, eyes shimmering. "Let's just agree that we've both been boneheaded, all right?" She nodded, heart pounding, as he wound his fingers through her damp hair. "Did you take a dip in the pond or something?"

She laughed. "Got into a fight with a water bottle."

Smirking, he pulled her closer, his lips brushing hers. "I like the wet t-shirt look on you." He covered her lips with his, smothering her protests and obliterating all thought. She bunched the hem of his shirt into fistfuls as he kissed her softly, then teased her lips apart with little nips before slowly swirling his tongue across hers. She inhaled and pulled away, blushing furiously, but needing to see his face, to know that he was here with her and never going away again.

She searched his dark eyes, even as they furiously traced the outlines of her face. "Come home."

His face softened, a glimmer of a smile breaking through the intense concentration. "I'm already here." Planting a gentle kiss on her forehead, he whispered, "Because I have you."

As she sank into his arms, content to rest there amidst the humming of the cicadas with the pecan trees rustling overhead, Cress knew that this was what she had always wanted. And she wouldn't take it for granted again.

Epilogue

L ate afternoon sunlight glinted off the rippling grass. On the front porch, Cress pulled the little tray table closer to her, then leaned back in the wicker chair and closed her eyes, enjoying the cool spring breeze.

When she opened them again, she let her gaze settle on the orchard, the long rows stretching steadily away, like the days in a year. The pecans stood proud and gleaming, the gentle blush of sunset falling to a velvet mist under their branches. They had come through the winter strong and healthy. And now, free to stretch their limbs and encouraged by the careful hedging they'd received, they burst into an abundance of new growth so green it shimmered.

The wind ruffled her notes, and she reached out to tuck the pages back down. Soon, it would be too hot to sit out here for long. But for now, she enjoyed the sound of trilling birds and thrumming insects as she worked on next year's plans. Champ stretched and whined at her feet in his sleep, conked out from his romp in the pond earlier. Telltale splatters of mud still coated his belly.

Behind her, the screen door creaked open, and the familiar thump of Jake's step sounded on the boards. She smiled to herself.

"Hello, husband."

A chair scraped across the porch toward her, and he plopped into it with a groan. His fingers wrapped around her hand and drew it to him. Tenderly, he kissed each knuckle, stopping to playfully fidget with her wedding ring.

"Hello, wife." He hung his ball cap over his knee and stretched out his legs with a contented sigh, looking at her. In the sunset's fiery light, his velvet brown eyes glowed with sparks of liquid gold. She could lose herself staring into his gaze. She'd never imagined enjoying just looking at someone as much as she enjoyed looking at her husband. And now she could look at him all she wanted.

A smile teased about his lips as he tugged at a curl that had escaped her ponytail. "You're so beautiful." He cupped the back of her neck.

"Mmm." She traced a finger up his arm. "Think a little flattery might soften me up?"

He leaned forward and planted soft, slow kisses up her neck that left her tingly and giddy. At her woozy look, he whispered in her ear, "Maybe."

She wrinkled her nose. "Maybe it would work better if you showered first." She shot a pointed look at his sweaty shirt.

He laughed and held up his hands in mock defeat. "Fair enough." They both knew the likelihood of her joining him in the shower was high. She tried to hide her smile as she looked back at the spreadsheets glowing on the screen of her new laptop, a Christmas gift from Gramps.

"Whatcha' working on?" Jake cast a languid eye at the screen as he lounged back in his wicker chair.

Excitement thrilled through her. Cress pointed at a line of numbers. "With the unexpected profit we got from this past harvest, we should be able to replant some of the thin spots in the East lot and a few rows in the new orchard with Creek grafts."

Jake sat forward, eyes focused now, as she clicked to another sheet. "I've just got to check some numbers to make sure it won't get us in a tight spot with insecticide and fertilizer."

He plucked his shirt away from his chest, wafting it in the air to cool himself, as she pointed again. "I can run this pretty easily in the morning and have us an answer, but I'm pretty optimistic." She turned and smiled at him, pride swelling in her chest. "Your bartering idea worked like a charm."

Jake's eyes widened. "My idea?"

She shook her head and motioned at the computer. "You know! Trading pecan harvesting for the crop dusting and whatnot."

Jake shook his head, confusion clouding his face. "That was just with Thomas and Floyd. Figuring out the profit share with all the rest of our neighbors … that was all you." He took her hand. "We couldn't have done this without you."

Embarrassment at his praise colored her cheeks. He touched her face, brushing her cheek with his thumb.

"Baby, be proud of what you've done. I am." She warmed at his words. No one supported and encouraged her like Jake. She wound her fingers through his, heart so full of gratitude for this incredibly kind, smart man who always made her laugh. She couldn't wait to see how life would unfurl for them. He kissed her forehead, her nose, then her lips, lingering and teasing until she was breathless. When she finally opened her eyes, he was grinning at her again.

"I'm going to go hop in the shower. Meet me upstairs?"

All she could manage was an *mmhmm*. His laughter echoed all the way inside. As Cress sat back in her chair, enjoying the delicious breeze cooling her flushed skin, she watched the pecan trees dance in the twilight and smiled at the thought of all the harvests to come.

* * *

*Get a glimpse of Cress and Jake's life after the Happily Ever After in "**All I Want for Christmas.**"*

Jake and Cress just want to spend a romantic evening together at Midnight Bluff's Christmas Festival. And this year, Jake has big plans for Cress' present.

But when things keep going wrong, he has to embrace the giving spirit of the season and accept the help of his neighbors in order to pull off a Christmas miracle.

*Read "**All I Want for Christmas**" today:*
https://susanfarris.me/free-reads/.

Taken For Granted: Midnight Bluff Book Two

It's easy to take love for granted in a small town...

Ellie Winters can conquer any challenge—except finding happily ever after.

When she teams up with Midnight Bluff's dreamy but gruff urban developer for her biggest job yet, she finds that more than the town needs a renovation.

Maybe it's time to let go of her past to see who her future holds. After all, even big-city boys can fall for small-towns.

Grant Emberson just wants to fix this town so he can get on to the next.

Too bad he needs the help of a cute-as-a-button realtor to win back the locals—and save his job. But the more time they spend together, the more he sees the future they could have.

Except with his career on the line, he can't afford to get tied down. So, why does he keep finding reasons to stay?

Taken for Granted is a sweet, small-town romance in the Midnight Bluff series with a pinch of laughter and a heaping helping of Southern sass.

Read It Now: https://susanfarris.me/taken-for-granted/

Also by Susan E. Farris

Fiction

The Gravedigger's Guild

Midnight Bluff Romance Series:
Nuts About You
Taken For Granted
Piece Of Cake
High Horse

Poetry

Heartwork: Poetry for Growth
Flooding the Delta: A Journey Through Things Found and
Forgotten

Acknowledgments

This book would not be possible without Dr. Eric Stafne of MSU Extension Services for being an invaluable resource. My eternal gratitude goes out to Dr. Lenny Wells of the University of Georgia for allowing me to ask him endless questions about pecan orchards and their care. One of the great pleasures of writing is researching and meeting knowledgeable people and both of these men are exceptional.

As always, a huge thank you to my beta readers Brenda, Kim, Dawn, and Josh for being my cheerleaders and speakers of truth through the writing process. And a huge shoutout to my editor, Domenica Pillo, for making this book shine.

To Pete, my one and only. You believe in my dreams and keep me grounded on days when I doubt everything I'm doing. You're my anchor and my supplier of coffee. When I don't know what I want for a cover design you gamely make me three different ones. I love you more than caffeine and sugar, and I can't tell you how thankful I am to have you in my life.

About the Author

~⚬⚬⚬~

Sweet stories with a Southern twang.

Susan Farris is a Mississippi author and poet with a passion for local stories and a deeply held belief that a cup of tea solves many of life's problems. Her favorite local places often appear in her books- along with her favorite foods!

When she's not wrangling words on the page, she loves to garden, play board games, or snuggle up with her three cats and two dogs while appreciating her husband's amazing cooking skills.

You can follow Susan on Instagram and TikTok (@author-susanfarris) as well as on Goodreads and BookBub.

Want the VIP treatment? Join the **Sweet Squad** to receive book news, short stories, and reading recommendations: https://susanfarris.me/free-reads/.

Subscribe to my newsletter:

✉ https://susanfarris.me/free-reads

www.ingramcontent.com/pod-product-compliance
Lightning Source LLC
Chambersburg PA
CBHW020941260626
47169CB00006B/1757